SAFE

The Shielded Series – Book One

By Christine DePetrillo

Kim,
Love grows in
the woods!

Christine
DePetrillo

Author Contact:
Website: www.christinedepetrillo.weebly.com

Facebook:
www.facebook.com/christinedepetrilloauthor

Christine DePetrillo

Dedication

To our future selves and all we deserve...

Chapter One

Dr. Foster Ashby leaned against the crumbling brick exterior of an abandoned building, trying to catch his breath. His heart drummed a frantic and untamed beat in his chest, echoing in his ears as he sucked in oxygen and struggled not to choke on the fumes in the air. They'd dropped a pepperblast a few feet from him, but he'd managed to duck into an alley before the noxious cloud enveloped him. The stinging vapors would linger though. He couldn't run back the way he'd come. Going forward was his only option.

I have to make it.

Lungs burning, he patted the small tablet zipped into the pocket of his gray cargo pants. If his research fell into the hands of his pursuers, all would be lost. He was close to an answer now. Too close to fail. Too close to disappoint the entire globe.

No pressure.

Foster rubbed his eyes, certain they were bloodshot, not only from the pepperblast but simply from being in the city. Running through dilapidated Boston took its toll on the body. The stink of trash and decaying carcasses—animal and human—made breathing difficult. Summer temperatures didn't help. Everything smelled as if it'd been marinated in sour milk then roasted on sun-scorched asphalt. The uneven pavement was tricky to navigate and hell on the feet. Something sharp had jabbed his heel through his black combat boots as he'd run through the city, and now his sock felt wet. He didn't dare stop to heal what was probably a deep gash.

Have to keep moving.

He picked his way along the alley, staying close to the building at his right. Fortunately the brick façade was continuous and offered good cover. Red bits of brick flaked off as his fingers trailed along the stone, sounding like rain pattering on the street. He'd loved the brownstone buildings in this part of the city where he'd lived before the Anarch attack. They'd been so cozy, nestled next to one another along the narrow streets, old-fashioned iron lampposts lighting the way for nighttime walkers on summer evenings. Boston had been such a historic city, filled with the sights and symbols of America's fight for freedom. Now it was no more than a wasteland.

Rubble and litter ruined the landscape. The sound of cars bringing people here and there no longer filled the day and night hours like a steady, healthy heartbeat. Instead an eerie quiet—an odd absence of city noise—hung over the skeletons of broken buildings. Business no longer thrived here. Social activity no longer thrived here.

Nothing thrived here.

Except for one area where Foster resided. His employer, Emerge Tech, owned the intact and enhanced building and allowed its employees to live there. The science-based company had taken over a section of the ruined city to rebuild its headquarters, erected fortress-grade walls with a security field around its assets, and had been operating as if the rest of the world wasn't in a total state of disarray. They were committed to solving the problems that were causing the chaos across the globe, but life within Emerge Tech walls and its security field was as close to normal as life got these days.

If I could get back there…

Maybe he'd be safe inside Emerge Tech's walls. Maybe he'd be leading the enemy right where they wanted to be led. Maybe he wasn't meant to survive the day.

Foster shook his head. He *had* to survive. Too many people were counting on his research. Too many lives would be lost if he didn't succeed. He couldn't quit now. Especially because he'd snuck out of the safety of Emerge Tech after his superiors had made it quite clear they didn't approve of his requested trip into the city.

But he needed samples. Samples that were too risky for anyone else to acquire. Patting the pocket of his cargo pants, he took pleasure in the fact that he'd been successful. Now he just had to get back to his lab.

As he decided to make a run for Emerge Tech, a bright spotlight lasered down to where he stood in the dim alley.

"Nowhere to hide now, good doctor," a digitized voice boomed from overhead.

The light was too bright for Foster to see its origin. He made a move to run again, but fingers dug into his biceps. He was yanked out of the light and through a hole in the brick wall behind him. The fingers felt small but strong against his bare skin. He made a move to turn around, but the fingers tightened painfully, so he stopped.

"Look," he started, "I know what you want, but I don't have the cure. I might never find it." Maybe if the enemy thought he wasn't close to finding the right recipe, they'd decide he wasn't a threat.

He expected a response. Something along the lines of, "You will have the cure soon." That was most likely true. Foster didn't make a habit of failing; however, he feared the rest of that sentence would be, "So you must die."

He wasn't ready to die. He had faith the world could be restored. He knew he was a big part of that restoration. He had to live and find the cure. He also wanted to be around to enjoy the new world that would be rebuilt in place of the shithole this one had become.

Instead, the only answer he received was the sound of someone breathing behind him. He strained to listen and didn't hear more than *one* set of inhales and exhales.

If there's only one of them...

Foster whirled around and sent his fist straight out. His knuckles immediately connected with something and a pained cry filled the dark space around him.

"Fuck," an angry female voice said. Spitting sounded followed by more cursing and a soft click as a flashlight flooded the area with white light. "You made me bleed, you ass." The beam of light turned to the cement floor where dark splatters zigzagged between Foster's black combat boots and a similar, smaller pair across from him.

While he was studying the blood spill, someone grabbed his shirt, brought his head down, and slammed it against a sharp, boney kneecap that appeared out of nowhere. The pain was instant and sent him to his knees. He reached out his hands to brace himself and debris on the floor cut into his palms. Now *he* was bleeding.

"There," the female voice said. "We're fucking even now."

Foster swung out his arms and grabbed onto the ankles of his attacker. Pulling with all he had, he swept her legs out from under her. She crashed to the ground, landing flat on her back. Her body made a sickening smack, but Foster didn't give a shit. She wasn't getting his research.

No one was getting his research. Not until he had the cure and not until he was sure it'd be going into the right hands—hands dedicated to saving lives. Emerge Tech hands.

He scrambled to his feet, grabbed the flashlight the female had dropped, and ran deeper into what remained of the building they were in. If he could get out the other side of it, he could avoid what might still be waiting in the alley and have a chance at getting to his domicile. He'd be safe on the other side of Emerge Tech's walls and its security field. He had to believe that.

His heel ached along with his palms and his head now, but he kept running. Moving had to be better than sitting with a target on his back. He rounded a corner, spilling into a better lit area where a wall was broken and let in daylight. His eyes took a moment to adjust to the light then he ran straight into the nose of a gun.

"I wonder if Emerge Tech will pay me regardless of your condition upon delivery." The female pushed the gun into his breastbone until it felt as if it were grinding a hole there.

"You're getting paid by Emerge Tech?" He backed up a step to rid himself of the gun prod and take a better look at his assailant.

"Yeah." She pushed a mane of reddish-brown waves out of her face as her tongue ran over the fresh split in her bottom lip. A split Foster had put there.

"And what exactly are they paying you to do?" Thoughts of betrayal flashed into his mind. The company he'd given everything to was out to get him? The company who had thrown funds his way to save the goddamn world wanted him dead? If he died, so did nearly everyone else. The enemy would win. Is that what Emerge Tech wanted?

"They're paying me to keep your sorry ass safe, though they are miffed you left their walls without consent. I can see why. People want you dead out here on the outside." She flexed her hand around the gun. "You must be important, Dr. Foster Ashby." Her face took on a disgusted expression as her hazel gaze combed over him. "Rich guys are always important. Or at least they think they are." She lowered the gun now and wiped at the fresh blood dotting her lip.

"And what? I'm supposed to just believe you're here to keep me safe?" Did she think he was that gullible? He may spend hours upon hours locked in his lab, but he knew not to assume everyone told the truth all the time. Especially not in the world of 2025. Honesty had gone down as hard as the buildings in the Boston. Trust was an antiquated notion. Extinct even.

Foster knew that first hand. His biggest enemy right now had once been his best friend. He'd worked long hours with Dr. Mikale Warres, a brilliant chemist at Emerge Tech. He'd assumed they'd been toiling after the same goals, believed in the same ideas.

He'd been wrong.

He wouldn't be wrong again. "Listen. I'm all set on my own here."

"Clearly." She scoffed. "You were about to be terminated in that alley, moron. I pulled you out of there and the thanks I get is a punch to the face." She wiped at her bloody lip again. A bloody lip that made her mouth look dangerous. She winced as she ran her tongue over the split.

Foster unzipped his pocket and plunged his hand inside.

"Hold it right there." She took several steps closer, her gun still trained on him.

He put his hands out to his sides. "My weapon is not in this pocket." He wasn't going to tell her he didn't have a weapon on him at all. She'd already called him a moron. She'd think he was downright insane for venturing into the city unarmed, but he liked to believe he was stealthy enough not to need a weapon.

Clearly that's not true.

But he hadn't realized Mikale was actively pursuing him. Emerge Tech had to have known, though, if they denied his request to go outside in the first place and then thought a bodyguard was necessary once they realized he was missing.

"I want to grab my tablet." Slowly, he reached into his pocket, his gaze staying on the nose of her gun, which didn't waver in the least. She obviously had experience holding people at gunpoint.

He pulled out his tablet. Tapping the screen, he found the program he wanted and stepped closer to her. He hadn't decided whether she was friend or foe yet, but he didn't need her blood creating a trail for his enemy to follow.

"Let me see your lip there," he said.

She backed up a few steps. "Get away from me."

"Do you enjoy donating your precious blood to the floor?" he asked.

Licking at the split again, she huffed out a breath. "It's just a few drops. Trust me, I've donated way more than that in the past."

"I'm sure." He held up the tablet. "You obviously know I'm a doctor. I can stop that bleeding with this. If you'll let me. It's perfectly safe. Watch."

He hovered the tablet over the deep scratches on his left palm and hit scan. A warmth radiated over the damaged skin and soon the cuts were completely healed. He did the same to his right palm then met her gaze.

She lowered her weapon and waved a hand toward her lip. "Hurry up then."

He stepped a little closer, careful not to put himself within range for her to do any damage to him. Lining up her lip in the tablet's screen, he hit scan and the program went to work closing the split.

Within seconds, she was healed and no longer bleeding.

She brought her fingers up to her lip and ran them back and forth. Foster was a little mesmerized by how full those lips were. Bodyguards weren't supposed to be this... this hot, were they?

What am I doing? He didn't have time to notice how beautiful this female was. He only had time to find the cure.

As he backed away, his heel stung, shooting pain up his entire leg. The pain brought him back to his current situation and out of the daydream of pressing his lips against this female's just to get a taste of her. He listened for a moment, but didn't hear sounds of anyone still in pursuit outside. Sinking to the ground, he sat and pulled off his boot and blood-stained sock.

"What are you doing?" she asked. "We have to keep moving and get you and your impressive brain to Emerge Tech."

"Ah, now I believe you." Shaking his head, he used his tablet to tend to the gash in his heel.

She folded her arms across her chest. "Now you believe what?"

Foster put his boot back on and stood, securing his tablet into the zippered pocket of his cargo pants. He studied her for a few moments. She wasn't much shorter than his six-foot-three frame, and her legs went on for miles. He'd definitely not seen a pair of black cargo pants and black boots look better. The army green tank top she wore showcased muscular arms and smooth caramel-colored skin. A tattoo encircled her left arm—a ring of stars—and Foster put a hand to his own tribal tattoo on his neck, swirling up around his right ear. He'd gotten his to celebrate life. Why had she gotten hers?

Why do I care?

"Now you believe what?" she repeated as she pulled at her bottom lip, looking a little impressed it had been healed so easily.

"Now I believe you were hired by Emerge Tech. My brain is important to them." Only his brain. He was pretty sure if he could download his brain onto a machine, Emerge Tech would have had him do so years ago. "My employer would pay someone to keep my brain safe."

"But not your body, huh?" She smiled now, and Foster wasn't sure if he should like it or fear it. "Too bad. I'm not sure what your brain looks like, but your body's definitely…" Her voice trailed off and her dark brows lowered.

"Definitely… what?"

She blinked and cleared her throat. "Definitely not disgusting." She pulled at a chain around her neck and presented a triangular metal tag. "Back to business. I'm Officer Darina Lazitter. This is my badge. I'm supposed to escort you to Emerge Tech safely. Your employer felt you were taking too long out here on your unauthorized visit."

Foster took the tag from her, tugging lightly on the chain so she had to take a step forward. Sure enough, it said the name she'd given him and her badge number along with the letters BPD for Boston Police Department.

He let the tag drop, and the chain landed between her breasts. Breast that were also definitely not disgusting, not that he was paying attention to those sorts of things. He had more important shit on his mind.

"I suppose we should stop beating each other up then," he said. "We're on the same team."

"I'm my own team," she said. "Always. I'll do the job and be on my way." She turned on her heel before he could reply. "C'mon."

Foster fell in step behind her. He'd follow her to Emerge Tech. Perhaps she knew an easier way to get there. One that wouldn't involve him getting blasted to pieces by Warres's associates. Thirty-six years old and he already had some artificial parts. He didn't need anymore.

And he certainly didn't need to be dead.

****

Darina knew she should keep a closer eye on her charge, but Dr. Foster Ashby was over six feet of solid, attractive man. The less she looked at him, the better. She didn't need to analyze how those gray cargo pants molded to his fine ass and long, toned legs. She didn't need to study how his black T-shirt emphasized a muscular chest and strong biceps. That interesting ink crawling up his neck to his ear definitely did not need her close inspection, and she was absolutely *not* wondering how the dark stubble surrounding his full lips would feel scraping along her bare skin.

Nope. She was focused on her mission of getting this guy to the safety of his employer, the wealthy Emerge Tech. Normally she didn't accept jobs like this, but times were tough, and she had Ezekiel to support. Sure, he wasn't her biological son, but that sixteen-year old meant as much to her as flesh and blood. He'd been with her since he was six and had been found living under a pier jutting out into Boston Harbor. She'd coaxed him to her with a chocolate bar, and the two of them had been together ever since. If getting Dr. Rich Scientist to Richer Emerge Tech beyond Richest Steel Walls would bring in some extra cash, then she was going to do it.

For Zeke.

"You know this city well." Foster's voice made the image of Zeke in the camouflage shorts and printed T-shirt he probably absconded from her best friend and neighbor, Ghared Timms, disappear.

"Lived here my entire life. All thirty-four years." Twenty-something of those years had been amazingly wonderful. She'd had her parents who loved her abundantly, her brothers Deo and Dixon with whom she was a triplet, and Ghared who was like another brother. Then she'd become a cop like her father and had enjoyed every day at work. Her colleagues were wonderful to be with, whether catching criminals or downing beers. It was as if she'd had *two* families. When she'd found Zeke, her happiness climbed to a new level because she now had someone to take care of, someone who depended on her.

Things had been fabulous in the city she loved.

Then the Anarch—a secret group of techhead terrorists—fucked everything up.

Grinding her teeth now, she led Foster down a set of narrow stone steps to the underground railway, inoperable since the Anarch unplugged the entire globe. What she remembered most about that night was how dark and quiet it had been. Not a single light anywhere. Not a single mechanical noise of any kind. Just complete blackness and absolute silence, both so intense it hurt.

With so much of the world dependent on electronic devices and the internet, the phrase *third world country* became *third world globe.* Hospitals couldn't run. Their generators only lasted a few days. Existing patients died and new ones couldn't get the care they needed. NASA satellites dropped out of space, crashing to Earth and crushing anything they landed on. Those satellites still remained where they'd fallen, looking very much like tragic monuments memorializing the Anarch attack.

Businesses tanked with no technology to keep them operational and no patrons to keep commerce going. Money simply stopped flowing just as electricity and water had. Prosperous cities around the globe instantly became cement jungles where people did their best to survive to see the next sunrise. Without modern inventions, people had gone insane pretty quickly. They'd forgotten how to be self-sufficient.

They didn't know how to live unplugged.

Savage behavior clawed at humanity's hold on civilization. A new way of living emerged.

It was called survival.

Darina could admit to missing the conveniences, but she'd managed. Even after the Anarch had been caught, no one knew how to turn everything back on properly. The techheads had left a nasty virus in the system, and geeks were still trying to sort it all out. If you knew the right people, you could get access to working technology today, but that was all underground stuff. Maybe someday the world would be up and running at full power again, but Darina had her doubts she'd live to see it.

She hoped Zeke got to, though.

After several miles of scurrying in the shadows like feral cats, Darina ascended a set of stairs, motioning for Foster to stay below until she signaled to him. He nodded, surprising her.

"What?" he asked.

"Nothing." She shrugged one shoulder. "I just expected you to be more trouble than you've been."

"Punching you in the face wasn't enough trouble for you?" He smiled, all perfect white teeth, and she wished he wouldn't do that. That was a dangerous smile right there. One that made her forget she didn't allow herself to have feelings for attractive men. Especially rich ones. Not anymore.

She'd had a few relationships in the past, but nothing that stuck. She didn't need one that stuck. She had Ghared and Zeke for company. After the Anarch attack, pockets of fighting broke out; she'd lost her brothers who were soldiers and had joined the battle without hesitation. They'd fought bravely, as did Ghared, but only Ghared returned home. Returned to what was left of home anyway. He'd been taking care of Darina and Zeke ever since, and they took care of him. She only had room for two men in her life, and Ghared and Zeke were the chosen two.

She'd let another man get close to her once. At least she'd thought she had. A stupid move. One she wouldn't be repeating.

This Dr. Foster Ashby was a job. A paycheck. Nothing more.

She climbed the last few steps slowly, scanning the open area at the top and holding out her weapon. Deeming it free of bad guys, she signaled Foster to join her. She watched all that black hair atop his head as he traveled up the steps. Her fingers got this wild notion to bury themselves in it, and she silently scolded those fingers.

Traitors.

She needed all her focus to finish this job and get back home to Zeke. The kid had endured one of his violent seizures right before she'd had to leave. Ghared had said he'd take care of it, but she'd hated leaving Zeke in that exhausted, confused, post-seizure haze. Every time he had one, she feared it would take him from her. Though he wasn't technically hers to begin with, after ten years of acting as if he was hers, she couldn't deny she loved him more than anyone on this screwed up planet.

After finding him under that pier and taking him home with her, the boy had obeyed her every word and clung to her like a magnet. Even now at sixteen, he preferred hanging out with her and Ghared rather than anyone his own age. He spent time with Ghared's niece, Mareea, whenever she visited Ghared, which was often, but he was still mostly Darina's boy, and she was totally okay with that.

She supposed he felt lucky to have been found by her and owed her something. Most genetically engineered castoffs—GECs—were imprisoned and scrapped for parts. Zeke had received the failed rating because of his seizures. Not his fault the DNA they combined wasn't a good cocktail, but the companies working in genetic engineering took their failures seriously. They weren't going to be responsible for putting substandard humans in the battlefield. Only the best test tube-grown soldiers were allowed to suit up and fight alongside enlisted men and women.

Zeke had not been considered the best so he'd been labeled a GEC as soon as he had his first seizure, but he'd escaped from the company that had made him to a life of living on the streets or under harbor piers. That had been better than being ripped apart for pieces to be used in other experiments. Dismantlement. If Darina wasn't so busy trying to keep herself, Zeke, and Ghared alive in the city, she would have lobbied against dismantlement. What a horrible notion.

Thinking of it now sent a shudder rippling through Darina. She couldn't imagine her life without Zeke. He was her reason for living.

Zeke was also her reason for traipsing around the city with a man who had a target on his back. And not just any target. Dr. Mikale Warres, famous chemist and current World's Most Wanted, was after Foster Ashby. Darina had to be out of her mind accepting this job. She didn't want to get tangled up with Warres.

But the money will keep us in the clear for a while.

Besides, getting behind the walls of Emerge Tech might get her some help. Help with Zeke's seizures. She'd heard word of a medicine that eased conditions like Zeke's. If she could get some of that medicine, maybe she could spare her boy the debilitating after-effects. He always said he felt nothing during a seizure, but when it was over and he wanted to do nothing but sleep, she knew the toll it took on his body.

Foster stood beside her now—a little too close for comfort, but she was supposed to be guarding him after all. Couldn't do that if he was far away.

"See that busted up subway car over there?" She pointed across the street to the charred car tipped on its side. It had probably been in motion when the Unplug happened and vaulted off its tracks up to street level. Dead passengers were most likely rotting inside if the stench riding the warm, summer breeze was any indication.

"Yes." Foster's breath skated across the back of her neck as he replied.

She ignored the sensations whispering throughout her body. "Let's make a run for that and reassess there."

"Okay." He took a stance, ready to run, and matched her pace perfectly when they took off.

Darina rather liked having someone beside her as they picked their way closer to Emerge Tech's walls. Nowadays, she was on the job by herself, seeking out low-life scum or, more recently, overseeing the removal of dead bodies from the streets. Unfortunately, the number of dead bodies had become too many to count.

Ever since Mikale Warres had unleashed his lethal plague while the world was still trying to recover from the Anarch attack.

A disease that devoured people from the inside out, this bit of fatal chemistry was worming through the globe's population. If it wasn't stopped soon, the pandemic would succeed in wiping out the human race, which was exactly what Warres wanted. He was obsessed with cleansing the planet and starting a new breed of humankind. Reports called him a "madman pursuing madmen," which wasn't altogether false. Lunatics wandered the wrecked streets of Boston every day. Some of them probably shouldn't be allowed to run about, but that wasn't for Warres to decide. He didn't have the right to end their lives, and so painfully, no matter how crazy they'd become. The police were working on containing those people and getting them help. Eventually the technology would be back full strength—Darina had to believe that—and the world would need as many people as possible to rebuild. That was the correct strategy.

Not repopulation, but reconstruction.

Certainly people like Ghared, Zeke, and herself hadn't lost their minds despite the lifestyle they were forced to endure. They were trying to help the cause. Ghared was a tech geek, working on rebooting, while she was policing the streets. Zeke often helped Ghared, and someday, she hoped he'd get the chance to contribute to society in whatever way he decided. They all deserved to live. And in a world where they didn't have to worry about contracting Warres's plague.

She shot a look over her shoulder at Foster. He was waiting for her next command. Ready to listen. Perhaps he deserved to live too. After all, the man was dedicating his life to finding a cure to the pandemic, but what were his motives? Fame? Fortune? The rich always wanted to be richer. Most likely he wanted to be the hero of the day.

Self-absorbed prick.

Huddling beside him behind the subway car, she said, "Emerge Tech is about three miles west of here. If we stay low and move fast, we can make it."

"Low, fast. Got it."

His eyes were an odd shade of pale green that reminded Darina of the plants her mother used to grow in her greenhouse before the Anarch attack. Before her mother, a robotics engineer, and her father, a cop, joined the search for the techheads and had lost their lives as her brothers had. Darina would have been there hunting or fighting at their sides, but she'd been injured in a hovercopter accident only a week before the world went dark.

Ghared still blamed himself for that accident, though she'd told him a hundred times it wasn't his fault. Flexing the fingers of her left hand now, she fought off old memories and heartbreak over things she'd had to do make herself whole again.

Focus on now.

If she had any hope of getting Foster to Emerge Tech, Darina had to use all her cop skills. Reliving the past—and her mistakes—was not the way to do that.

They made their way west, sticking close to building remains and moving like phantoms. Foster kept up effortlessly, never complained about their pace, and didn't question any of her decisions. The smart rich guys she'd encountered did not behave like Foster Ashby at all. They were all too eager to assume she didn't know the first thing about anything and made it their duty to enlighten her. They were manipulative and believed the world revolved around them.

Well, maybe not *this* world. This world barely kept turning on its axis anymore, but whatever. Every wealthy male she'd had the bad luck to come across had treated her like an object, one they could do with as they pleased.

And yeah, she'd let that happen. Once. But she'd gotten what she wanted out of the deal too. Sort of. That was how life rolled sometimes.

Again she flexed the fingers of her left hand, watching the ring of stars tattoo waver under the movement of the muscles in her forearm. She'd always been a woman who did what had to be done no matter how much it sucked.

She glanced at Foster. Now she was doing what had to be done to keep this guy safe. She was always keeping someone safe. Zeke, sometimes Ghared and his niece, sometimes random people on the streets, and today, a genius doctor.

A damn sexy one.

The walls of Emerge Tech came into view before she had too much time to think about Foster as sexy. Distracting thoughts. Her line of work didn't blend well with distracting thoughts.

"Thanks," Foster said. "I can take it from here." He made a move to walk past her to the gates.

She grabbed his arm and jerked him back. "My orders are to bring you to your domicile." She reached into her pocket and produced the keycard the CEO of Emerge Tech had given her when she'd accepted the job.

Foster eyed the keycard then shook his head. "I don't need an escort."

"I didn't ask if you needed one. You've got one, and that's that."

He pursed his lovely lips, all the muscles in his face tensing as he regarded her with those piercing green eyes.

A flash of heat zipped through her body. *Summer temps and running through the city.* That was all. It had nothing to do with the intensity of his gaze.

"You're persistent," he said.

"I'm thorough. This is my job." She checked to the left, then the right, and led the way to the gates.

Foster followed, and she let out the breath she'd been holding. She was minutes away from collecting one of the biggest paychecks in her career, *and* she'd be inside Emerge Tech's walls. She didn't want to have to deal with Foster if he somehow ruined either of those end results. The money she'd receive for delivering him would go a long way in keeping her, Zeke, and Ghared fed and if she could get her hands on something to help Zeke's seizures, that would please her like nothing else ever had.

To not have to see her favorite person in the world suffer... hell, she'd do anything for that.

Chapter Two

"How in Hell did we lose him?" Dr. Mikale Warres pounded his fist on the dashboard in front of him. What good was a cadre of R81 Podsters if you couldn't catch one man with them? The sleek, single-person craft was bullet-shaped, fast, and should have been able to track prey like Foster Ashby without incident.

Yet, here I am. Empty-handed.

"Sorry, boss," a voice piped into Mikale's earpiece. "He isn't showing up on any scans."

"He didn't just vanish." *Imbeciles.* He'd probably have better luck ditching his associates and hunting Ashby on his own. "I'm heading to Emerge Tech walls. That's where he's going."

"But their security field will zap you, sir. You'll be fried."

This was true. For most people anyway. But Mikale wasn't most people, and he couldn't let Ashby get into the safety of Emerge Tech's defenses. The good doctor had been bold enough— or stupid enough—to come out into the city, and Mikale wasn't wasting that mistake. Only one thing stood in the way of his plague reaching its intended goal—Dr. Foster Ashby. Mikale planned to take care of that little detail.

Today.

"I'll go on foot," he told his associate. "You and the rest of the team head back to the base."

"But sir, you shouldn't go anywhere near Emerge Tech. It's not safe for you."

Mikale let out a roar. His associate was right of course. He was a wanted man. "Fine." No time for arguments. "Take a contingent and get Ashby before he makes it back inside ET's walls."

Flicking off his earpiece, he jetted his Podster to a former parking garage and landed. It may not be safe for him to go to Emerge Tech, but he could still comb the streets, hoping Foster was still wandering. He holstered his gun, attached two pepperblasts to his belt, and ran for the stairs. Most of them had crumbled to no more than a steep, bumpy ramp so he tested the iron handrail. Finding it still pretty solid, he straddled it and slid down. He used this system for four flights then jumped to the pavement of the bottom floor. A cloud of dust stirred up under his boots, and the crunch of rubble echoed off the remaining concrete walls of the garage.

Taking a moment to get his bearings, he headed west. With each pound of his boots, an image of Foster splashed into his mind. Being schoolmates together. Studying long hours together. Shooting to the top of their class together, Foster at number one and Mikale at number two. Emerge Tech hiring them both right out of school. Working side by side on perfecting prosthetic limb technology. Recognition. Awards. Wealth. They were golden boys.

Together.

Then some punkass techhead terrorists flicked the "off" switch and the world was plunged into the early 1900s. Fortunately, Emerge Tech had the means to build itself back up... and protect itself and its employees. He and Foster hadn't changed their lifestyles all that much. They'd still lived in great comfort. They'd still had prestigious jobs, doing the work they loved. They'd had wounded soldiers aplenty, desperately needing prosthetic limbs after fighting broke out and the search for the Anarch stretched on. They'd still been golden boys, though the world was neck deep in pandemonium beyond the walls of Emerge Tech.

Then Mikale's mother got sick. She lived on the outside, and he often visited her, but the city had become a place unfit for an aging woman. Mikale petitioned to have his mother brought inside the walls, but Emerge Tech refused.

"If we start taking people in, where do we draw the line?" they'd asked. "We have important work to do here. We can't be distracted from our goals."

"But it's my mother," Mikale had said. "I can't leave her out there."

Still, Emerge Tech wouldn't bend, so he'd begun to take her supplies—food, clothing, medicines. When they'd caught him, they terminated his employment without a second thought. He hadn't had a chance to say goodbye to Foster.

And Foster never contacted him.

His mother's condition worsened without the medicines, and he had no materials to make her well again. He couldn't bear to see her suffer and did the only thing he could do to relieve her of her suffering.

He wasn't sure he could do it at first, but the pillow slipped easily over her face while she slept. She struggled as she fought for air, but Mikale was so much stronger than she was. He held her in place until she no longer moved beneath his hold. When he removed the pillow, peace had crept onto her features.

Mikale wandered the beat-up streets of Boston, barely surviving. The fighting raged on while the world struggled to plug itself back in, but he wasn't a soldier. He was a chemist, a scientist. His brain was his only weapon. The more he saw what the Anarch had done to the human race, the more he became convinced the world needed a significant reboot. A total purge and repopulate.

So he set to work. Using unsavory methods, he acquired more wealth and built his own empire.

And his plague was pure genius.

A vicious virus that infiltrated the body's internal organs, turning them to powder, similar to acid's effect on metal. A steady breakdown of elements until rust flaked off like orange snowfall. The blood-filled dust seeped through the pores and eventually the body shut down, leaving a shell of a human to decay wherever it dropped.

Once a good chunk of the human race was gone and the globe was cleansed, repopulation could begin.

If Foster didn't succeed in bringing a cure, of course.

Mikale knew Foster succeeded in most everything he did... except maintaining friendships it seemed.

"Not this time, Ashby," he growled. "This time things are going to go my way."

They had to. He'd worked tirelessly for too long to see his mission fail. After his mother's death, he'd found her diary. A tablet containing her personal thoughts about everything from the best way to clean a stain off her favorite sweater to whether or not God existed. The woman did superficial and deep with equal amounts of careful attention and detail.

One line, though, had snagged him. One line that propelled him into action after reading it. One line that fueled him.

I've done my best with Mikale, but he deserves better.

She had been proud of him when he worked for Emerge Tech, but after he got fired, she'd felt she'd gone wrong somewhere in his upbringing. She'd blamed herself because he'd been worried about her. Her guilt ate at Mikale's soul.

But things would be better once his plague took full effect, and the world could start again.

His ex-best friend wanted to stop all that with his cure.

Foster Ashby had to die.

****

He'd made it beyond the walls. Technically, *they'd* made it. Darina hadn't left his side since they'd been granted access at the gates. Foster understood it was her job, what Emerge Tech had paid her to do, but it was totally unnecessary. He wasn't in any danger within his company's domain. They wanted him to succeed with the cure as much as he wanted to succeed, even if they were pissed he'd left without their approval. He could have parted ways with Darina at the gates.

"Seriously," he said now. "My domicile is right there. Why don't you head to the main offices to collect your payment?"

"I will." Darina fingered her weapon in its holster at her hip. "As soon as I see you to your living room, I'll be on my way."

Foster puffed out a breath, realizing by now it'd be a waste of time arguing with her and her determination. "Fine."

He quickened his pace, eager to be rid of her.

That's not true.

She'd gotten him to his destination without either one of them being pummeled by pepperblast or bullets. No one had plucked them from the streets. It hadn't even seemed as if they were being pursued anymore. Darina knew the city layout and had done as she'd promised.

She'd kept him safe.

He probably wouldn't have made it on his own. Not that he wasn't capable, but his enemies weren't dummies either. They had a leader with an intellect that matched his own. They'd be able to anticipate his moves. Plus, most of his brain was focused on trying to find the cure. He wasn't paying attention to anything else.

Also not true.

Darina was something he'd been paying attention to since she'd hauled him into that abandoned building. Paying too much attention to, in fact. She threw the unknown into the mix. He didn't need that, but here he was, pushing his key into his door, opening it, and not wanting her to leave now that she'd completed her mission.

But I have my own mission. One that couldn't afford distractions.

He turned to face her. "Thank you."

She gave him a tight nod then glanced over his shoulder. "Mind if I check out the place. Cop instincts tell me to search the area."

He stepped aside to let her pass and didn't mind when her shoulder rubbed against his chest. Even after sprinting through the streets, she smelled good. Like aloe, maybe? Following her inside, he closed the door behind him and watched as she wandered around his living room.

"You live here all by yourself?" She lifted one dark eyebrow at him.

"Yes."

She frowned and shook her head. "Figures."

"You think it's too much for one man?" He folded his arms across his chest and leaned against the wall by the door.

"It *is* too much for one man." The disgust in her voice perturbed him.

He swung one arm out. "I've worked hard for all this."

"I work hard too, Dr. Ashby." She peeked down the hall and went left.

He followed her. "And yet you live in a tiny domicile?"

"Miniature," she said as she peeked into his bathroom and bedroom. "Doesn't even qualify as a domicile."

"Alone?" He followed her to his office and library.

"What?" Her eyebrows lowered as she turned and stared at him. Even slightly pissed off, she was gorgeous. All that reddish-brown hair looked soft, and Foster had the urge to bury his fingers in it as he feasted on that long, slender neck of hers. Her eyes were an unusual hazel, concentric circles of green and brown around black pupils. Her eyelashes were full and feathery.

"Alone. Do you live alone in your miniature non-domicile?" He was overstepping his bounds, but an unexplainable drive to know more about her prevailed.

"No. My son, Zeke, lives with me." Her features softened. "He would love this place."

And his father? But Foster didn't ask that particular question. Too prying. Instead he asked, "Who watches the boy while you're busy being a bodyguard?"

"He's hardly a boy anymore," Darina said, a slight smile on her lips that made Foster's throat go dry. "He's sixteen, and most likely hanging out with our neighbor, Ghared."

"I see." *Just a neighbor?*

An awkward silence stretched on as she scouted around the rest of his place. She moved gracefully and quietly, offering Foster the chance to appreciate her female form. She had curves right where a woman should have curves and muscles right where a woman trying to survive in 2025 should have muscles.

She pointed to a door across the living room. "What's behind there?"

"My lab."

"You have a lab in your domicile?"

"I work around the clock, Officer Lazitter. Emerge Tech thought it would be convenient and more productive for me to have a lab right here."

She left that one alone and went to one of the large windows. Bracing her hand on the wall, she peeked out but reared back when she saw the view.

"Don't like heights?"

She shook her head and turned from the window.

He grinned at her sickly expression. "And here I was thinking you didn't have any weaknesses."

"Shut it or I'll knee you in the head again." With that threat, her badass aura returned.

"You're only allowed one of those." Though he wouldn't mind if she wanted to put her hands on him in other ways.

"I never said I was playing by *your* rules." She brushed some dirt off her pants.

"Can I get you something to drink or eat?" After all, the woman did run through the filthy city with him, some of it with hot summer sun beaming down on them. She was getting payment, but that wasn't from him directly. He wanted to show his gratitude. Other ways to do that kept creeping into his subconscious the more he looked at her, but he had to keep it polite and professional.

"You have clean water?"

"Of course." His response made her scowl, and he immediately regretted his superior attitude. "My apologies. I didn't mean to sound like a—"

"Rich bastard?" she finished. "You probably can't help it. You are, in fact, a rich bastard." She gestured to his domicile.

"Rich, maybe," he said as he filled a glass with water at the sink in the kitchen then handed it to her. "Bastard, definitely not."

She made a noise as if she didn't believe him and drank the water. When she tipped her head back to get the last of the drink, Foster had to look away for fear of descending upon her exposed throat. All caramel-colored smooth skin in one long line... no, that was too damn tempting, especially because he hadn't touched a real woman in so long. She clearly wouldn't appreciate an advance from him though, rich bastard that she assumed he was.

Handing him the glass, she said, "Thanks. Good luck with your work, Dr. Ashby. We're all counting on you."

As if he needed the reminder.

She started for the door but turned around before reaching it. "What were you doing in the city anyway? Why leave the safety of this place when your employer clearly didn't want you to? I mean, there's a plague raging out there. One you specifically are aware of."

Foster chewed his bottom lip. It wasn't any of her business why he was on the outside, but something inside him didn't want her to rush off. Explaining his trip to the streets would get her to stay a few more minutes. He rather enjoyed having a live, flesh and blood female in his domicile. She was far more interesting than the hologram partners he turned too every now and again to take the edge

34

off. They were programmed to bend to his wishes, his demands.

Officer Lazitter didn't strike him as one to bend. She'd challenge and question. Why did he find that so arousing?

He unzipped his pocket and extracted his tablet. "You obviously know I'm working on a cure for the plague."

She nodded as she approached him. "They say you're the only one who can find it."

"That may be so," he said as he sat on his couch and motioned for her to do the same.

She hesitated for a moment, appearing to have an internal conversation with herself, then walked over and lowered to the cushion beside him.

Trying his best to ignore the physical reactions her close proximity caused, Foster fired up his tablet and scrolled through pictures. Finding the one he wanted, he angled the tablet toward her.

"I needed this," he said, deciding a picture of the sample would suffice. He didn't want to risk showing her the real thing still buried in his other pocket.

She took the tablet and stared at the red powder. "Is this… ?" She squinted at him then back to the image. "Is this from a body?"

He nodded. "I need samples of what the plague does to the human body in order to test my cures."

"Surely someone else can get this for you." She handed him the tablet and shifted over on the couch, no doubt wondering if he were contagious after being close enough to an infected body to collect such samples.

"Why risk getting the plague myself you mean?"

"Yeah, if you get it, then we're all screwed." She gathered all that hair of hers and twisted it into a knot at the base of her neck. Her face was even more beautiful now that her hair didn't hide it.

"I'm not going to get it."

"We all hope we're not going to get it. Zeke and I are super careful and stay away from the active zones. Ghared too, but that's no guarantee. We're all at risk."

She shuddered a little beside him, and Foster now wanted to find the cure more than he did before. For people like Darina and her son. People just trying to live their lives the best way they could, considering the circumstances.

"I'm not going to get it," he said again.

"Money doesn't make you immune, rich bastard."

"No, but being a GEC does."

****

"You?" Darina rubbed her ear as if it had suddenly been taken over by an alien technology that made her hear things that couldn't possibly be true. "You're a GEC?"

Foster nodded once, his eyes focused on the tablet resting on his thigh.

"And GECs are immune to the plague?"

"Yes. The plague targets DNA code that genetically engineered individuals do not have."

"*All* GECs are immune?" Zeke? She didn't have to worry her Zeke would get the disease?

"Every last one of them. It's impossible for us to contract the disease. Our bodies can't host it."

36

He wiggled the tablet in his hand where the image of the red powder was still on the screen. "I could roll around in this stuff and not get sick."

Darina sifted out a long breath. Zeke wouldn't get sick. One worry off her gargantuan list of worries. Excellent.

"Does Warres know GECs are immune?"

Foster shook his head. "I don't believe so. If he did, he'd already have unleashed a new strain to target us. Most GECs are in hiding, so I think he hasn't considered them."

"How do you know all GECs can't get the virus?"

At this question, Foster shifted uncomfortably, as if he didn't know what to say or he was hiding something. Typical. Rich bastards didn't know the meaning of the word *truth.*

"I just know," he said.

"Tight-lipped on that, but just tossed it out in the open that you're a GEC. Why would you tell me? You don't know me." That was dangerous information to share with someone he'd just met. As he'd said, most GECs were in hiding. She prayed every day no one ever found out about Zeke.

"I don't know why I told you." He shrugged one shoulder, looking a little shy, and she instantly got the feeling Dr. Foster Ashby didn't have many human connections. "Maybe because you're a cop. Maybe because you got me back here safely. Maybe because the secret is eating me up inside. Maybe because I trust you for some reason."

Darina stood. Sitting so close to him on his couch had suddenly become way too personal. "You can't trust anyone."

"You won't expose me, will you?" He followed her to the door, a note of unease in his voice now.

She turned to face him. He was close again and the clean smell of him swirled pleasantly around her. She had to raise her head a little to look him in the eyes. His green gaze was intense, zeroed in on her eyes, locked. One step forward by either of them and their lips could touch.

Why am I thinking of touching his lips?

No time for that stuff. And hadn't she told him not to trust anyone? That went double for her. Especially stupid to trust a rich bastard.

But smart to see if a rich bastard can help me.

"I won't tell anyone if you can do something for me," she said.

"A bargain?" His eyes dropped down to her lips. "Name it. I owe you for your protection today."

She waved that off and ignored how her body had heated under his gaze. "Emerge Tech has that debt covered." Maybe it hadn't been such a terrible job either. She'd learned Zeke was safe from the plague. Valuable information indeed. "My son…"

"Zeke?"

He'd been listening.

"Yeah, Zeke." She brushed some stone dust off her tank top and wondered if she looked like a city rat. Here in Foster's tidy domicile, she felt like a giant dirt stain. "Well, he has these episodes. Seizures. They come on out of nowhere and exhaust him."

"He's epileptic?"

Darina nodded. "The seizures are awful to witness. His eyes go blank, his entire body tenses up, and the shaking is wild." She shook her head, trying to clear the image of Zeke in full seizure mode. Unfortunately, that image would never clear. Every time she looked at him, she saw him in this state and wished she could take the experience away for him.

"How long do the seizures last?" Foster hadn't stepped back at all, hadn't given her any space, and she needed some. Desperately.

But she didn't move either.

"When he was younger, they were short, lasting only a few moments. He'd be a little sleepy, but a short nap would revive him, and he'd be back to his usual self. Since he was about thirteen, however, they started happening more often and lasting longer. Afterward, he's shot. He'll sleep for a whole day and have no appetite. Sometimes his speech is slurred."

"Sometimes the onset of puberty can worsen the condition," Foster said. "Does he have any memory issues after a seizure?"

"He says he doesn't remember having the seizure, which in my mind is a good thing." She swallowed loudly, her throat stinging. "Seeing him like that is... difficult." Blinking rapidly, she fought to keep her tears to herself. No reason to come unglued in front of Dr. Rich Bastard.

Only he didn't seem like a bastard. Not the way he was listening to her and asking relevant questions as if he truly intended to help her.

When his hand rested on her shoulder, she jerked back, hitting the door behind her. He immediately retracted his hand, looking at his palm as if he wasn't quite sure how it had gotten on her shoulder in the first place.

"I can give you medicine to prevent seizures. I just need a few minutes to make it. Can you wait?" He put both his hands in his pockets now.

Did he put his hands away for him or for me?

"I can wait. Thank you."

"It's no trouble." He stepped away, heading for the door he'd said led to a lab. Looking over his shoulder, he asked, "Actually, do you want to see how it's made?"

Something inside her definitely wanted to see Foster at work. "Sure."

"This way." He took his tablet and punched in a code Darina couldn't see. Waving the tablet over a black rectangle by the door unlocked it. "Lights." At his voice command, lighting flooded the room beyond the door. "After you." He gestured for her to go in first then followed right behind her.

The walls were covered in huge touch screens with some panels covered in text. Others had complicated equations Darina couldn't begin to understand. Along another wall were shelves with bottles, boxes, and jars. She couldn't read half of the scientific words emblazoned on the sides and felt dumber than she had in a long time.

Out on the streets she considered herself intelligent. She knew where everything was, how to get food and other supplies, how to track a criminal, and a whole host of other useful skills.

In this lab—in Foster's world—she knew shit. They lived in different universes.

"Maybe I should wait out there." She pointed through the door to his living room.

"Is this room making you uncomfortable?" He paused in selecting bottles and jars from the shelves.

"Being inside Emerge Tech's walls is making me uncomfortable." Normally she wouldn't admit such a thing to anyone.

"Shouldn't it be the other way around?" he asked, setting his materials on a long table in the middle of the lab. "Living out in what's left of the city is tough. In here, it's easy. We have everything we need and most of what we want. It's clean. It's safe."

"It's not real."

He stopped in his work and stared at her. "It feels pretty real to me." He ran his hand along the table in front of him. "This table is real." He grabbed the bottle by his hand. "This bottle and its contents are real." He pointed his hands at himself then at her. "I'm real. You're real."

"But it's a lie, Doc. Outside Emerge Tech walls and its security field, the world is crumbling, brick by brick, body by body."

His dark eyebrows lowered. "Not if I can help it." His determination made her want to believe. Want to hope the world could be saved by this man.

He finished making the medicine and poured it into a bottle, sealing it with a dropper cap.

After cleaning his workspace, he skirted around the table to her position by the door, which she hadn't left. He took her right hand and pressed the bottle into her palm. His hand was warm and solid, and the contact tightened places deep within Darina's body.

Closing her fingers around the bottle, he said, "One drop of this a day and Zeke should be seizure free."

"No seizures at all? Really?" She met his gaze and was again struck by the color of his eyes. Such a strange light green. Had his genetically engineered cocktail made those eyes on purpose? Or had it been one of the many mistakes genetic engineering also made?

"Really." He led her out of the lab, commanding the lights off and locking the door behind them. "That should last you for a while. If you need more, you know where to find me. I can let the guards at the gates know you're allowed in."

"Thank you." *Why was he being so nice? Why wasn't he a rich bastard like the rest of them?* He couldn't be as perfect as he appeared. Something had to be wrong with him.

"Why were you cast off?" Her boldness was probably going to get her kicked out of his domicile, but she had to ask.

The sad smile on his lips made her chest ache, and she wanted to take the question back. He stepped into his kitchen and retrieved something by the sink. When he was back in front of her, he held out a bottle exactly like the one he'd given her for Zeke.

"You have seizures too?" No wonder he was so willing to help.

He shook his head. "I used to have them. I don't anymore and neither will Zeke." Worrying his bottom lip between his teeth, he asked, "He's a GEC too, isn't he?"

Something in his eyes made her nod once.

"Your secret is safe with me, Officer Lazitter. It takes a special brand of bravery—or stupidity—to take in a GEC." He offered her a slight smile that had her entire body buzzing. "Either way, I respect people like you who care for people like me. I wouldn't be here today if someone hadn't taken me in as you've taken in Zeke."

What made her think closing the distance between them and throwing her arms around him was a good idea she'd never know, but it happened before her logical brain could stop her. When his arms came around her back and he squeezed gently, she thought maybe it hadn't been a mistake at all.

They stood like that for a few moments before common sense kicked in and she released him. He held on for a second longer then dropped his arms.

"Thanks again," she whispered, her gaze tracing lines along the tattoo on his neck.

He motioned to the tattoo. "I'll tell you why I got this if you tell me about yours." He took her hand and traced the ring of black stars on her left forearm.

She closed her eyes as the pad of his index finger ran along the stars. She allowed herself to enjoy the caress for a moment. How long had it been since someone had touched her? Too long, and never with such tenderness. Her last official relationship had ended horribly, but what had she expected? Few good things existed in the world anymore.

Opening her eyes, she said, "Another time, Doc." She turned and opened his domicile door.

With a deafening roar they hadn't been able to hear inside, scorching orange flames reached out from the hallway and threatened to grab her.

Chapter Three

Foster grabbed Darina by the upper arms and yanked her back into his domicile, swinging the door shut.

"He's here," she said, patting out the smoking leg of her cargo pants.

"Probably not him personally. He's not that stupid. Unfortunately, Mikale Warres is brilliant."

"Yeah, but he lacks street smarts." Darina grinned, making him want to have her in his arms again. That embrace had been completely unexpected, but thoroughly welcomed. "We need to get you back to the outside if Warres's crew is inside."

"We?"

She faced him, her hazel eyes pinning him in place. "Look, I want a better world for Zeke. You've already helped with this medicine." She patted the pocket on her cargo pants. "If you can cure the world of the plague, you need to do that. You can't do that if you're dead."

She jogged across the living room and, with a deep inhale, peered out the windows. Craning her head up, she asked, "Are we on the top floor?"

"Yes. The roof is right above us."

"You have direct access to the roof then?" She walked back toward him.

"In my office." Foster led her to the room and opened the closet where a set of steps spiraled upward.

"Phone?"

He dug out his tablet, punched in the security code and opened his phone app. "Who are we calling?"

"Our ride. We need out of this building before that fire brings it down or Warres's men get to you."

"Emerge Tech has its own defense team." Foster held up his tablet. "I can just call them."

Darina shook her head. "I'm not sure we can trust Emerge Tech right now."

"They don't want me dead."

"The company doesn't, but perhaps an individual does."

Maybe she had a point. There were people who agreed with Warres's plans. Certainly some of those people could be within Emerge Tech's walls. It was unlikely, but this wasn't a time to play with the odds.

"Do we have time to wait for a ride?" He handed her the tablet, a little shocked he'd actually let another person touch the device. Normally, it was on his person at all times and he guarded it with his life.

Why do I feel so comfortable around her? It didn't make a bit of sense.

"The pilot I'm going to call doesn't exactly know how to drive slowly." She flexed her left hand, the ring of stars tattoo undulating on her skin.

"Can we trust him?" Hadn't she just told him to trust no one?

"He's one of two people I trust." Her thumbs hovered over the screen. "The question is, where will we go? Warres can get to you in the city or in here. He's proven that today." She frowned. "Why hasn't he come after you before?"

Foster puffed out a breath as he raked his hand through his hair. How much should he tell her? "Warres and I used to be very tight. I don't think he *wants* to kill me, but he knows I'm getting close to finding the cure. Letting me live is no longer an option for him." Sad to think his former best friend had put a mark on his head. At one point in their lives, their friendship was all they'd had. They'd kept each other going, challenged each other, reached new levels unthinkable in science.

Now the closest thing he'd had to a brother wished him dead.

An overhead sprinkler sprayed water down on them, and Foster scrunched up his shoulders against the artificial rain. Darina pulled him into the stairway where there were no sprinklers.

Wiping his face, Foster said, "I have a place we can go, but it's not local."

What am I doing? He never let anyone go where he was thinking. That place was for him and a small group of... friends. Officer Darina Lazitter was *not* a member of that small group.

And she wasn't exactly a friend.

She narrowed her eyes. "How 'not local'?"

"Vermont."

Muscles in her face tensed as she considered his reply. "It'll have to do."

"I can get myself there. You should leave. It's not safe to be around me." He didn't want to endanger her life. She had a boy depending on her, a boy whose life she'd changed with her care. If Darina was taken from Zeke because of him, Foster would never forgive himself.

She shook her head. "I haven't finished the job. You're not safe yet."

"Surely getting me here was good enough." Though he didn't want her to go. Not at all. Sharing his burden with someone lightened the load.

"I don't do 'good enough,' Dr. Ashby." She tapped on his tablet's screen then reached past him to close the closet door, sealing them in the stairwell and keeping out the dark smoke that had crept into his domicile.

"Call me Foster, please." No need for formalities if they were going to be spending more time together. *How much time?* And why did he want that?

"So we're friends now?" She rolled her eyes. "Is there anything in your domicile you absolutely need to complete your work?"

He gestured to the tablet still in her hand. "That's all I need."

"Light traveler. Excellent."

The tablet vibrated, and she looked down at it. "My buddy, Ghared, will meet us on the roof in five minut—"

A loud siren cut off her words. The sound banged around in Foster's head, making him wince. He spent so much time alone, sequestered in his lab, that his ears weren't used to such noise.

Darina, on the other hand, sat on one of the steps, looking totally unaffected. She grinned up at him. "This is nothing," she yelled. "You should hear Zeke snore after a seizure."

He actually laughed. His domicile would be consumed by flames any moment now. Warres's men were probably nearby, waiting for the building to crumble and confirm his death. His research could fall into the hands of the enemy, and the human population would be wiped out by the plague, but here he was in a stairwell, laughing with a police officer he'd only met hours ago.

What is happening?

He'd thought the world had gone mad after the Unplug and Mikale unleashing his disease, but clearly Foster had only, just now, lost his mind.

The siren stopped, and he checked his ears for blood while Darina waved his tablet at him.

"Here," she said. "I don't want to be responsible for this. I'll protect you, but *you* have to protect your research."

"Delegating. Smart." He shoved the tablet back into his pocket and prayed it'd be safe as he zipped it closed. "Were you a cop before?"

"Before the Anarch? Yeah."

"Did you join the search for them or the fighting?" He could easily picture her engaging the enemy head on, guns blazing.

She shook her head and got a faraway look in her eyes, then she met his gaze. "No. I would have." She flexed her left hand as she had before. "I was… injured at the time."

He waited for her to say more, but she didn't. Instead she glanced up the stairs. "Let's get to the roof."

She led the way and Foster stayed close behind her. At the door to the roof, Darina hesitated.

"Don't think about it," he said. "As far as your mind knows we're on ground level."

"Ground level, yes. No way we'd plummet to our deaths at ground level." She nodded and proceeded out the door. "Of course, we could die in an all-consuming fire instead."

"Not on my agenda for today." He nudged her toward the middle of the roof in hopes flames would not blow the door behind him clear off its hinges.

Darina took out her weapon and scanned the area, squinting up to the sky. "C'mon, Ghared. I don't like being out in the open like this."

Seconds after she'd uttered the words, a light droning grew in volume. Before Foster could ask a question, a hovercopter appeared out of nowhere and wobbled over the roof.

"Let's go." Darina's voice was full of authority, as if she did this sort of thing all the time.

Maybe she does. How would he know? He didn't know anything about her. Only that she was a cop—probably an amazing one. She had a son she saved from dismantlement and obviously cared about greatly. She didn't like rich bastards.

That last one bugged him. Yes, he was rich. Emerge Tech paid handsomely for the work he did. He had all the major comforts of the wealthy. As he'd told her though, he wasn't a bastard.

At least I try hard not to be.

Was it possible he didn't realize he was, in fact, a bastard? Had he been avoiding that categorization? Had he been too wrapped up in his work to see he was an asshole? Did being wrapped up in one's work make someone a bastard?

What does it matter?

Bastard. Not a bastard. The only thing that mattered right now was staying alive long enough to finish the cure. He was too damn close to fail.

Darina's hair whipped around as the hovercopter touched down on the roof. She ran for the aircraft and ripped open a door on the side. Turning back toward him, she waved him over.

Foster hadn't been aware of the distance between himself and Darina. He'd fallen behind in his bastard-not bastard internal debate. As he looked at the hovercopter, however, he groaned. The vehicle appeared to have been patched with parts from about twenty different machines, none of them matching or exactly fitting together with a perfect seal. It didn't look as if it could stay up in the air for very long.

And how had it gotten past Emerge Tech's walls and security field?

He was about to tell Darina he'd organize for other transport, but she'd already hopped into the hovercopter. She clearly had faith in its ability—and its pilot's ability—to get them the hell out of there, despite her fear of heights. She leaned forward to the cockpit where Foster now realized *two* people sat, not just the pilot. When her head popped back out, she waved him over again with a *hurry up* expression on her face.

And he wanted to hurry up. He really did. He wasn't imagining the growing heat beneath his feet. If he stayed any longer, he'd be toast.

But letting these people into my sanctuary?
He didn't like this.
He didn't like being dead more.

Foster sprinted toward the hovercopter. When he reached it, an explosion vibrated the building beneath him. He stumbled and fell to the roof a few yards from the waiting aircraft, banging his forehead when his arms didn't move fast enough to prevent the impact. As he attempted to get to his feet, the roof caved in to his right. He rolled to his left and gazed up at the sky clouded with smoke and ash. The sky inside Emerge Tech's walls never looked like that. The air purifiers made the sky an ever-present blue, intense and reminiscent of a summer Boston afternoon circa 2015.

The black plumes of smoke mesmerized him. He couldn't blink, couldn't move. A fleeting thought that this was the end made regrets rocket through Foster's mind.

Why hadn't he abandoned the city altogether and stayed in Vermont?

Why had he worked so hard and played so little?

Why hadn't he at least tried to find someone to love?

Too late. He was meat cooking on the rooftop now.

A tug on his arm made him angle his head toward the still-waiting hovercopter. Darina crouched by his head, her hair a wild storm around her face—her beautiful, concerned face.

"C'mon, Foster!" she shouted above the roaring in his ears.

His name sounded wonderful coming from her lips. He wouldn't mind hearing her say it again. Sitting up, he waited for the roof to stop spinning, but that didn't seem to be happening. He brought his hand up to where his forehead had hit the roof and his fingers came away bloody.

"Shit."

"A little flesh wound. You can zap heal it on the hovercopter," Darina said. "We're all going to have major flesh wounds if we don't get the hell out of here like now."

Foster rolled to his knees, trying desperately to clear his head with no success. He managed to stand and focused on the rickety hovercopter and what he could now see of the long-haired pilot.

A short beard surrounded the pilot's jaw, but a long slash ran through the scruff along his right cheek. No hair grew there, indicating it was probably the remnant of an unpleasant injury. He was solid and a bit more muscled than Foster. A sleeveless gray shirt that revealed a full sleeve tattoo on his right arm covered his torso. The ink appeared to start under the shirt somewhere and from what Foster could see, it looked like a barbed-wire design with... with... were those skeletons trying to free themselves from behind the wire?

Okay then.

The guy had a pair of headphones around his neck and his icy blue stare said, *I'll mess you up if given the chance.*

"Time to jet, Foster." Darina reached out her right hand and wiggled her fingers. "Do you trust me?"

Another explosion rattled the building beneath them as flames shot out of the ventilation system.

He didn't have the option not to trust her.

****

Why did Darina want Foster to take her hand so badly? She couldn't make sense of her need to keep this guy safe. Sure, she'd kept people safe for most of her police career, but something was different when it came to this doctor.

Maybe it had something to do with the medicine in her pocket—medicine that could significantly improve Zeke's life. Maybe it had something to do with the fact that Foster hadn't hesitated when she'd asked him about helping with the seizures. Maybe it had to do with Foster being a GEC like Zeke with the same affliction even.

Maybe it had to do with the way he'd looked at her when he'd traced the stars around her forearm in his domicile.

No time for this.

"Foster, c'mon. This roof isn't going to hold much longer." She took another step closer, wary of the gaping hole in the roof beside Foster. Heat and smoke poured from it as well as other places on the roof.

He reached forward and put his hand in hers. With a tug, she pulled him to his feet and they ran to the hovercopter.

She didn't let go of his hand. Not when she climbed into the craft. Not when he climbed in right behind her. Not when they settled in their seats. Not when she signaled to Ghared to get the hell off that roof.

The hovercopter ascended vertically, leaving Foster's building a flaming beacon below them. Banking around the neighboring buildings, the craft jetted toward Emerge Tech's walls.

Foster let go of her hand then to lean forward to Ghared. "Those walls have a security field above them."

"Yeah, no shit." Ghared shot him a sideways glance. "But I got in, didn't I?" He reached over and smacked the leg of his copilot—Zeke.

Darina had been surprised to see Zeke in the hovercopter, but Ghared told her he hadn't wanted to leave the kid behind so soon after a seizure. She immediately regretted calling her buddy for help, but he was the only one who could get them out of there in one piece.

She loved him for not leaving Zeke behind, even if the kid looked pale and groggy in his seat now. His dark mass of hair was sticking out at odd angles as if he'd been ripped out of a death-level slumber, which he no doubt had been. She fought the urge to pull Zeke into the back seat and into her lap, wanting nothing more than to comfort him.

Foster leaned back in his seat beside her. "Is our pilot's confidence warranted, or should I be concerned?" He touched the gash on his forehead and frowned at the blood dotting his fingertips. He unzipped his pocket and extracted his tablet.

"I wouldn't have called someone incompetent for help. I make a point of only associating with useful people," Darina said, watching Foster power up his tablet and attempt—unsuccessfully—to doctor the gash in his forehead.

She slid closer to him and held out her hand for the tablet. After he slid it into her hand, she focused on lining up the injury in the tablet's viewfinder. She absolutely did not notice how beautifully green his eyes were or how long his dark eyelashes were or how wonderfully that black stubble framed his tempting lips. She barely registered the artistic way his tattoo swirled up from his neck to his ear. Nope. Didn't see a thing.

Grumbling to herself, she scanned his wound and it sealed itself. She reached under the pilot's seat and grabbed a first aid kit, which no doubt was an antique to Foster. Rummaging around in it, she found a cleansing wipe and gave him one to wash the blood off his forehead.

As she stowed the first aid kit back under the pilot's seat, she said, "You'll live."

"Thanks." His voice also sounded as if he had tried—and failed—to not notice anything about her face as she'd tended to him.

Nodding, she peered out the front window of the hovercopter as Ghared approached the walls and security field. Her buddy's work-roughened hands tightened on the yoke as he rocketed them toward the place where the walls met at a ninety-degree angle.

"Number Two." He poked Zeke in the arm and the kid jolted in his seat. "You only agreed to come with me if I let you engage the field infrared camera. Quit napping. It's time."

Darina smiled in the backseat. Zeke was forever bugging Ghared about flying. Whether it was building crafts, operating them, or enhancing them, the kid wanted to know it all. She knew

Ghared let Zeke fly his crafts sometimes when he thought she wouldn't find out. Didn't he know she always found out? She didn't stop the boy's secret flight lessons though. Who knew when Zeke might need to know such skills? She wasn't going to get in the way of something that could potentially save his life or the lives of others.

Like right now.

Zeke lifted his head from where it had been resting against his seat. "Ready. Just tell me when." He yawned, his voice scratchy, and again a maternal wave crested over Darina.

"This is your son?" Foster craned his head a bit to get a better a look at Zeke.

Darina nodded.

"Give me the medicine." He held out his hand, looking at the bulge in her pocket where the bottle was tucked.

"What? Now?"

"It works immediately."

She dug into her pocket and handed the bottle over to Foster. He leaned to the front seats again as he unscrewed the top and drew some of the liquid medicine into the dropper attached to the cap.

"Take this," he said to Zeke.

Zeke's dark brown eyes flicked to Darina, an unspoken question in his expression. They talked like that often. No words, just tilts of eyebrows, slants of lips, twitches of muscles.

"It's okay," she said. "He's a doctor. That medicine will help."

"You told him about me?" A note of accusation laced Zeke's words.

"Only because I thought he could help you," Darina said.

"And she thought right." Foster reached the dropper full of medicine farther forward. "Take this, and you'll feel brand new."

"Nothing feels brand new anymore, pal." Ghared shook his head and glanced back at them. "Where the hell did you find this guy, Darina?"

"Ghared," she warned.

"Fine." He let out a few mumbles she couldn't hear, but whatever he'd said made Zeke laugh.

Foster still held the medicine dropper between the front seats. "Hey, it's up to you, kid. You can take it and feel awesome or not take it and feel as if you're stuck in quicksand."

At that Zeke snapped his head all around to look at Foster.

"I always tell Mom I feel as if I'm in quicksand after a seizure." He looked at Darina. "Did you tell him that too?"

"She didn't have to tell me," Foster said before she could answer. "I know."

Ghared glared back at Foster now, his icy blue eyes narrowing, and Darina wished Foster would shut up. Didn't he know to keep his personal information personal? She could almost hear the millions of questions popping into Ghared's head.

"Take it, Zeke." She took the dropper from Foster, grabbed Zeke by the jaw, and squirted a drop of the medicine into his mouth.

"Mom…" Zeke coughed and gave her one of those teenage looks—one that said he wasn't a baby and didn't wish to be treated like one.

"Sorry, but I want you to feel better so you can do what Ghared's asking you to do. We'd like to not get fried at the wall."

"That tasted horrible," Zeke said, sticking his tongue out.

"I didn't have time to add flavoring." Foster sat back, his shoulder pressing against Darina's, making heat creep over her body again.

"I think what my son means to say is 'Thank you, Dr. Ashby,' right, Zeke?" She shot the kid a pointed look.

Zeke had the good sense to look embarrassed by his lack of manners. He turned in his seat to see Foster better. "I'm sorry. Thank you, Dr. Ashby."

"Give that medicine a few seconds and you'll be out of that quicksand. Promise." Foster folded his arms across his chest and looked out the window.

Ghared continued on his path to the corner of the wall as Zeke readied the infrared camera. From where Darina sat, it looked as if they were heading for a crash with the security fields above the walls, but she knew better. She'd been flying with Ghared enough times to know he had many tricks up his sleeve... even if the shirt he wore right now had no sleeves.

"Now, Z," Ghared said.

A high-pitched whine filled the interior of the hovercopter. It didn't bother Darina, but Foster stiffened beside her. When she looked up at him, his jaw was clenched, his eyes closed. She warred with her hand, which thought sliding onto his thigh would be the right thing to do.

It was not.

She ended up clamping both of her hands on the back of Ghared's seat and applauded herself for remaining sensible.

Barely.

"Whoohoo!" Ghared roared as he spiraled the craft downward.

Foster's hands went to the back of Zeke's seat now, his entire body braced for whatever it was he expected to happen.

"Hey," Darina said, her traitorous right hand resting on his shoulder. "Are you okay?" She was the one who didn't like heights, yet Ghared's flying never made her nervous. She was completely safe in his care, even if he didn't always think so.

When Foster met her gaze, the depth of his green eyes drew her in, and she had this crazy desire to be alone with him.

"Yeah, I'm okay." He let out a sarcastic chuckle. "I just always imagined committing suicide in a less brutal way than flying, purposely, into a security field."

How many times had he imagined committing suicide? From the looks of his domicile, he lived the good life. What reason could he possibly have for wanting to end his existence?

"We're not going to die today." She squeezed his shoulder and reluctantly let her hand fall away.

A double whoop from the front seats made both Darina and Foster look out the cockpit window. Darina had to admit it did look as if they were headed for direct impact with the field, but doubting Ghared or Zeke would be a waste of time.

Together they would get them past Emerge Tech's walls and security field unscathed.

After that, she didn't know what was going to happen.

Darina didn't love that uncertainty. She'd kept herself and Zeke—and to some extent, Ghared—alive by always having a plan and plotting her next moves. Now the only thing she knew for certain was she had to keep Foster from falling into Warres's hands.

Because no one should be in Warres's hands.

"Got it!" Zeke reported a series of numbers.

"Roger that, kid." Ghared tipped the hovercopter on its side, and Foster slid in his seat to spill over to Darina's side.

She was about to tell the doctor to stay on his own side, but Ghared flipped the hovercopter back to horizontal, and suddenly they were on the outside of Emerge Tech's walls, beyond the security field, flying over the gray and broken streets of Boston.

"Up high, Z!" Ghared held his right hand out to Zeke and they slapped hands in celebration.

"What just happened?" Foster asked. "I may have closed my eyes. Are we dead?"

Zeke turned around in his seat, his skin a healthy shade of caramel, his dark eyes wide and alert. "Total opposite of dead, man." He looked at Darina. "He was right, Mom. I feel great!"

Her heart swelled to quadruple its normal size at the sight of Zeke's smile. He was more alive than she'd ever seen him.

Foster, on the other hand, looked a tad green.

"We made it," she said softly, touching his shoulder again. She had to stop touching him. "We're on the outside."

He peered out the window at his right, down at the ruins of the city below them. Raking a hand through his hair, he said, "How did he do it?"

Darina knew how he did it. The security field that extended from the top of Emerge Tech's walls was a giant dome of invisible panels. Each panel had its own coding. Ghared used his tech geek skills to hack the code, but it could be tricky to find which panel had shut down. The infrared camera could locate the dead panel. Unfortunately only one panel could be shut down at a time, and flying through it involved some crafty maneuvering.

Nothing Ghared can't handle.

"Can't give away my secrets," Ghared said from the pilot's seat. "Just know that I have many talents." He glanced back at Foster. "And trust me, you don't want to know about most of them."

"Where are we going?" Zeke asked, saving Darina from having to say anything about the possessive and protective vibes coming off Ghared in tsunami-style waves.

She raised her eyebrows at Foster. "What do you say, Doc? Where are we headed?"

Foster's shoulders rose then fell as he inhaled deeply. He appeared to be mentally reviewing his options, which she knew were few. He had to stay away from Emerge Tech and the city streets. Warres had found him in both settings. He also needed a quiet, remote place to continue his research and find that damn cure.

"Can this poor excuse for a hovercopter make it all the way to Vermont?" he asked.

"Hold it right there, asshole," Ghared said. "Insult my bird again and you're getting ejected."

"No one's getting ejected," Darina said, "but I do advise against insulting our phenomenal pilot."

"Have I told you I love you?" Ghared asked, reaching his hand back to squeeze Darina's knee.

"Not today," Darina shot back, noting how closely Foster watched the interaction. She and Ghared said I love you all the time, and they did love each other, like siblings. In the aftermath they'd been left in, they'd built a screwy little family. One cop, one jack-of-all-trades tech geek soldier, one teenage GEC. They took care of each other and had survived this long. They had to be doing something right.

But Foster probably didn't think they were doing anything right. His lifestyle couldn't have been more different than theirs.

"I can continue my research into the cure at my Vermont property," Foster said.

"Vermont it is then," Darina said. "Make sure we're not followed, Ghared."

"That sounds like a green light to drive aggressively." Ghared wiggled his eyebrows at Zeke.

Foster's hands went white-knuckled on the back of Zeke's seat. "Something tells me I should have taken my chances back there in that burning building."

Darina shook her head. "No, that was certain death." She gestured to the pieced together hovercopter holding them. "Flying in this to Vermont for hours out in the open has only a half certain death rating."

Foster looked a little freaked, but the left side of his mouth turned up in a slight grin—a grin Darina wouldn't mind seeing again.

Chapter Four

Mikale paced in his office. Sometimes that space felt like a kingdom. Roomy, inspiring, productive. Today was not one of those times. Today it felt as if the walls were closing in on him. He'd traversed the perimeter of the room about twenty times and still none of his associates were calling in. How hard was it to take down one man?

Foster is good, but not that good. The man knew science, not evasive maneuvers. He had no tactical skills. He wasn't a fighter.

Mikale had searched the streets leading to Emerge Tech, but found no traces of Foster, so he'd returned to his headquarters, not willing to risk going beyond the walls himself.

His tablet buzzed on his desk. *Finally.*

He tapped the earpiece wedged in his ear. "Give me good news."

"What if I don't have any?" Dugan, one of his trusted associates, asked.

"Goddammit, Dugan." He peered out the window of his office. They'd been operating out of an abandoned warehouse outside Boston for months now. The exterior of the building looked as decrepit as its neighbors, but inside had been totally remodeled. The space was filled with state-of-the-art equipment most people wouldn't dream of getting their hands on, but Mikale had his connections… and his money.

"I don't know what happened to him," Dugan said.

"The camera footage you shared clearly shows his burning domicile building and its collapse. If he was actually inside—and we don't know that for sure—how could he have gotten out?"

"He had help, sir."

"Help? From whom?" As far as he knew, Ashby worked alone. He reported to Emerge Tech and had colleagues, but he never worked with partners—not since they'd been partners.

"Check your tablet."

Mikale walked to his desk and sat at the high-backed chair. He tapped the screen of his tablet and watched as pixels arranged themselves into the face of a woman. A breathtaking woman with unusual hazel eyes and auburn hair that framed her face. Her skin was a lovely caramel shade. She had a fierce look on her face, but he couldn't help noticing how full her lips were.

With lips like those…

His body tightened in spots he'd neglected since unleashing his deadly plague. Taking down the human population required all of his attention. He'd forgotten the simple pleasures. This woman made him remember pleasures… not all of them simple.

"Who is she?" he asked, though something about her looked familiar. Something in the eyes.

"Sending info now, sir."

A data file came up on the tablet. He scanned it, reading aloud. "Officer Darina Lazitter,

Boston Police Department. He's hooked up with a cop?"

"Think she's playing the role of bodyguard. One of our guys obtained footage of her and Ashby at Emerge Tech's gates earlier today. Maybe she was hired by the company," Dugan said. "Some of our people reported a hovercopter taking off from the roof of Ashby's building before it crumbled."

"And where is that copter now?"

"That's the thing, sir. We had sight of it heading to the security field, then it was gone."

"Gone? It can't be gone, Dugan. Hovercopters don't just disappear. Certainly not one a simple cop has access to. And I don't think Emerge Tech would have access to cloaked crafts."

Mikale thought about his collection of vehicles in the garage adjacent to their warehouse base. He loved anything that rolled on the ground, flew through the air, or swam through the water. He knew how to drive them all too. If he didn't have invisible vehicles, no one else did.

"I don't know. The copter was there one moment, then poof. The next moment it was nowhere. Maybe they flew into the security field and got fried."

Mikale shook his head though Dugan couldn't see him. "No. Even if the cop didn't know about the security field, Ashby would. He's lived within Emerge Techs walls long enough to know it's protected by more than the physical walls."

"Maybe the cop knew another way in and out. We have our ways so the cops probably have theirs."

That was possible, but in a hovercopter? Mikale got his team in and out on the ground. Having worked inside Emerge Tech's walls, he knew how it ran and what its weaknesses were. It also helped that one of his projects as an Emerge Tech employee had been working on those walls. All Mikale had to do was memorize the code for one of the panels and it was as if he had his own key.

As Dugan had said, though, that was an on-the-ground way in. Less liable to be spotted on the ground than taking an airborne route. It would also take some pretty sophisticated flying to get through a single dead panel in the security field above the walls, assuming someone else had been able to hack the code.

"So we have no idea where Ashby and his bodyguard are?" Mikale clenched his teeth.

"Not at this time, sir, but we're optimistic."

"Glad someone is."

"We'll find them."

"If you don't..." He let that thought go unfinished, knowing Dugan could fill in the blank for himself.

Mikale ended the call and removed his earpiece, tossing it to the desktop in disgust. Rubbing his forehead, he tapped his tablet and opened a picture of his mother. Laurette Warres had been a formidable woman, raising Mikale on her own. When she'd fallen ill, all his brilliance did him no good in trying to save her. He regretted what he'd had to do instead.

He could build impressive prosthetic limbs with Ashby, but stopping his mother's body from withering away was beyond his grasp. She'd given him everything, and he couldn't give her a simple thing like life.

Doesn't seem fair.

He was working on justice though. Justice for her death. Justice for getting kicked out of Emerge Tech. Justice for Ashby's attempt to stop his plague from doing what it was designed to do. The planet needed a cleansing and who was Ashby to stop that?

Mikale stood and looked out the window again. "You can't hide forever, Foster."

****

The hovercopter hummed along as Foster's thoughts bounced around his skull. Over the last few hours, he'd done about a thousand things wrong. He'd almost gotten caught on the city streets by Mikale's associates while obtaining samples from bodies afflicted with the disease. He'd divulged his secret of being a GEC to someone he'd just met. He'd mixed medicine and administered it to a patient he hadn't checked physically or given an official diagnosis. He let two other strangers in on his GEC secret. He'd agreed to let his new acquaintances into his Vermont sanctuary. He was about to put the lives of the others who lived in Vermont in danger.

And he couldn't forget his growing attraction to his bodyguard. An attraction he should be pushing right out of his mind. Immediately.

He glanced at Darina without moving his head, hoping to be discrete. She was looking out the side window of the hovercopter, her right knee pushed into the back of the pilot's seat so her leg dangled. Her right boot wiggled.

Is she as nervous as I am?

Probably not. Officer Darina Lazitter didn't strike him as the type to get nervous over anything.

Except her son.

Foster regarded the back of Zeke's head. What had prompted Darina to take in a GEC? Especially one who had seizures. He knew firsthand how difficult it was to live with someone with that condition, never mind keep a GEC hidden. Foster had been genetically engineered at six years old. He'd escaped from the company that had created him and survived on the streets for two years, alone until the woman he considered his mother, Carielle Ashby, had taken him in.

He'd just had a violent seizure and was sleeping under a highway overpass when Carielle drove by in her land cruiser. The first image he had upon waking was of massive spiked tires.

"You look like shit, kid," she'd said when she hopped down from the driver's seat.

He hadn't said anything. He'd learned a while back that the less he talked to people the safer he was. As tough as life on the streets had been, the alternative—getting hacked to pieces by the company that made him—was far less attractive.

"You hungry?" she'd asked.

Of course he was. Ravenous.

She'd held out her hand. "The streets are no place for a kid, even one like you. I can give you food and shelter and a place to grow up to be something, but you have to work at it. I don't give something for nothing, got it?"

For some reason, Foster had taken her hand and let her pull him to his feet. He was still dizzy from his seizure so he stumbled into her. She caught him easily and held him for a moment. It had been the first hug he'd ever received.

It wasn't the last.

Carielle had stuck to her word. She'd cared for him along with several other GECs, kept their secrets, and made sure they all got proper schooling. When she'd gone off to fight after the world went black, Foster had an unshakable feeling she wouldn't be coming back. She'd been the type to give her all for the cause.

When he and the other GECs who had come to know her as their mother learned of her death, he'd felt both sadness and pride. She'd made a difference in his life and in the world. He'd never forget her.

That was why he'd built his Vermont sanctuary—the sanctuary he was about to expose to people he wasn't entirely sure he should trust yet.

Send me a sign, Mom. Not that he believed in signs. Signs weren't scientific.

"Relax." Darina's voice made Foster jump.

He angled to face her, willing himself to at least appear relaxed. "What makes you think I'm not relaxed?"

She laughed, her face turning into something truly artistic. "Instinct makes me think you're not relaxed, Doc." She slid her right leg down and turned to lean against the hovercopter's door so she faced him. "I can *say* you can trust us," she waved her right hand out to encompass herself,

Ghared, and Zeke, "but you're not going to trust us until we *show* you why you can."

"You kept Mikale's men from grabbing me. You got me out of a burning building and out of Emerge Tech," Foster said. "You've probably already shown me."

She shrugged one shoulder. "Sometimes people take a little more convincing."

"Well, I believed you were motivated to protect me because Emerge Tech was giving you a hefty paycheck to do so." He looked out the window for a moment then turned back to her. "But now... who knows what is going on back there? Mikale might decide to demolish Emerge Tech altogether. He has his reasons for wanting the company to go down in a fiery blaze."

"I read somewhere they fired him for stealing. Is that true?"

"Yes, but he was in a situation. His mother was ill, and Emerge Tech wouldn't let Mikale bring her inside their walls so he could care for her. He stole supplies to take to her. When he got caught, he was fired immediately."

"What's the status of his mother?"

"I heard she was dead."

"You and Warres were partners at Emerge Tech?"

Why did he suddenly feel as if he were in an official interrogation?

"Yes."

"And after he got fired..."

"We didn't speak anymore."

"Some friend." She gave him a disgusted look.

"Maybe there's more to it than you think, Officer Judgmental."

Her lips turned up, and he forgot to be pissed at her assumptions. "We have some time to kill. Tell me the story."

Foster settled into his seat and raked his hand through his hair. He needed a shower and a drink. Maybe the drink should come first. He traced the outline of his tablet in his pocket and waffled over the right way to begin the tale.

"Mikale got fired. Emerge Tech has a policy that as soon as you are no longer an employee, you must leave the premises immediately. They actually have security escort you out. A team boxes up your personal shit and sends it to you. You can't have any interaction with any colleagues, friends, no one as you leave.

"I watched Mikale walk by our lab. I stepped out and called his name, but the security guards shook their heads and kept walking, ushering him along. Mikale looked back once, and I figured that was his way of telling me we'd catch up later."

Foster cleared his throat, the memory of his best friend and partner being shoved out like a criminal upsetting him all over again. True, he shouldn't have been stealing supplies, but times were tough and his mother was seriously ill. The company could have been more sympathetic, especially considering the excellent work Mikale Warres had done for them.

"After I finished working for the day," Foster continued, "my plan was to head over to Mikale's domicile which was right next to mine. I wasn't thinking he'd be kicked out of there too. Only Emerge Tech employees get to live inside the walls.

"At the last minute, I got pulled into an emergency meeting regarding the blackout. We were working on getting power back to the rest of the globe and were close to figuring it out—Mikale and I in particular." He looked at Darina here. "I'm not bragging."

"I didn't say you were." She motioned for him to continue.

"The meeting lasted hours, and by the time I got to my domicile, Mikale's was totally empty. I mean, cleaned out. No trace that he'd ever lived there." Foster felt as if he were reliving that terrible day all over again as he told the story. Not his favorite day. "When I got to my domicile, a handwritten note was stuck to the door."

"What did it say?" Darina leaned closer, either to hear him better or because she was interested in the story. Her eyes were so focused on him he felt a little like a specimen under a high-powered microscope.

"It said, *Find me.*"

"But you didn't find him?" Her voice had a note of accusation in it. She didn't know. She wasn't there.

"No, I didn't. I couldn't."

"Why? Didn't you know where to find him? If you guys were such buddies, wouldn't you know where to look for him on the outside?"

"Am I on trial or something here, Officer Lazitter?" He folded his arms across his chest.

A slow grin curved her lips, and any hope he had of getting angry with her sifted into the seat beneath him. How many men had she reduced to mere ash with those lips?

"Not on trial." She shifted in her seat, threw a glance to Zeke in the front, then focused back on him. "I'm just trying to understand what went down."

"Trying to decide whether I'm worth protecting or not."

She gave a little shrug. "Maybe."

He supposed that was fair. "I did know where to look for him, but Emerge Tech wouldn't let me go. They gave me two choices. Look for Mikale and suffer his same fate or don't look for him and continue to work on solving the biggest problem the globe had ever faced. Would you have chosen differently than I did?"

Darina shook her head. "The world needed you more than Warres did."

"That's what I thought. Originally." He rubbed his forehead. "But if I'd gone looking for him, maybe he wouldn't have unleashed his disease while the globe was trying to get back on track from the Anarch assault. Maybe I could have reasoned with him. Maybe I could have gotten him back into Emerge Tech to work on getting everything back online again."

"Maybe, maybe, maybe," Darina said. "Can't play the What If game, Doc. If we do that, we'll have to go all the way back to what if the cops had caught the Anarch before they unplugged us all." She blew out a breath and drummed her fingers on her knee.

"Wait a minute." Foster leaned toward her now, the small space between their seats growing smaller. "The cops knew about the Anarch?"

"They had tried to shut the world down more than once, but they were a tricky bunch to track down. Amazingly we were only able to find them after they zapped all our tech."

"Old-fashioned methods sometimes work the best."

"Simplicity is often the most valuable tool."

"If you two are done trading philosophical quotes," Ghared interrupted, "I believe we've just crossed the Vermont border. Now what, Ashby?"

Foster peered out his window at the treetops below. While Boston and most cities had fried with the blackout, the fighting, and Mikale's plague, the woods of Vermont had remained miraculously immune. Most of the people who lived in Vermont had moved to the woods to get away from the bustle of crowded city life. They lived simply off the land and didn't give a shit about the latest technology. With acres and acres of land—mostly filled with trees—between properties, the plague hadn't spread as quickly either.

Vermont was the perfect safe haven.

And I'm bringing these three into it. Foster hoped he wasn't making a colossal mistake.

****

Darina couldn't remember the last time she'd seen so much green in one place. Probably not since she was a little girl and her parents owned a cottage in Maine on a gorgeous lake. They'd spent summers there. She, Deo, and Dixon were wild children, running free—and often barefoot—

through the grass, playing hide-and-seek in the woods, swimming like fish in the refreshing waters of the lake.

That seems so long ago.

She felt as if she'd lived a hundred lifetimes since those carefree days when she had her whole family together and survival wasn't her main goal. Back then, she and her brothers had been invincible. Now every day brought more challenges to her existence such as what they were going to eat next, staying plague-free, catching the next person to go crazy on the streets, protecting genius doctors from people that wanted to kill them. Deo and Dixon had been cheated out of their futures too. Shit, she missed them.

Zeke turned around and gave her a smile.

At least I have him. And Ghared. She had people. She wasn't totally alone. Sometimes, however, when she stared at the cracked ceiling in her tiny bedroom at night, she felt alone and burdened.

And furious.

She hated what her life had become. She hated that Zeke had to live in the world that now existed. She hated that she didn't have time to do anything else but hunt down bad guys or, as in the case right now, protect what appeared to be the good guy. She hated that there wasn't anything else to do anyway. She hated that everything had depended so heavily on technology that one flick of the proverbial switch had upended the entire globe. She hated that people were dying because some crazy chemist had a warped mission of cleansing and restarting the human population.

She hated that sometimes she thought his mission wasn't a bad idea.

"Can you get us lower?" Foster asked, leaning toward Ghared. "I'll be able to pick out my property if we're a little closer to the ground."

She looked out the window again. Every once and a while, a break in the treetops indicated cleared land. Off to the east, mountains pointed up at the hovercopter, and Darina had an urge to climb to the top of one and scream her lungs out. Maybe then she'd be rid of the perpetual frustration swirling inside her.

"Descending," Ghared said. "Zeke, what do you have on radar? Anyone following us?"

Darina smiled. Though Ghared wasn't a cop, he thought like one. Actually, he thought like a soldier—and a tech geek—and that was even better sometimes. She was glad to have him as backup on this assignment that had become much more than an easy paycheck.

She probably should have let Emerge Tech take care of its own people. The huge company had been under fire for erecting its walls and seemingly shutting out the outside world, but Darina knew its employees were working on solutions. They couldn't do that if the plague reached them. They couldn't do that if they didn't have labs to work in. They couldn't do that on broken down city streets. She was probably one of the few people who got it. That didn't mean she liked it. The idea of rich bastards and bitches living the high life while she and the rest of the regular folk lived like homeless wretches didn't sit well in her stomach.

But if they can bring change for the better…

If they could do that, they'd be an answer to a prayer.

"No one is following us," Zeke reported, a note of confidence in his voice. Flying with Ghared always made him happy. The kid was good at it too.

"There." Foster shot his arm into the front between Ghared and Zeke's seats. "To the northwest. See that open patch and the lake?"

"Got it. Can I land in the open patch?" Ghared asked.

"Yes."

Darina pushed closer to her window. She squinted at parallel lines etched into multiple fields adjacent to the open patch. "Are those... are those rows of crops?" She turned back to Foster to see him smiling.

He waved his hands, wiggling his fingers. "Be prepared to be shocked and amazed, Officer Lazitter."

I'm already aroused. Why shouldn't she add shocked and amazed to the list? What other long forgotten emotions could Dr. Foster Ashby bring to the surface in her?

Ghared lowered the hovercopter in the open patch and guided Zeke through post-flight checks while Darina climbed out from the back. Foster met her on her side of the craft as he stuffed his tablet into his pocket and zipped it closed.

Grabbing her arm, he stopped her from taking a step toward the fields. "I think we need a little group meeting before I let you all loose here."

"You make it sound as if we're animals."

Foster shook his head. "Not animals, just the unknown. I'm not the only one who lives here." He rubbed a hand down his face. "In fact, out of everyone, I live here the least." He looked past her and a dreamy expression washed over his face. "I hope to change that one day."

Ghared and Zeke joined them, and Foster addressed them all.

"This property is sanctuary for me... and some others." He looked at Zeke and gestured between the two of them. "Others like us."

"GECs?" Zeke eyes brightened as he looked around. "Where are they? How many?"

"Fourteen." Foster glanced at Darina, waiting for her to... waiting for her to what? Tell him he was crazy for harboring fourteen GECs? Who was she to say a damn thing? She harbored one, but if she found more, she'd take them in too.

Besides, he had them hidden away where no one would look for them. He was playing the game way better than she was.

"How long have you had them?" Ghared asked.

"Different lengths of time, but all of them have been here for at least five years." Foster stepped ahead of them. "And I've never had guests like you. I just got off the phone with one of them, letting her know we were on our way, but that doesn't mean you're going to get a warm welcome." He scratched at his slight beard. "I'm not sure *I'm* going to get a warm welcome."

Releasing a breath, he walked toward a stone path and as soon as Darina could tear her gaze away from the way his cargo pants showcased his toned ass, she looked at Ghared and Zeke.

"What have we gotten involved in?" Ghared asked, waves of protectiveness coming off him.

"I don't know." Darina reached for Zeke's hand. "But you feel better, right?"

"I feel fantastic. Whatever he gave me totally lifted the fog." He pretended to search her pockets until she slapped his hands away. "Tell me there's more of it."

"There is." She arrowed her thumb to Foster, still walking. "He's got it. I handed it back to him after administering some to you in the hovercopter."

"Then we're going wherever he is." Zeke jogged past Darina and Ghared, his long legs allowing him to catch up to Foster easily.

Darina watched Foster clap Zeke on the back when he noticed the kid next to him.

"Are we being stupid?" Ghared asked.

"When have we ever been stupid?"

"This is true." Ghared elbowed her. "C'mon."

She stopped him and tugged him around to face her. "Thanks for coming to get us."

"You know I'll always come when you call, Darina. We always have each other's backs." He leaned back and checked out her ass. "And may I reiterate that your back is really something?"

Now it was her turn to elbow him. "Sometimes I think all that flying you do has turned your brain to mush."

He stuck his finger in his left ear, pulled it out, and inspected it. "Nothing leaking out yet."

With a gruff chuckle that crinkled up the scar on his cheek, he jogged ahead as Zeke had, and now Darina watched all three of them as Foster pushed open a wooden gate. Curious as to what waited beyond that gate, she sprinted up the path, arriving just as Zeke and Ghared passed through.

Foster held open the gate and motioned for her to go first. "Rich bastard or gentleman?" he asked so only she could hear.

"Haven't decided yet."

"Let me know when you come to a conclusion." He followed her and closed the gate behind him. After unzipping his pocket, he extracted his tablet. "Wait here, please." Stepping away from them, he tapped the screen of his tablet and put it to his ear.

Darina couldn't hear what he was saying, but imagined he was telling someone to clean up all evidence of illegal activity. She nearly laughed aloud at that. *Ridiculous.* Foster Ashby was as clean as they came.

At least she hoped he was.

Chapter Five

Foster led Darina, Ghared, and Zeke to the main house. He'd called Estoria, the first GEC he'd offered sanctuary to, and told her to gather the others in the great room. Best to do the introductions all at once. Better to outnumber the outsiders upfront. He wanted to trust them wholeheartedly, but that would be pretty stupid. He and the others had gone undetected as GECs all this time by not being stupid.

And then I go and tell three outsiders I'm a GEC. Nice going. What had caused the false sense of trustworthiness when it came to Darina? Was it false? Was he picking up on... on *something?*

Hell, he hated having doubts. He hated putting his fellow GECs at risk. He hated being out of the lab. He hated how his gaze kept roaming to Darina as she silently followed him, taking in her surroundings. Cop instincts most likely. She was probably looking for the quickest way to leave should the need arise.

Why did that thought bug him? He didn't want her to want to leave.

Shaking his head, he led them up the half-log front steps, pausing when Ghared crouched to inspect the stairs more closely.

"Did you make these?" he asked, squinting one eye at Foster and looking like a 17th century pirate with his long hair, scruffy beard, and scarred cheek.

"Some of them," Foster said, noting how Darina's eyebrows rose over her beautiful eyes. "Then I showed others how to make them. People, even GECs, like to have a purpose."

"Can you show me how to woodwork?" Zeke asked. "There's no wood in the city to make stuff. I'm sure I can trade one of my skills for a lesson."

"Oh yeah?" Foster said. "What skills do you have? Aside from copiloting hovercopters, that is." He gave the kid a smile and was rewarded with a megawatt one in return.

Ghared slung his arm around Zeke's shoulders. "This guy here? There's nothing this guy can't do." He gave Zeke a little playful shove to which the boy responded with an equal shove. They pretended to scuffle with each other until Ghared got Zeke in a light headlock and messed the boy's dark hair.

Something unwrapped in Foster's chest at the familiar way Ghared and Zeke interacted. While Carielle had shown him unconditional love, a strong bond with a male role model had not been part of Foster's early years. Sure, he'd learned guy stuff along the way on his own—he had an aptitude for learning after all—but to have had a living, breathing, experienced male show him the ropes? Well, that would have been fantastic. He tried to be that for some of the younger male GECs on the Vermont property, but *being* the role model wasn't the same as *having* one.

"If you really want to learn, I'd be happy to show you," Foster said.

"He really wants to learn," Darina and Ghared said at the same time. A look passed between them—one also born out of familiarity.

What's the deal with them?

Darina was clearly a gorgeous, intelligent woman. Ghared appeared to be a healthy male. A healthy, tall male whom Foster was sure would get some looks once introduced to the others. The guy had a ruffled, ex-military look, and he knew what he was doing in a hovercopter. He was different, and the others hadn't had a great deal of different in their sheltered lives in Vermont.

Had Darina sampled that different?

He shouldn't care. None of his business. In fact, now that he'd arrived safely in Vermont, Darina, Ghared, and Zeke didn't have to stay. They hadn't been followed. He'd be fine here.

He kept those thoughts to himself.

"Foster?"

Turning around, he found Estoria at the front door, a nervous look on her face. *Shit.* He didn't want anyone to be anxious.

"Estoria." He gave her a wide grin, and her expression relaxed as she smiled back. "I've brought some visitors."

"I can see that." She peered past him, her eyes wary again. "What are you doing?"

"We're not going to hurt you," Darina said, causing Estoria to jump at the sound of her voice.

"Foster said you're a cop?"

Darina nodded from her position on the stairs. She seemed to understand that any sudden moves might spook Estoria. "I am. That's my son, Zeke, and that's Ghared."

"He a cop too?" Estoria jutted her chin out to Ghared.

"No," Ghared answered, his voice gentled. "Retired soldier. Though the serve and protect mission still applies." He winked at her, and Estoria's tensed shoulders lowered slightly.

"Did you get the others together?" Foster asked, stepping to the door and opening it. He motioned for Darina, Ghared, and Zeke to follow him.

All three of them moved together, slowly, carefully. He liked how much they were respecting the fact that Estoria was not yet comfortable with their presence. He didn't blame her for feeling that way. He hadn't given them many opportunities to interact with outsiders, but it was safer that way.

Some GECs like himself and apparently Zeke could hide among regular people. They looked like everyone else—except when in the throes of a seizure. Fortunately, medicine could hide that too.

But some GECs had visible and... unique traits. He always hated the word *imperfections*. In about ten seconds though, his visitors would see what had gotten Estoria cast off after her engineering.

Though they wouldn't understand at first.

Estoria backed up to let them all in. With pursed lips, she flicked another wary glance at their guests then looked back at Foster. "Almost everyone's in the great room."

"Good." He turned back to Darina. "This way."

But Darina was already studying Estoria. "How far along are you?" she asked.

Estoria patted the mound at her belly, a protective motion. "A week shy of nine months."

"So you could give birth at any moment." Was that longing in Darina's eyes? She blinked, and whatever Foster thought he'd seen was gone. "Congratulations."

"Condolences is more like it." Estoria shut the door behind them and took a different route to the great room.

Darina looked at Foster. "What's that about?"

"She's been nine months pregnant once every year since she hit puberty."

With a quick glance toward Zeke who had walked farther into the house, Darina lowered her voice. "I thought GECs were infertile."

"They are. Estoria got cast off because she's not and because she doesn't need a male to become fertilized."

"Well, that's handy."

"Not when every single one of the babies is stillborn after nine months of her carrying them."

Darina's mouth dropped open a little. "How awful."

Foster nodded. "I tried to help her, but she immediately became pregnant again. Her body insists on going through the cycle once every year no matter what." He scratched his whiskered jaw. "I want to work on her situation more, find a solution, but—"

"The world keeps needing you to work on something else," Darina finished.

"Yeah."

"Must get annoying."

"Slightly."

Darina looked to where Estoria had disappeared. "Should I apologize to her?"

"You didn't do anything wrong. How could you have known what her situation was?"

She shrugged one shoulder. "I still feel like an ass."

"No need. I'll smooth things over with her. She's been here the longest and is probably pretty angry with me for bringing you all here."

Stepping closer so Foster couldn't inhale without catching a teasing whiff of her, she said, "Why did you let us in? I could protect you in any number of neutral places. Bringing us here makes it…" She looked up to the ceiling and chewed on her full bottom lip as she thought.

"Personal?"

"Very."

"This is the only place I could think of that would allow me to continue my work. I have everything I need here. I have to find the cure. Soon."

She glanced down the hallway to where Zeke and Ghared had wandered. "How does this place even exist?"

"Do you remember reading about how the entire nation used to be like this? Simple. Self-sustaining. Natural. Do you?"

"Yes. It never seemed real to me, but we had a lake house and I got a taste of it, of this way of living." She pointed out the hall window where a few GECs were finishing up in the closest garden and heading toward the house. "I just didn't think places like this could still be found."

"The government wants you to think that."

She let out a short laugh. "I wouldn't be surprised if that were the truth. I always suspect the government is up to something. If I hadn't seen the effects of Warres's plague in person, I'd think that was something the government invented as well."

"Unfortunately, there's nothing fictional about what Mikale has done."

"Then we'd better get on with things." She brushed past him to join Ghared and Zeke.

Foster took a moment to figure out what he was going to say to his... his *people*. They trusted him to look out for them. If they didn't live in Vermont, they'd be out on the streets just as he had been as a young boy. Maybe someone would have taken them in, but that didn't happen often.

Most of the time, runaway GECs got caught and that never ended well.

Foster rubbed his right thigh, remembering when he'd been caught at age twenty. He'd gone so many years without being found, and then one night, he was crossing the college campus to get to his next class, so caught up in the notes he was still studying for an exam, he hadn't heard their approach in the darkness. About thirty yards from the door to the building, he'd been slammed to the ground; his tablet of notes fell from his hands and skidded along the pavement like a skipped stone.

The black night had gotten suddenly blacker. The way his head had hit the ground had caused an awful ringing in his ears. Loud and constant, the noise had paralyzed him somehow. He couldn't move. He couldn't fight back.

Then another sound took control—the buzz of a reciprocating saw.

To this day, loud noises hurt his ears and gave him phantom pain in his thigh where his leg had been severed from his body.

"Foster?" Darina's voice pulled him from his past.

Shaking his head, he pushed the memory aside. Now wasn't the time to think about old wounds. Instead it was time to allay the fears of his comrades then bury himself in his lab.

That cure wasn't going to find itself.

****

The house itself was a marvel. All natural woods, stone accents, and rustic charm, Foster's *home*—for this was much more than a city domicile—made her feel as if she'd stepped into the pages of a history book on early America. The artwork hanging on the walls of the hallway belonged in a museum, and she stopped to take a closer look at one. A red barn sat in a field gone yellow after the harvest. The sky was a shade of blue that no longer occurred in the city and puffy white clouds cast shadows in the field. Trees with gold, red, and orange leaves rose tall behind the barn like an autumn embrace. Darina wished she could climb into the painting.

"Estoria painted that." Suddenly Foster was standing right behind her, his breath pushing wisps of her hair forward. The urge to lean back into him disturbed her.

I don't lean on anyone.

People leaned on her. That was the way it had to be.

Or is it?

She shook her head. It had to be. The world they lived in wasn't made for happily ever afters where people gave and took in equal measures. Stupid to think for a moment such a life was possible. Not now anyway. Maybe someday.

"She's got a real talent." Darina motioned to the painting.

"That barn is on the property," Foster said, not taking a step back, not giving Darina the space she required. "It looks totally different in the summer. I'll show you later."

Would that tour be a private one? Did Darina want it to be?

Not going to answer that.

Too risky. She turned to face Foster and exhaled the breath she'd been holding when he took a step back and motioned to the room where Zeke and Ghared already stood at the threshold.

"Should we wait out here?" She indicated the hallway.

Foster shook his head. "Best to hit them fast and get it over with." He offered her a smile that sent a warm buzz through her body.

She made a note to ignore that warm buzz. Warm buzzes were distracting, and she was technically still working on keeping Foster safe.

"C'mon." He put his hand on the small of her back and edged her into the room. The touch was light, but she felt it everywhere.

Inside the great room, people were on couches and chairs. The room itself was welcoming with its earth tones and leather furniture. The atmosphere, however, was the exact opposite of welcoming. Darina's cop instincts darted her gaze to all four walls, noting exits, windows, possible weapons. She made eye contact with each person, quickly counting fourteen total, just as Foster had said lived here. All of them were adults, but some of them younger than her and Foster.

Estoria sat toward the back of the room, her large blue eyes zooming in on Zeke standing next to Ghared. Was the sight of a teenager—a child—painful to her? Darina couldn't imagine giving birth to stillborn babies once a year. She'd never given birth herself, but she'd considered it now and then. Of course, the world as it stood now was no place for a baby.

"Okay, everyone," Foster began, "nice to see you all." He moved to the middle of the room and turned in a circle to see the assembled group.

A few hellos came back to him, but the tension hung heavy above them.

"So I know I've broken my own rule by bringing these guests here, but it was necessary." He cleared his throat, his hands going into his pockets as he continued moving to see everyone. "As you know, I've been working on a cure to the disease my former colleague released into the air. While on a run into the city to collect samples, I was pursued by some of my colleague's associates."

Estoria's hand went to her mouth, and a few gasps slipped from those listening intently to Foster.

"You're going to get killed," Estoria said. "You're going to get killed, and we won't even know about it. You're gone too long from here,

Foster. When are you going to realize you should stay here with us and screw the rest of the world?"

Darina admired the woman's fire. The Boston Police Department could use fire like that. If it accepted GECs.

"Essie, we've been over this before. I can't turn my back and allow the globe to suffer." He rubbed the back of his neck, looking exhausted. "Not when I can do something about it."

A few people sitting closest to Foster nodded their agreement, but Estoria's hardened expression didn't change.

"I'd like to introduce Officer Darina Lazitter, her son, Zeke, and her friend, Ghared…" Foster looked to Ghared.

"Timms. Ghared Timms." He gave the group his best see-I'm-harmless smile.

Darina had to fight to keep a straight face. While her buddy had never shown any aggression toward her or Zeke, she knew he had a temper that could strip the skin right off his opponent and the muscles to match. Looking at him trying to be non-threatening was comical, especially with the slashing scar across his cheek and that barbed-wire and skeleton sleeve tattoo. She'd been there with Deo and Dixon when Ghared had gotten that tattoo. Actually all three of the males had gotten tattoos that day. Deo and Dixon had gotten identical wolf head tattoos except for the eyes. Deo had opted for yellow eyes, Dixon red.

Ghared had offered to let her pick his tattoo because he felt guilty she'd been injured with him in his hovercopter. At first, she'd selected a delicate fairy sitting atop a sunflower. She'd been busting his balls, but he'd been ready to let that be the image. When she'd told him she couldn't be friends with a man who had a fairy on his forearm... or a man who carried guilt around, he'd scrolled ahead on the tattoo artist's tablet until he landed on the barbed wire and skeleton design.

"What about this?" he'd asked. "Can you be friends with a guy who has this?"

"Forever," she'd replied.

Flexing her left hand now, she looked at Ghared standing next to her.

He elbowed her and whispered, "Stop it. I can do soft and cuddly."

She did laugh quietly at that, and Ghared smiled along.

"You two are going to get us kicked out before the day ends," Zeke said, giving them both a stern look.

"We'll behave," Ghared said, grinning at the kid.

Zeke's expression relaxed, and a look of curiosity took over the boy's face as he scanned the people in the room. What must it be like to finally be among people who were also genetically engineered? Zeke never talked about being a GEC, and Darina was in full support of considering him to be just like her. That was often hard to do when he was overcome by a seizure, but thanks to Foster, those days could be a thing of the past.

She glanced to Foster's pocket where the outline of the medicine bottle protruded. She'd have to get that back from him along with a copy of the ingredients. She never wanted Zeke to suffer from a seizure again.

"I wouldn't be standing here right now if Officer Lazitter hadn't come to my aid in the city. She helped me elude my pursuers and got me to Emerge Tech safely." He paused in his movement around the room. "Until my domicile within Emerge Tech walls was consumed by fire." He held out his hands to quiet the group when they started talking all at once.

"Officer Lazitter is also responsible for getting me out of harm then and Ghared and Zeke here flew us all to Vermont. I stand before you now in one piece thanks to these three individuals."

Thirteen sets of eyes—Estoria still wouldn't look at them directly—flicked to Darina, Ghared, and Zeke. An awkward moment of silence stretched on until one of the GECs got up from his seat and held his hand out to Darina.

"I'm Roben. Thanks for bringing the big guy back to us." He smiled pleasantly as Darina shook his hand.

"It's my job." She didn't particularly care for being in the spotlight.

"And you did it well." Another man stood and approached her. "I'm Pike. Welcome."

Darina shook his hand as well and soon a line of people formed in front of her. She, Ghared, and Zeke shook more hands than any of them probably ever shook in their lifetimes. Each person was nicer than the next. Some of them looked like ordinary humans. Others, like Estoria, couldn't hide their bad genetic code. Skin conditions causing odd complexions, limbs that weren't formed correctly, strange coloring in the eyes, and other unusual traits

SAFE

comprised the group. Foster had his work cut out for him if he ever hoped to help them all.

When the meet and greet wound down, Foster dismissed the group, promising to check in with each of them later. Darina admired the way the GECs regarded him as their leader and the authority exuding from him was damn sexy. This job would be easier if he was an old, ugly dude.

Foster Ashby, unfortunately, was the total opposite of an old, ugly dude, and she couldn't stop noticing that fact.

"Roben," Foster called as the man passed by.

"Yes?"

Resting a hand on the man's shoulder, Foster asked, "Could you show Ghared and Zeke around? I want our guests to feel comfortable here. They might," he shot a quick look at Zeke, "even want to be put to work."

Ghared slung his arm around Zeke's shoulders. "Me and the kid don't shy away from work, do we, Z?"

"Nope." Zeke's eager smile could have powered a hovercopter for eons.

Darina's heart almost couldn't take the joy she felt at seeing him so happy.

"What about Darina?" Ghared eyed Foster suspiciously. "Shouldn't she get the tour too? It will help her keep your ass safe if she knows her way around and sees if we need to fortify this place."

"She's getting a tour," Foster said. "I'll handle it."

Ghared's blue eyes narrowed to thin slits. "See that's all you *handle*, buddy."

Darina gave him her own narrowed glare. "Ghared."

"What? I didn't fly you here so Dr. Smooth could put the moves on you."

"Gross." Zeke looked away, shaking his head.

"He has no time for moves, Ghared. Besides when have you known me not to be able to take care of myself?" She threw her hands on her hips.

"Well, there was that one time..." He shot her a teasing grin.

"Get out of here." She turned to Zeke. "Mind your manners," she said, feeling the need to mother him suddenly.

"I'll keep him in line," Ghared said, giving her a wink.

She watched them go off with Roben who had already launched into tour guide mode.

"He'll either intrigue them with every detail of this place or bore them to death," Foster said, standing close to her again.

"I've yet to see either of them bored to death."

"Good." Foster looked down to his boots for a moment, then met her gaze. "I hope I wasn't being presumptuous in assuming you'd allow me to give you a private tour."

She looked at the already empty great room around them. "So just us?"

He nodded slowly. "I wanted to give you my full attention."

"Right. Good. I should probably stay close to you anyway. To protect you. Keep you safe, you know." Did she sound as stupid to him as she did inside her own head?

Get it together, moron.

"Staying close sounds like a good plan to me." He smiled and Darina's knees felt not quite capable of holding her weight. "This way."

He guided her down the hallway that led to a huge kitchen and dining room. The slate tile floor, in various shades of gray with a few reds mixed in, continued into the dining room where stone wainscoting met mustard-colored walls.

"Some of the people here are in charge of cooking. We're mostly vegetarian," he said. "We grow everything right on site so anything prepared in this kitchen is good for you and tastes absolutely wonderful. Pike, who you met a few moments ago, is one of our best chefs, but many of the others know their way around this kitchen too."

"Do you cook?" The vision of him surrounded by ingredients, slicing, dicing, chopping, made her suddenly hungry... and horny.

"When I have time, which lately is never." He gazed longingly at the stove. "Do you?"

"No. Generally, after I get my hands on food, Ghared cooks for me and Zeke." She shrugged. "I forget to eat half the time." Right now, however, devouring something—or someone—was definitely on her mind.

"You wouldn't forget to eat if you lived here. You'd look forward to eating. Everything that comes out of this kitchen tastes incredible."

Everything?

She couldn't stop her gaze from combing down the length of Foster.

He caught her and smirked. "Wondering what I'd taste like?"

His candor caught her off guard. "Oh... umm... I..."

Laughing, he said, "You don't have to answer that. I couldn't resist." He motioned to a door at the back of the kitchen. "C'mon. We have enough daylight left to see the grounds."

"Lead the way." Hopefully to a wide open space where she didn't have to be so close to him.

She fell into step beside him instead of letting him lead, but maintained at least a seven-foot gap between them. He showed her all the crops they grew—everything from strawberries to things she'd never heard of. He explained they used science to create hybrid produce they could grow in Vermont's climate or in the property's many greenhouses. His description shouldn't have turned her on, but the guy was a freaking genius. Darina had no idea she'd find brilliance so damn attractive, but holy shit, she did.

Foster led her to the barn she'd seen in Estoria's painting. The woman had really captured the building, and Darina felt a familiarity when looking at the structure.

"What are these flowers?" She fingered tall, orange blossoms that lined the barn. Nothing in the city was that vibrant.

"Those are day lilies. They're all over this land." He said it like they weren't anything special.

Darina disagreed. Crouching to touch her nose to the fragrant petals, she asked, "You don't like them?"

"I guess I don't really think about them. They're so abundant here."

"They'd sure make the city look better."

Foster picked one bright blossom and tucked it behind Darina's ear. "And you make them look better."

They stood in front of each other for several silent seconds, their gazes connected, and Darina's pulse drummed in her ears.

"Do you have animals?" she asked, hoping to get back to the tour and away from the way Foster's staring made her feel.

Blinking slowly, Foster said, "Sheep, horses, cows, chickens." He ticked off the list on his fingers. As he ushered them into the barn, something barked behind her, its low raspy, neighing making her turn around.

A large, four-legged creature loped toward her with long strides. Black and white with big, pointed ears and a long muzzle, the critter's pink tongue lolled over the side of its mouth.

"What in the world is that?" Too big to be a dog. Too small to be a horse. Darina had never seen anything like it.

"Oh, that's Homer." Foster stepped around her and threw his arms out by his sides. "Hey, boy!"

Darina held her breath as Homer bounded toward Foster and knocked him down.

"Homer!" she yelled, fearing Foster had been hurt.

"No, no. I'm okay. He's just saying hello." Foster reached his arms up as he lay on the floor in the barn and scratched the sides of the mammoth beast's head. "Homer's a dorse—combination dog and horse. Rescued him too. Did you know the government dabbled in hybridization of animals as a warfare option?"

"I did not." What else didn't she know? "So he's a GEC too?"

"Yep. He got cast off like the rest of us here. Dorses didn't learn commands well, so the government didn't want them." He gave the critter a few extra scratches. "But he's got a home now. He's a good fellow with a big heart. Did you miss me, Homer?"

That big pink tongue unrolled and sloshed across Foster's face.

Darina laughed as Foster struggled to his feet, still petting Homer. "You're soaked."

"Homer gives the best kisses." He raised an eyebrow at Darina. "So far anyway."

Chapter Six

Emerge Tech Building Crumbles to the Ground.

Now there was a headline Mikale could applaud. Official news wasn't broadcast any longer, but freelance writers often penned stories of interest and circulated them underground. Mikale's sources had picked up this story, and he loved knowing his associates had been the ones to cause the blow to the world's largest, functioning corporation. Of course, no one else would know his people were the catalyst for Foster Ashby's domicile to be reduced to soot, but he still reveled in the satisfaction of knowing he'd run the doctor out of his protected cocoon.

"Nowhere is safe, Foster."

His former colleague, however, had done a good job of disappearing. That fire should have scorched him and ended Mikale's primary obstacle in completing his mission. The help Foster was receiving had to be phenomenal.

Mikale had spent the day gathering intel on Officer Darina Lazitter, but it'd only taken him moments to know she was the one. For his plan to work, he needed not only to cleanse the planet of the humans now in existence but repopulate the vacated planet as well. To achieve that phase of his mission, he needed a suitable—no, an *exceptional*—female with which to mate. His specifications for such a female had been detailed, and he feared he might never find what he needed.

Until he received the lovely officer's file on his tablet after losing Foster in the city.

She was beautiful, intelligent, resilient, had a glowing police work record, and just looking at her picture made Mikale's whole body respond. For some reason, he felt as if he knew her already. She was... familiar and enthralling. The women he normally interacted with didn't even begin to offer him stimulation.

A soft knock sounded on his office door, and he knew that would be yet another woman who would fail miserably at arousing him.

Still, a release was a release. He was tense and nothing let him unwind like sex.

He got up from the couch and answered the door. A short, blonde woman leaned against the wall opposite him. She wore an almost transparent sleeveless dress in shimmery silver that complemented her fair skin nicely. By regular standards, she was gorgeous.

By Mikale's standards—ones only solidified after seeing Darina's picture—this woman was mediocre at best.

"Are you Mikale?" Her voice was on the high side and sounded a little fabricated. She was merely trying to be what she thought he wanted. He had to give her points for effort.

"Yes. Come in." He stepped aside and let her pass.

She smelled like flowers, and he wondered how she'd managed that. No flowers grew in the city. As far as he knew, the only place to get flowers was within Emerge Tech. Scientists there grew them to use in cures.

Or deadly plagues.

The ground petals of some flowering plants could be toxic. Mikale knew exactly which ones.

"My name is—"

He silenced her with a finger to her pouty lips. "You name isn't necessary, love."

Her brows lowered, and for a minute, Mikale thought she was going to give him trouble. Though he paid for the activities these women provided, some of them insisted on being treated in a civilized manner.

He wasn't feeling very civilized today.

The woman shrugged, grabbed the hem of her dress, and slowly peeled the garment from her body. She dropped the dress on the floor, and standing in only silver high heels, she cupped her own breasts then swept her hands over her stomach, and down to her thighs.

Widening her legs, she asked, "Do you want to touch me first or watch?"

Options. He liked options.

"Touch." The sooner he finished with her, the sooner he could get back to searching for Foster and the good officer.

He took the woman's hand and led her deeper into his office. After removing his clothes, he sat on the couch, rolled on a condom, and pulled her down onto his lap. She wiggled slightly to get comfortable, and Mikale closed his eyes, instantly picturing Darina in her place. That had him going rock hard in record time.

Deciding to keep his eyes closed and not spoil the image, he coasted his hands over this woman's shoulders, down her arms, around to her breasts, which filled his palms to overflowing. Using only his fingertips to guide him, he continued traveling over her body until he felt the heat of her ready core. He dipped a finger into her wetness and reveled in the deep, throaty moan she released.

What sounds would Darina make?

He couldn't wait to find out. That day would come. He'd make sure of it. Together they'd build a new human race, and he'd have that future his mother had always wished for him.

He buried his length inside this woman sitting atop him, but it was Darina's name that looped in his brain. It was her surrounding him. It was her digging her fingernails into his shoulders. It was her gasping in pleasure. It was her bringing him to the edge and pushing him over as he thrust into her again and again.

"Wonderful."

The sound of the other woman's voice wrenched him out of his fantasy. He opened his eyes and stood, giving her barely enough time to dislodge herself from him.

"That was amazing." She fluttered her eyelids at him as she sat on the couch and folded her legs beneath her.

"And now it's over." He picked up her dress and handed it to her. "You can go now."

She opened her mouth to protest, but he turned away, and whatever she was going to say died on her lips. She must have gotten up because he heard the sound of skin shifting on leather. A few huffing breaths escaped from her as she slipped on her dress, and her heels clicked on the floor. Their quick *tap-tap-tap* let him know he'd pissed her off.

The slam of his door let him know he'd probably done more than piss her off.

After removing the condom, cleaning up, and getting dressed, he settled at his desk and brought up Darina's picture on his tablet. She probably had too much patience to get so pissed over nonsense. She definitely reminded him of someone, but who? Tracing the edge of her jaw, he vowed to find her.

Find her and claim her.

****

Foster had shown Darina almost every corner of the cultivated property from the farmland and gardens to the greenhouses to the hydro-electric station that ran off the powerful stream cutting through the land to the field of solar panels used as additional energy. He'd taken her into the woodshop where Roben and some of the others who were skilled with building things worked. They'd toured an outside area where a ring of smaller cabins sat, and he'd explained that some of the GECs chose to live together, while others had their own places.

He only had two more spots to show her—his lab and the rest of the main house. His house.

"What do you think so far?" He wasn't sure what was going through her head. She'd been quiet through most of the tour, only asking practical questions about electricity, water, and roles and responsibilities of those who lived there.

She stopped walking. "It's impressive. I mean, you've got a self-sustaining community here, Doc." She turned in a circle, looking out at the land around them. "And if you can build this here…"

"It can be built elsewhere," he finished, nodding. "It takes time and hard work, but it can certainly be done. It could easily be unplug proof. Fuck the Anarch and what they did to the globe."

"I like the sound of that, but in order to prove it can be done to the government," she turned back to him, "you'd have to provide evidence."

She fit the pieces together perfectly.

"And if I provide evidence, I have to reveal this place." Foster shoved his hands in his pockets. He couldn't recall how many times he'd had the internal debate on this very dilemma.

"And all those you keep safe here would be at risk."

"I'd like to think the government would look beyond my illegal harboring of GECs in light of the fact that we could have a solution to rebuilding our nation here, but you and I both know it won't go down that way."

"Emerge Tech wouldn't help?" she asked.

"Emerge Tech serves the government, just as all the other corporations had before the Unplug, the fighting, and Mikale's plague. When Emerge Tech was the only one left standing, the government took more control of it. After the Unplug, we only worked on restoring technology. During the fighting, we worked on weapons. When the virus was unleashed, I got assigned to find a cure. We've been reacting, not looking for solid solutions."

He ran a frustrated hand through his hair and Darina stepped closer. Throughout the tour, she'd been careful to keep a distance away from him. Had it been because of the Homer's kisses comment? He probably shouldn't have said that, but she'd been standing there, looking truly intrigued by Homer, and he couldn't help himself. As that silly dorse slobbered all over him, he'd been wondering how much slobbering he could get Darina to do.

"My line of work is similar," she said softly. "I get sent out to deal with people who have already become criminals. Wouldn't it be damn nice if I could get them before they broke the law? If I could stop them from making stupid choices?" She shuffled her boots in the stones on the path. "But people are probably always going to be making stupid choices."

"Probably. It's human nature."

She squinted a hazel eye at him. "It is in a genetically engineered human's nature too."

"Indeed." He motioned to the main house. "Up for seeing my lab?"

"Sure. Then we have to talk security. This place, though remote, is also wide open."

As the sunset outside colored the darkening sky with deep pinks and purples, he led her into the house and down a set of narrow stairs behind a bookcase off the kitchen.

"Someone was thinking of security when building this lab though," Darina said from behind him.

"I thought it best." He waved his tablet by a screen at the door to his lab and the door unlocked. Pushing it open, he said, "This is where I'll be spending most of tonight. The sooner I can find this damn cure, the sooner I can make Mikale's plague a thing of the past. If people weren't so afraid to come out into the city, maybe we'd have a chance at rebuilding everything we once had."

"Only better."

He liked the determined glint in her eyes. "Only better."

She wandered deeper into the lab when he held the door open for her. "This is set up like the lab in your domicile."

"It's more efficient to organize every lab in the same way."

"Neatness must have been a trait they were after when genetically engineering you folks," she said. "I'm told teenagers are supposed to be messy, but Zeke is so tidy. Except for his hair. That he won't let me touch."

"But you've tried?" He smiled, picturing Darina attempting to give Zeke a haircut.

"He used to let me buzz cut it for him, but when he turned fourteen, that was it. I no longer had haircutting rights." She shrugged one shoulder. "I think he asks Ghared to trim it for him now and then, but I don't pry into their beauty regimens."

She circled his worktable and paused at one corner, leaving a side between them, keeping her distance as she had for most of the tour.

He'd had enough of that distance.

Walking slowly so as not to cause her to step back, he joined her at the corner. "And what's your beauty regimen?"

"Me?" She looked up at him. "I just wake up looking this good, Doc."

The grin on her lips was too much to resist. He took another step closer, and when she didn't back up, he reached out a hand and pushed her hair off her neck.

She swallowed loudly, her eyes locked on his.

"You do look good," he whispered. "You also know how to save a guy's life."

"Twice," she said, holding up two fingers.

"Twice." He nodded. "I should probably say thank you." His other hand went to her waist and tugged her closer.

"Unless you want me to think you're a rich bastard."

"I told you I'm not a rich bastard." He stroked the pad of his thumb against the silky caramel skin of her cheek and stopped breathing altogether when she put her hands on his hips.

"Prove it."

His lips were on hers faster than his mind could tell him to stop. Just as he'd thought, her lips were soft and intoxicating. When she opened her mouth, granting him access, he nearly fell at her feet.

She must have sensed his weak knees because she backed him up to the table and pushed him against it until he sat on the edge. She was a little taller than him now, and she took command of the kiss, going deeper, taking more.

He was perfectly willing to give her more.

Wrapping his arms around her waist, he corralled her against him and feasted on her mouth. She tasted like danger and security all rolled into one. He was both scared to death and comfortable as hell in her presence. How could she stir such different emotions in him?

Probably because the last woman you touched was merely a hologram.

Being as busy as he was, Foster didn't have time for the company of women and most of them didn't have the tolerance for his single-mindedness when it came to working in his lab. Holograms didn't nag him to spend more time with them. They didn't require much attention or conversation.

They also didn't feel half as good as Darina did in his arms right now.

He tangled his fingers in her hair and she let out a little moan that surged through him like an electrical charge. The heat from the flames in his domicile had been nothing compared to the fire sparking wildly inside him now.

She hooked her left hand onto the back of his neck and gave him a few more sizzling kisses before breaking free of his hold. Breathing as heavily as he was, she said, "If they bred you to be a phenomenal kisser, they succeeded. Superbly."

He loved the flush on her cheeks, the puffiness of her lips, the tousled hair on her head. He'd caused all three of those and wanted to affect her in so many other ways.

"And you do kiss better than Homer," he said.

She shoved him, and he grabbed her left arm. He traced the ring of stars as he had back in his domicile. "These are hot."

"As is this." She fingered the tribal swirls inked up his neck and around his right ear.

"Does kissing like we just did mean we're now able to swap tattoo stories?" He didn't know why he wanted to know the reason for the stars so badly, but he did. He actually wanted to know everything there was to know about her.

Darina was quiet for a few long minutes, then she slid onto the table next to him, her feet dangling. She rested her left hand on her thigh and wiggled her fingers. "This isn't my original hand."

Gently, he lifted her hand in his and inspected the star tattoos more closely. Sure enough, a thin seam was just below them. "A prosthetic?"

She nodded, taking her hand back. "It's what happens when you go thrill seeking." She outlined the fingers of her left hand with her right index finger. "I'd been flying with Ghared, before the Unplug when the biggest thing we had to worry about was how we'd spend a Saturday. Carefree and clueless, you know?"

Foster didn't know, but he nodded anyway so she'd continue.

"Ghared banked around a skyscraper at a near ninety degree angle as he'd done a billion times." Her brows lowered and her prosthetic hand curled into a fist. "Unfortunately the skyscraper he'd chosen that day had a bridge connecting it to its neighboring building and he couldn't avoid crashing. He ended up with a concussion and was cleared for military duty a few days later when the world went dark."

"But you weren't so lucky."

"Nope. My hand had gotten crushed so badly I had to give it up. Ghared felt awful, but it wasn't his fault."

Still, Foster had the urge to find Ghared and pound on him. If the guy had been more careful, nothing would have happened to Darina. He didn't like the idea that she'd been in pain.

"Can I see something?" he asked, holding his palm out for her hand.

She rested her hand in his and he held his tablet over it. With a few taps on the screen, he confirmed what he had thought. "It's one of mine."

"What?"

He ran his finger along the smooth skin on the back of the prosthetic hand. "It says right here, *ET-FA-98732*."

"And that means?"

"That means Emerge Tech, Foster Ashby, limb number 98732. I made this… or at least the design for it."

She held her hand up, looking at it as if seeing it for the first time. "Well, for what I had to do to get this, I'm glad I ended up with the best."

He desperately wanted to ask what she had to do, but was almost positive it had to do with why she thought all rich men were bastards. He was fighting to stay out of that category so he didn't ask. Not now anyway.

Clearing her throat, she said, "Now you. What prompted the neck and ear tattoo?"

"Would you believe a similar trauma to yours?" He lifted his right leg and shook his booted foot. "This is also a prosthetic. One of mine too and the reason I went into that line of work to begin with."

"How much of it?"

He slashed his right index finger along his upper thigh and Darina's eyebrows rose.

"That much? Wow. What happened?"

"In college, someone found out I was a GEC. The manufacturer tried to reclaim what was theirs."

Her hand went to her mouth. "Oh, Foster. They tried to… take you apart?"

"Right on campus. And not gently either, but I managed to escape. Minus one leg. The woman who'd taken me in, as you've taken in Zeke, picked me up when I called her and after some time of healing, Carielle arranged for a prosthetic leg. They were poorly designed then. I made it my mission to improve them."

"So if you almost died because your GEC secret was discovered," she began, "I have to ask again why you told me, not knowing me at all? Why risk being ripped apart again?"

He shrugged. "I don't know. It just felt right to tell you." Since Mikale had left Emerge Tech and had gone down the dark path he'd chosen, Foster had a hard time finding the best in people. Something in Darina, however, gave him hope that good people still existed.

Darina studied him for a moment then rested her prosthetic hand on his thigh. "You did a good job on this. Thanks."

He put his hand atop hers. "It was a selfish goal, but I'm glad someone like you benefited." He pointed to his tattoo. "Anyway, I got this after losing my leg. The design is ancient, and it means *survival*."

"I like it." She reached over and pressed her lips to the design.

Before he could respond to that gentle kiss and steal more, she hopped off the table. "I should go find Zeke and Ghared. You should get some work in." She pointed to the worktable. "Mind if I walk around the property again and plan my security strategy?"

"Of course not." Though he didn't want to be without her presence even for a short while.

"Good. See you later."

"Count on it."

****

Darina slumped against the lab door after she'd closed it behind her. Foster had nearly kissed her senseless in there. *Damn.* She'd been with a few guys here and there, but only one had ever made her mouth—and other parts—feel so electrified. And she didn't think about that guy anymore. Well, she tried not to. He had a way of cropping up in her mind on occasion.

But Foster put a new memory in there. A crazy wonderful memory. One she wanted to revisit as soon as possible.

She put her hand to her chest where her heart still drummed, overwhelmed by the physical reactions Foster's kiss had caused. Seeing this amazing property and sharing stories with him about their traumas had done something to her.

She felt as if she *knew* him.

"Well, this is dangerous." Never a good idea to become involved with someone you were supposed to protect. It took your mind off the goal. It distracted you. It made you care beyond getting a paycheck.

Not that she was convinced she'd be getting a paycheck anymore. She had no way of knowing whether Emerge Tech had survived the fire or not. Would they be pleased she'd gotten him out of their walls or angry she'd allowed him to get so far away?

Shaking her head, she decided not to worry about money right now. As long as she and Zeke were on this property, they wouldn't have to worry about food, the only thing she really used money for. Besides, she couldn't put a price on the experience Zeke was having amongst other GECs. That was an opportunity only being here could provide.

After ascending the stairs and pushing open the hidden bookcase door, Darina inspected the main house's kitchen more closely until a few GECs filtered in with baskets of food. They told her to stay and were perfectly cordial, but she continued on to the great room. It had one exit which she discovered led to a deck facing a majestic mountain range in the distance.

"The White Mountains in New Hampshire," a voice said below the deck.

She peered over the railing to find Pike standing there. "They don't look white."

He laughed. "This is true. In summer they are pretty damn green, aren't they?" He climbed the deck steps and stood next to her. "Your tour with Foster all over?"

"Yes. I'm scouting around now, deciding how to best keep him safe."

Pike appeared to consider her words carefully before saying, "Some of us wish to help with that."

"How many is 'some of us'?" She wasn't opposed to getting help, especially from these people who knew the property and appeared to care deeply for Foster. After kissing him, she understood how easy it would be to care deeply for him.

But she was going to ignore that. She had to.

Pike looked up to the sky, raising one finger for each name he ticked off. It was then Darina saw what his genetically engineered *problem* was. He only had three fingers and a thumb on each hand. She wondered what else might be wrong with him. A shortage of fingers didn't seem like enough to be cast off or ripped apart. What was enough really? And why should the government decide?

"About eight of us to start," he said. "Smart folks. Strong too. And we know the property well."

"Any of you know how to use a weapon?"

At this, Pike grinned. "Sweetheart, most of us were bred to use a weapon."

"Oh. Right." *Great. Idiot.* "Are there weapons on site?"

Pike nodded. "Foster is a pretty peaceful guy, but he's the complete opposite of dumb. He knows the world that exists out there isn't altogether friendly. This place makes that world fade away, but it's still there."

How she wished that weren't true.

"Okay, can you round up those who want to get involved and the weapons so I can see what we're dealing with?"

"Can do. Let's meet at my cabin. Fourth one in from the left. Fifteen minutes."

"Copy that." Before Pike could leave, she asked, "Have you seen Zeke and Ghared?"

"Last I saw, Roben was getting all poetic about the solar panels." He rolled his eyes and jogged off.

Darina headed for the solar panel field, but stopped when a scream rattled the woods to her left. Sprinting in that direction, her weapon drawn, she searched the trees. When a second scream pierced the air, this one ending in a pained wail, she called out. "Who's there? Are you okay?"

Another cry sounded and Darina quickened her pace through the brush. She broke through the brambles and nearly stepped on Estoria curled into a ball, writhing on the ground.

"Are you in labor?" she asked, getting to her knees beside the woman.

"Y-y-yes." Estoria cradled her stomach. "Just catch it. Just catch it."

Without thinking, Darina rolled the woman onto her back and bent her legs. Blood soaked the earth, and though Darina had not assisted in the birth of any babies, she knew this was all wrong. Way too much blood.

"Just catch it." Estoria's voice was breathless, her face contorted in pain.

"I'll catch it," Darina assured. "You push."

"I'm so… tired." Estoria let out a wail, but pushed as well.

The baby's head became visible and Darina prepared to receive the child. With one final push, the tiny human plopped into Darina's waiting hands.

It didn't move.

It didn't breathe.

It was purple.

Estoria flopped back onto the ground, her arms covering her face. "It's dead, isn't it?"

After checking for a pulse and finding none, Darina said, "I'm afraid so." Her throat was tight, her hands shaking. She saw a great deal of death in her work, in the city, in the world they lived in, but to hold a dead baby? Well, that was something she never wanted to do again.

"Just once," Estoria sobbed. "Just once, why can't one of them survive? Why do I have to be this way?" Tears rolled down her cheeks. "Was it a girl or a boy?"

"Girl." Darina struggled with whether or not to put the baby down to comfort Estoria.

"That makes ten girls, ten boys."

"You've given birth to twenty children?" That made Darina's vagina hurt.

"Yes. It started when I was fifteen. I'm thirty-five now."

"Foster mentioned he tried to help you with this condition."

"First we tried terminating the pregnancy. I reconceived immediately after. Next we tried a full hysterectomy. All the parts grew back within a month. Not only can I fertilize myself, I can apparently regenerate organs. That should be a good thing, but it's not. It's so not." She sat up and held

119

her hands out. "Give her to me." When Darina hesitated, she said, "I've held every one of them."

Nodding, Darina handed over the tiny body. She had to look away when Estoria pressed a gentle kiss to the baby's forehead.

"Thank you for coming to my aid." Estoria looked at Darina. "I wasn't nice upon your arrival, but you helped me anyway."

"I understand Foster bringing us here was a bit of a shock."

"He's only ever brought GECs here, and he hasn't done that in ages because there aren't any new ones being made. We value the privacy he's given us here." She rocked the baby as if it were alive in her arms. "If his enemies get hold of him, however, we'd be pretty pissed about that."

So would I.

"I'll do my best," Darina said.

"I know you will." Estoria got to her feet, swaying a little. Darina reached for her, but she held out a single hand. "I'm okay. I'm going to bury this sweet girl with the others."

"Do you want some help? Do you want me to get Foster?"

"No. I'm fine. There's nothing he can do anyway. Smart as he is, he can't fix my heart which breaks every time I give birth. Nine months of loving the new life inside me only to see it dead." She squeezed her eyes shut, tears collecting on her lashes.

"I'm so sorry, Estoria." Darina wished she could do something for this woman whose shoulders hunched as she walked away with her lifeless child tucked against her bosom.

"Mom?" Zeke's voice cut through the anguish.

Darina turned to see Ghared and Zeke approaching, with Homer galloping alongside them. She didn't wait for them to arrive. Instead, she jogged up to Zeke and threw her arms around him.

"Whoa." He stumbled back but put his arms around her in a return embrace. "What's this for?" He released her enough to hold her at arm's length. "Is that blood on your shirt? Are you hurt?" He looked her over with worried eyes.

Ghared was immediately at her side, nudging Zeke back. "Who did this to you? Where are you bleeding?" He lifted her tank top, but she slapped his hands away.

"It's not my blood." Both males exhaled loudly in relief as Homer came up and sniffed at her shirt then licked her arms. Rubbing the dorse until its eyes squeezed shut, she said, "I came upon Estoria over there and she gave birth. The baby was dead just as Foster said it would be."

"Poor girl," Ghared said.

Zeke pulled her into another hug. Bless him. "That had to be tough to witness."

She nodded against his shoulder then craned her head back to look him in the eye. "I know I didn't give birth to you, but you know you're mine, right? I love you as if you're mine."

He gave her one of his full blown smiles—the ones that were like sunshine in the gray city. "I know. You're mine too, Mom. Always."

Ghared threw his arms around both of them. "This is so beautiful." He made his voice all weepy, and the three of them ended up laughing as Homer nudged his way into their circle.

With an elbow to Ghared's stomach, Darina broke up their little huddle. "Okay, back to the business at hand."

"Protecting Doctor Cure the World?" Ghared made a face Darina wasn't sure how to interpret.

"Protecting Foster, yes. Pike told me there are others here who want to join the team and they have weapons."

"Excellent. The more eyes and guns we have here, the better."

Darina wondered if more eyes meant fewer opportunities for kissing the good doctor. It probably did. It definitely should.

But it wasn't what she wanted.

Chapter Seven

Foster surveyed his worktable covered in various bottles, beakers, and strewn about ingredients. He tapped a finger on the edge of the table while he waited for his latest cure attempt to mix in the centrifuge. He already had a Petri dish ready with some of the powder sample he'd taken from an infected body in the city. He'd tried four other formulas this evening, but none of them affected the sample the way he wanted them to.

None of them were The Cure.

The centrifuge stopped spinning and he carefully removed the vial. Taking a medicine dropper, he sucked up the solution and squirted a few drops onto the sample. He slid the Petri dish under his high-powered microscope and peeked through the eyepiece.

Some bubbling occurred.

The red powder turned pink.

The pink gelled, solidified.

Foster held his breath. *Please work. Please.*

The gelled sample fizzled then turned to black ash.

"Fuck." He slammed his hand down on the table, making all the bottles and beakers rattle like glass chimes in the wind.

Picking up his tablet, he hit the microphone app and said, "Test #4773, solution successfully reversed red powder to pink gel consistent with normal human organs. After regeneration, however, sample was reduced to black ash." He sniffed and wrinkled his nose. "And there's a sharp, unpleasant odor."

He tossed his tablet to the table and stared at all the ingredients he had already tried. The combinations were endless. He'd need a thousand lifetimes to test them all.

No. Just be smart about the test combinations.

Some things could be eliminated. He could narrow the parameters.

He could do this, dammit. He could keep innocents from dying.

He had to.

But not tonight. His eyesight had gone blurry with concentration, and his back and neck hurt from being hunched over the worktable for so long. He didn't even know what time it was.

Had Darina finished outlining her security strategy? He'd had to push her out of his mind while he worked. Not an easy task by any means. Especially not after kissing her as he had. He was surprised she'd let him kiss her. Darina didn't strike him as a woman who let anyone do anything to her.

So she must have wanted *that kiss. My kiss.*

That thought filled him with satisfaction despite his failed cure attempts tonight. What else might she want from him?

Deciding he'd like an answer to that question, he powered down his equipment and capped any opened bottles. He'd come back to the lab early tomorrow and work nonstop until he found that damn cure.

After making sure his tablet was in his pocket and his lab was locked, he climbed the stairs and wandered into an empty kitchen. Darkness hung outside like a black curtain over the main house, but he heard voices. Following the sound, he found Darina and Ghared talking to a group outside on the deck under the floodlights. Homer was lounging on the deck by Ghared's feet. Foster listened for a few moments from the shadows of the great room.

"So is everyone set with what quadrant they are covering when?" Ghared asked, sounding like a military general.

A few confirmations filtered through the group.

"I think the schedule we've agreed upon will offer continual coverage without taxing any of us. We'll always have someone fresh on guard, especially around this main house," Darina said. The official tone to her voice made Foster instantly hard. He'd had no idea that a woman in charge would be such a turn on for him.

A shrill chiming sounded and Ghared pulled a tablet out of his pocket. The man stepped off the deck and roamed away a few steps. Homer got to his feet, stretched his hind legs, and followed the man.

Darina's gaze followed Ghared then focused back on the group. "Okay, let's get the first watch set up on the perimeter. Second and third watches go get some sleep."

Muffled agreement sounded and the group dispersed. Some of them didn't go far and Foster assumed they were the first watch. The others headed for their cabins. Something warm swelled in his chest at his people's—his *friends'*—willingness to protect him.

Darina caught him standing at the door. "Hey."

It was a simple greeting, but the way she said it, the way her eyes scanned over him, made it seem like the most intimate greeting in the universe.

His gaze traveled down to the blood on her tank top. *Blood?*

"What happened?" He stepped out onto the deck and pointed to her shirt.

She looked down. "Oh, that's from Estoria. She gave birth earlier. I asked if she wanted me to get you, but she declined."

Foster raked his hand through his hair and leaned against the railing beside her. "Was it another stillborn?"

Darina nodded. "A girl."

Wanting to change the subject to keep from feeling frustrated he couldn't help Estoria, he scanned the assembled people fanned out around the house. "Looks as if you've made a security team."

"They volunteered to be one. I'd be foolish to refuse their help. They know the land, they know how to defend themselves, and you mean a great deal to each one of them." She folded her arms across her chest. "I almost *want* Warres to show up."

"Why hasn't anyone gone after him?" Foster asked. "Wouldn't it be easier?" If he were in police custody, maybe they could get the damn cure right from him.

"There are people assigned to trying to locate him, but as you've said, he's brilliant. No one can find him. We can't even get our hands on his minions." She puffed out a frustrated breath. "Our best bet is neutralizing his plague. I think that will bring him out into the open if he knows we can reverse his handiwork." She glanced up at Foster. "Any luck on that front?"

"Not today. Sorry." His shoulders slumped.

She reached out a hesitant hand then gripped his forearm. "You'll get it."

"What if I don't?"

"I'll kick your ass."

He laughed, tension leaching out of his body.

"Hey, that was supposed to be a threat. No laughing matter."

But when he looked at her, she was smiling and thoughts of kissing her rushed into his mind again.

As if reading his thoughts, she warned, "We're not alone out here."

Not *I don't want you to kiss me.* That encouraged him. "Then let's go in there." He pointed to the main house.

She opened her mouth to reply, but boots on the deck steps interrupted her, and she peered around Foster. "Ghared? Everything okay?"

"When is everything ever okay?" He ran his hands over Homer who had apparently nominated the man as his new best friend. "That was Mareea." He looked at Foster. "My niece. Her mother, my dumbass sister, has been gone for five days."

"That's long even for her," Darina said. "Mareea is worried?"

Ghared scrubbed a hand down his face and around his whiskered jaw. "Yeah. She's convinced this is the big one."

"Big one?" Foster asked.

"The time my sister doesn't come back at all." Ghared sighed. "I've got to go back, Darina."

"Of course." She waved a hand to the team surrounding the main house. "We've got things under control here."

Ghared threw a look at Foster then turned his gaze back to Darina. "You're sure you'll be all right."

"Are you doubting my skills, man?" She grinned and gave him a light punch in the shoulder.

"Never. I do, however, doubt his ability to keep his han—" His words got cut off by Darina's hand over his mouth.

"Do not finish that sentence unless you want to fly home with a black eye," she said.

"I'll second that," Foster said, though he rather enjoyed that Ghared could see something happening between him and Darina. It meant Foster wasn't imagining that spark.

Ghared moved Darina's hand and stepped around her to get toe-to-toe with Foster. The guy wasn't taller, but he was wider and had a wild look in his eye. One that made that scar on his cheek even fiercer. Foster wasn't sure what to expect next.

Homer growled and Foster was glad to see the dorse's loyalty still resided with him.

"If you hurt her in any way, Ashby, any way at all," Ghared warned, "a black eye will seem minor compared to what I'll do to you."

"Okay." Darina got between them. "That's enough. We're all on the same side here. Remember?"

So she's joined my team. Foster remembered her saying she was her own team this morning.

She backed Ghared up several steps, and Foster smiled over the fact that she wasn't backing *him* up anywhere.

Ghared picked up on that too and gave Foster another warning. This one was silent and in the form of a dagger-sharp glare.

Message received. He wasn't guaranteeing he'd listen to it, though.

"You want me to take Zeke back with me?" Ghared asked, turning his icy blue gaze back to Darina.

She faced Foster, and he readied to give her the bottle of seizure medicine still in his pocket. "If it's all right with you, Foster, I'd like Zeke to stay. He's enjoying being with other GECs. It's good for him."

"Completely fine with me. He's welcome here." Having her son stay felt like a big win for some reason. Foster liked the kid and wanted the chance to talk to him more.

"You have a way we can reach each other?" Ghared asked. "If I hear something in the city about Warres or if you need me?"

"I can give you the number for my tablet, but you have to memorize it," Foster said. "I'm not writing it down, and I don't want it stored in your tablet."

He rattled off the number and Ghared repeated it several times, committing it to memory.

With a hug and some whispered secret in Darina's ear, Ghared disappeared into the darkness.

"He won't fly directly home from here, will he?" Foster asked.

"Give him some credit, Foster," Darina said. "He's smarter than that."

Foster nodded, a muscle spasming in his sore neck as he did so. He brought his hand up to massage the ache, but the twitching continued.

"Your neck hurt?" Darina asked.

"It's from leaning over my worktable for so long." He turned his head one way then the other, looked down, looked up, but the ache persisted.

A low rumble sounded a short distance away and after a few gaspy revs of the engine—and a few loud dorse neigh-barks, Ghared's hovercopter ascended. He hadn't put any lights on, and Foster knew he'd been foolish to worry the man would be detected. Ghared Timms might not give a shit about Foster's safety, but he wouldn't want to lead the enemy to Darina.

When the engine noise died away and Homer came loping back to the deck, Foster felt Darina's hand on his. "Maybe I could help you with that neck pain. You know, in there." She motioned to the darkened main house.

He didn't need to hear that suggestion twice to know it was a fantastic idea. "Homer, let's get you put to bed, buddy."

"I'll take care of it," a voice said from below the deck. A whistle sounded and the dorse took off.

Taking her hand in his, Foster turned toward the house and led her inside to the great room.

Darina cast a glance to the wall of windows. "Do you have a more private location?"

Without a word, he tugged her down the hallway to his library. He wanted to scoop her up and take her to his bedroom but knew she'd find that too forward. That was what a rich bastard would do. Take command without regard for the other person's wishes. He was determined not to play that role.

"This room okay?" he asked.

She took in the floor to ceiling bookshelves, crammed with various genres of literature. He liked the look of old-fashioned books, though most of his reading—which he didn't have time for anymore—took place on his tablet. An oversized couch upholstered in soft suede took up the center of the room while a walnut desk stood in front of a large window. Two smaller suede chairs flanked a reading table sporting a lamp in the corner.

"This room is perfect." She pushed him to sitting on the edge of the couch then climbed behind him.

Just having her that close aroused him. When her hands kneaded the muscles at the base of his neck, he slipped into an alternate world.

One he didn't want to leave.

****

Foster's shoulders were broad, and as her hands kneaded them, Darina could think of only one thing—removing his shirt so she could touch

131

his bare skin. The desire to feel him against her own skin overwhelmed her. Never had she wanted fabric to disintegrate so badly.

A low moan escaped from Foster as she worked on a particularly hard knot at the base of his neck. His fingers gripped the edge of the cushion he sat on, and Darina wondered if he wanted to get naked as much as she did.

Only one way to find out.

"You're really tight up in here." She poked her index fingers into his trapezius muscles. Taking in a breath, she let it out slowly and decided to go for it. "Take your shirt off so I can—"

Foster yanked his shirt off before she finished her sentence. "Don't even care what your reason is." He grinned at her over his right shoulder.

Hopefully someone would come by and mop the melted puddle she'd become behind him on the couch. Between his grin, the gorgeous pale green of his eyes, the bare expanse of his back, and the sexy way his tattoo swirled down over his shoulder, she was quickly losing her grip on reality. Surely, she'd slipped into a fantasy.

"Are you going to drool over me or rub some aching muscles, Officer Lazitter?" he teased.

"I don't drool."

"I think if the roles were reversed right now, I'd definitely be drooling." He started to turn around, but she gripped his shoulders to keep him facing forward.

"We'll see about reversing roles in a little bit." That made her hot between her legs, so she shook her head and focused on the task of relieving his muscle pain. "Let me know if I'm hurting you."

"I don't mind a little rough treatment." Again, he looked at her over his shoulder, his mouth turned up, and she wanted to throw herself at him.

Massage. Focus on the massage.

She walked her fingers around his tattoo, fighting the urge to trace the design with her tongue. His skin was warm against her right hand and as she moved around his shoulders, up his neck, down his back, his muscles loosened, his body relaxed. Well, she imagined there might be at least one spot on his body that wasn't so loose, wasn't so relaxed.

Fanning herself for a minute with her hands, she dove back in and continued rubbing him until he felt like soft clay under her grip.

"Feeling better?" she asked when he took in a deep breath and sifted it out, his spine sagging a bit.

"If I say yes, will you stop touching me?" He took her hand from his shoulder where she'd rested it and tugged until she had to move to his side. Sliding back on the couch, he pushed his shirt off his lap and raised a hand to fiddle with the ends of her hair. "Because I definitely don't want you to stop touching me."

The way he was looking at her right now set fires inside her body. All-consuming. Inferno-level. Magma rising to the mouth of the volcano. Seconds to eruption.

"I'm glad I decided to keep you safe personally. Some others wanted to shadow you, you know."

"Is that what you're doing? *Shadowing* me?" He traced circles on her bare shoulder, his pale green eyes settling on her lips.

"Yes." She climbed onto his lap and smoothed her palms over his chest. "I think it's best if I stay very, very close to you."

His pupils doubled in size as his arms came around her waist. "To keep me safe?" He pulled her a bit closer and the heat between their bodies exploded.

When he pressed his lips against the curve of her neck and trailed a course along her shoulder, she thought maybe she needed someone to keep *her* safe. Safe from falling for this guy.

"Your safety is the Boston Police Department's top priority." Her voice was husky and didn't sound like hers at all.

Foster slid the shoulder strap of her tank top down and lightly nipped at her collarbone. A sound came out of her she'd never made before. One of longing and arousal, and if he stopped now she'd cry. Truly.

His fingers slithered up into her hair, lightly scraping her skull as they moved and causing goosebumps to rise on her skin. Her hands pulled off her tank top without her consciously telling them to do so.

The groan that ushered out of Foster made her feel sexy—something she didn't feel often. She was so busy trying to keep herself, Zeke, and

Ghared from losing the battle in the city that she'd lost touch with her own needs, her wants.

Doctor Foster Ashby was definitely something she wanted.

"So beautiful." His words were uttered on a whisper, like a secret meant only for her to hear.

She wanted to tell him he was beautiful too because, holy shit, he was, but Darina found her ability to formulate complete thoughts and convey words had been lost. Her body was in charge now, and it wasn't giving up control any time soon.

Foster shifted so she was spread out on the couch. He leaned over her on his elbows, mere inches between their chests. "Do you believe in seizing the moment?"

"Yes." The couch was soft beneath her. The man was hard above her. A wonderful sandwich she found herself in.

"Good. So do I."

His mouth crashed down on hers, possessive, devouring her as if she were dessert in a world that no longer served anything sweet. He slid his left thigh between her legs and pushed up enough to have her writhing beneath him.

Damn. She couldn't remember the last time she'd wanted something so damn much. Well, she could, but she wasn't going to think about that right now.

Seize this *moment.* No living in the past.

Her hands came around Foster's back, her fingernails grazing his skin, marking him, claiming him, willing him to do the same to her. She'd had no idea how badly she wanted someone to claim her. Aside from Zeke and Ghared, her life was solitary. She'd fooled herself into thinking that was how she wanted it. No doubt it was safer that way. Less people to worry about. Less likely someone would discover Zeke. Less likely to catch Warres's plague. Less chance of her heart getting stomped on. Again.

But it's also less adventurous, less fun, less living.

Her hands slid between them, reaching for the zipper on his pants. He sat up and gave her better access, his chest rising and falling with his rapid breathing—breathing that matched hers. She felt dizzy, out of control, alive.

"Darina." The word came out on a breath as she freed his impressive erection, her own arousal growing exponentially as she imagined Foster burying himself deep inside her.

His hands went to her pants now, his fingers slowly pulling her zipper down and hooking on the waistband, tugging downward. His fingertips scraped along her hips, and she arched her back, allowing him to slide the pants past her ass. He paused, his eyes darkening as he took her in, seeming to commit her body to memory.

The anticipation. Was. Killing. Her.

"Please, Foster." She didn't make a habit of begging for anything. Begging was a sign of weakness, but tonight she didn't care. She wanted Foster Ashby. She'd beg for him.

He grinned, a slow upturn of his magnificent lips, and she reached her arms up to bring him back down flush against her. His arousal rubbed along her wet, ready folds, and she nearly cried out, wanting desperately for him to fill her.

"We don't need any protection, do we?" She somehow had the presence of mind to ask this question.

"I can't impregnate you," he said softly, something sad creeping into his gorgeous green eyes, "and I'm immune to disease." He cleared his throat. "Not that I think you have any diseases… I… uh… I meant I can't give you anything." His cheeks pinked, and she wanted him even more if that were possible.

She closed the small distance between them and caught his mouth with hers. Her tongue tangled with his and each stroke had her vibrating with need.

He cupped her face with one hand, the gesture tender yet possessive, and Darina was ready.

So ready.

"Mom?" Zeke's voice, though muffled, cut through the lustful haze and they both froze.

"Shit," Darina hissed.

"He's in the hallway." Instantly, Foster lifted himself off her and struggled with zipping his pants.

"Something in the way there, Doc?" she teased as she wrestled her own pants back up.

He laughed, raking his hand through his hair and squirming back into his T-shirt. Handing Darina her tank top, he dropped a light kiss on her lips and whispered, "Promise me we'll try this again. Please."

She smiled and opened the door. "We'll see."

"Tease." He followed her out of the library.

"There you are." Zeke marched down the hallway, splitting a glance between them.

Oh, damn. Don't let him do the calculations here.

If Zeke figured out what was going on—or worse still, if she had to know that he'd figured out what was going on—she would die a thousand deaths.

Without having had the actual sex.

Tragic.

Zeke stopped about a yard in front of her. "Ghared had to leave?"

"Yes." She smoothed the front of her tank top, wondering how I-almost-had-amazing-sex she looked.

"Mareea?" Zeke's dark eyes softened on her name.

Darina had noticed Zeke spent more time with Mareea than usual lately. Did he have feelings other than friendship for the girl? She was a sweet teenager who loved her uncle to pieces. Of course, he was the only one who paid any attention to her from her family. Her mother—Ghared's sister, Lilia—was a rotten woman, full of hate and illegal substances. Darina herself had arrested the chick twice, but she knew how to play the game and usually got an early parole. As a cop, Darina didn't mind so much that the woman got out of jail so frequently. What pissed her off was how she treated—or didn't treat—her only daughter.

It wasn't right.

"I hope Mareea's okay," Zeke said.

Darina rested her hands on his shoulders. "You know Ghared will make sure she's okay."

He gave her a half-smile. "That's true." He looked over her shoulder at Foster. "You have an amazing place here, Dr. Ashby."

Darina eased out a breath. Zeke wasn't going to question what she'd been doing in that library with Foster.

Crisis averted.

But her arousal was still at a dangerously high level. She was going to have to do something about that. A shower, perhaps?

Now she was picturing water droplets gliding down Foster's impressive body. Not helping.

"I'm glad you like it here," Foster said, his hand digging into his pocket. He held the bottle of medicine out to Zeke. "You should take this. You'll need another drop tomorrow. Still feeling awesome?"

Zeke nodded. "Better than awesome." He took the bottle and held it up, wiggling it slightly. "Thanks." He pocketed the bottle and looked at Darina. "Are you overseeing the first watch out there?"

"No." She glanced back to Foster, who was standing close enough she could feel his heat on her backside—a heat she had been feeling on her *front* side only minutes ago in the library. "I'm guarding Doctor Ashby personally. The folks out there on the perimeter watches are our first line of defense.

She hoped that was the only line of defense they'd need.

Chapter Eight

"Are we staying in this house if you're guarding Dr. Ashby yourself?" Zeke asked around a yawn and a stretch of his arms above his head.

Darina scratched her forehead, and that simple movement captivated Foster. Good thing she was standing in front of him. Otherwise, Zeke would see one powerful erection straining to bust out of Foster's cargo pants. He'd need a visit from one of his hologram women later, not that any of them would be able to compare to having Darina in his arms, ready and willing and real. To have been that close to burying himself inside her and not being able to was torture.

"I guess I didn't think about where we would crash," Darina said.

"So like you, Mom." Zeke rolled his eyes but smiled at her. "Too busy working to think of mundane things like sleeping."

"Evil—"

"Never sleeps," Zeke finished. "I know. I know." He looked at Foster. "She should have that tattooed on her."

"Well, it's true." Darina crossed her arms over her chest as she faced Foster. His gaze immediately went to her breasts which swelled a bit at the low neck of her tank top. She followed his gaze, smirked, then dropped her arms. "Where can Zeke and I bunk?"

Foster had ideas on where Darina could bunk, and all of them involved being right by his side. He envisioned her hair splayed out on his pillow while he leaned over her and possessed her body, her mind, her very soul if he could manage it. It would be a challenge, but one he couldn't resist.

"Foster?" She poked him in the stomach, a slight smile on her lips. "A room for me and the kid?"

"Right." He blinked the image of her naked body out of his mind and turned around. "Follow me."

He led them past the library—a room that would now be counted among his favorites—and paused at two doors at the end of the hallway. Pointing to the second one, he said, "That's my bedroom." He desperately wanted to finish that sentence with, "and won't you please join me in there, Darina?" Instead, he indicated the first door. "This is a guest room you both can stay in. I think you'll find it has ample space, yet is still in close proximity to mine. You know, so you can oversee my safety. Personally."

Zeke's hand was on the doorknob, while Darina blinked up at Foster, her hazel eyes full of the same fire Foster felt in his entire body.

"Check it out, Mom." Zeke had stepped into the room, and Darina broke eye contact with Foster to follow him.

The guest room was painted a deep hunter green and the walls sported several of Estoria's paintings of deer. Two twin beds were perpendicular to one wall, while wide windows comprised most of the wall opposite them. Those

141

windows offered a prime view of the massive waterwheel Roben and some of the others had built along the stream. When the windows were open as they were now, the rhythmic shush of water dumping out of the waterwheel's buckets drifted in on the gentle summer breeze like a natural lullaby.

The quilts on the two beds were a soft brown, almost like deer hide, with embroidered evergreen branches and pinecones. The bedside tables, the headboards, and a high-backed rocking chair had all been handmade by Roben in an old Shaker style. No one ever stayed in that room, so it still smelled of freshly milled pine.

"What a cozy room," Darina said, running her fingers along the softness of the quilt on the closest bed.

"There's a bathroom through there." Foster pointed to a door by the closet. "Help yourselves to any supplies you find. Make yourselves comfortable."

Zeke had gone to check out the bathroom then let out a gleeful whoop when he discovered the shower. Peeking his head out the door, he said, "I call first to shower."

"Go for it. You stink worse than me anyway," Darina said, laughing.

Zeke's mouth dropped open, but when he sniffed his underarm, he made a face. "Ugh. You're right." He closed the door and a second later, running water sounded.

When Zeke started singing—quite well actually—Darina turned to face Foster. "You sure know how to make a teenage GEC happy. First seizure medicine, now a shower. He'll never want to leave."

Never want to leave. That didn't seem like a bad idea to Foster. What if they all stayed on this property? What if they forgot about the world outside its boundaries? What if they lived the rest of their days, blissfully happy, right there?

"It's a nice thought," Darina said, reading his mind, "but we wouldn't be able to live with ourselves if we didn't do what we could for the rest of the population."

"Damn." Foster took her hand and tugged until her front was pressed up against his front. "Maybe after we save the world then?"

"We'll see." The second time she'd given him that reply. It was enough to keep him hoping.

"Wouldn't you be able to better protect me if you stayed in my room with me?" It only made good security sense.

"That would be the best scenario," Darina said, bringing a finger up to trace along his tattoo, "but what kind of mother would I be if I left Zeke all alone in a strange place for the night?"

"Ah, the responsible parent role. I can't argue with that, now can I?" Foster brushed her hair from her face and dipped his head to nibble on her earlobe.

She breathed out a needy noise that touched Foster deep inside. "No, you can't." Pushing up on her toes, she pressed a kiss to his cheek and whispered, "Good night, Foster," into his ear.

Slipping out of his hold, she stepped to the door and leaned against it. When he walked by, he paused and hooked his hand on the back of her neck. "If you have any trouble sleeping, any trouble at all, I'm right there." He pointed to the door to his room.

"Good to know." She nudged him into the hallway. "You're going in there now, right?"

Foster nodded.

"And you'll stay there all night?"

Again, he nodded.

"Good." She pulled out a small flashlight from her back pocket and walked down the hallway to the great room.

After two quick flashes of the light, Foster heard voices. When Darina returned, she had two others with her—Rasha and Hydec. Foster had found these two GECs on this very property, deep in the woods, about ten years ago. Cast off because Rasha's blood didn't clot properly and Hydec's skin couldn't tolerate direct sunlight, the pair had found each other and had set up a camp together. Foster had given Rasha a blood thickener and Hydec a high-potency UV sunblock, but they'd decided to stay with him instead of trying to blend into society. Rasha had proven to be an outstanding farmer, and Hydec was a wall of muscle who could lift just about anything.

"Rasha and Hydec are assigned to guard your door tonight," Darina said, her voice official. Again, the authoritative tone sent ripples of desire through Foster.

"It is our great honor to help," Hydec said. "We owe Foster so much."

"I've told you a million times," Foster said, "neither of you owe me anything." He turned to

Darina. "Rasha and Hydec helped me build this main house and the cottages."

"Here's to hoping your guarding skills are as good as your house-building skills." Darina clapped them both on the back, checked their weapons, and saluted Foster. "Nighty-night, Doc."

She stepped into the guest room and with a quick look to Foster, she shut the door.

"She's different," Hydec said.

"Different," Foster said. "That's one word for her." He could think of several others and they all had to do with how sexy she was, how she made his blood rush around in his veins.

He stared at the guest room door for a moment before snapping out of his fantasies and walking to his own bedroom door. Looking at Rasha and Hydec, he said, "Thanks for what you're doing for me."

They both nodded solemnly as they took up posts on either side of his door.

"Foster?"

He stopped with his hand on the doorknob and squinted into the dark hallway.

"Show yourself," Hydec said, his hand on his weapon as he flicked on the hall light.

Rasha was in a ready position as well, and Foster didn't like seeing his normally peaceful friends look so fierce. Of course they all had that in them. They were bred to be soldiers after all. Their DNA had been specifically engineered to heighten their fight response.

Still… he didn't like it.

"It's just me." Estoria stepped closer. "Do you have a minute, Foster?"

"Of course." He touched Rasha's shoulder to get her to lower her weapon. "There might be a need for a talk about who is the enemy and who isn't."

"I don't think we should underestimate Warres," Hydec said. "We have no idea what his plans may be."

"I agree." Rasha stowed her weapon, but her posture remained tensed and ready for action.

"So do I," Foster said, "but no one on this property is the enemy. No one."

He reached for Estoria's hand and tugged her to the great room. Rasha and Hydec followed close behind and stood at the doorway. This guarding thing was going to get annoying.

Unless it was Darina guarding him. Personally. All the time. That he could live with. That he *wanted* to live with.

"How are you feeling?" he asked Estoria, pushing thoughts of Darina from his mind. Or trying to anyway.

"Just the usual tiredness and sore muscles." She shrugged and slumped onto one of the leather couches, patting her stomach. "I can already feel things resetting themselves though."

"This one was a girl, right?" Foster took a seat beside her.

"Yes. A little angel." She buried her face in her hands, her shoulders shaking as she cried.

Foster collected Estoria into his arms as he had after every stillborn baby she delivered, twenty by his count. "Oh, Essie." He smoothed her long blonde hair, still damp from the shower she must have taken before coming to the main house. "I wish I knew how to help you."

She looked up at him. "I know you do, Foster. I know." She wiped her eyes with her hands, sniffled, then squared her shoulders. "I want to apologize."

"Apologize? For what?" He was the one who should be apologizing to her. All these years and he'd never been able to find a way to relieve her of her condition, of her bad genetic engineering.

"For the way I acted with your guests. I was less than welcoming." She sniffed again and wiped away a few leftover tears. "I don't know why I was like that." She lifted watery blue eyes to him.

"I know why you were. I just paraded them in without checking with anyone. That was rude on my part." He rubbed her hand between his.

"You don't have to check with us, Foster. This is *your* place. You can do whatever you want here."

Foster shook his head. "No. That's where you're wrong, Essie. This is *our* place. It belongs to all of us. We've made it what it is together. I couldn't have accomplished all we have here on my own. It takes our combined skills to keep it functioning the way it does. We're a... we're a..."

"A family?" she finished, a hopeful arch to her eyebrows.

"Aren't we?" He couldn't think of another word to describe the relationships between everyone on the property. It seemed to fit. He wanted it to fit.

"I suppose we are." Estoria pulled on her bottom lip as she thought. "And if we are a family,

Darina and Zeke should gain membership. Zeke helped Setton harvest blueberries and the boy is a total sweetheart. He makes me wonder what any one of my sons would have grown up to be." She rubbed her hand over her now flat stomach. "And Darina… she didn't hesitate one second to help me when I was giving birth in the woods. She was very kind."

"She's amazing." Foster couldn't stop the words from spilling out.

Estoria's hand clamped onto his forearm, her eyes wide. "You like her."

"I enjoy her company, yes."

Her lips twitched up at the corners. "Enjoy her company. Hmm. Okay."

Foster poked her side, and she swatted his hand away.

"I think you more than enjoy her company, Foster. And that's okay, you know? You're allowed to think about yourself every once in a while."

If only that were true.

****

Finally Mikale's associates had brought him something useful. He turned on his flashlight. The teenage girl standing before him was tall and thin with long waves of chestnut hair. In the pre-Unplug world, she would have been that girl every boy was after, but in the world of today, she was another hooded sweatshirt trying to survive on the streets. Her face was pale, her blue eyes a bit bloodshot, and she shook visibly as Dugan held her by the arm.

"I'm not going to hurt you, child," Mikale said, shining his flashlight on the floor at her feet. Her sneakers were torn and faded. "So far you've followed my instructions magnificently. Keep that up and this will all be over before you know it."

A sob worked its way out of the girl's throat, and Dugan had to catch her as her legs buckled beneath her.

Mikale made a shushing noise as he walked over to her. He slid a chair over. The seat was ripped and a putrid shade of green, but he hadn't decorated the place. He wouldn't be in that place if given the choice. It was cramped and hot and sported an odor he could barely tolerate.

But tolerate it he would. For the cause. To meet his objectives.

"Sit, sweetheart." He motioned for Dugan to let her go, and the girl's body poured itself onto the chair as he turned on a dim overhead light and shut off his flashlight.

She'd pulled the frayed sleeves of her sweatshirt down over her hands as they rested on her thighs. A large hole in her tight black pants revealed her right kneecap. Her skin looked smooth, and Mikale fought the urge to touch her. Clearly, she was already terrified, and all they'd done was hunt her down, pluck her from her domicile, and make her tell them what they wanted to know.

At first, the girl had been tight-lipped, refusing to give away any secrets whatsoever. A few threats on her person and her family took care of her reluctance to cooperate. She'd made the phone call they'd asked her to make, said what she was told to say, and now they waited.

"Wouldn't you be more comfortable without that sweatshirt?" Mikale wiped his own brow. "It's at least eighty-five degrees in here." Though the sun had set hours ago, the temperature had not cooled.

The girl shook her head and hugged her biceps, retreating deeper into the sweatshirt.

A shame. Certainly a nice figure hid beneath the ratty garment. A peek would have passed the time and gotten Mikale's thoughts off Officer Darina Lazitter. He felt as if he knew her intimately already after having gone through her tiny living space. She didn't own many items, but what he'd found intrigued him.

A photo. A paper one. Three beautiful children with caramel skin all looking to be about the same age. The intel his associates had managed to dig up on the good officer stated she'd been the only girl in a set of triplets. The picture had to be of her and her brothers. All three of them were smiling, summer sunshine spilling behind them as they sat on a wooden dock, water rippling at their feet.

Books. The old-fashioned print ones with covers and pages. Titles like *The Collected Works of Edgar Allen Poe* and *Seventy-five Ways to Immobilize Your Opponent* sat on a dusty shelf above Darina's bed. A bed that was especially tidy in a dingy apartment with its sheets and blankets tucked in strict military fashion.

Clothes. Mostly tank tops and cargo pants. One whiff of the garments and Mikale knew the woman herself would smell even better.

He couldn't wait to meet her in person, though he still couldn't shake the familiar feeling seeing her image created.

She had some making up to do for the trouble she'd caused Mikale by hiding Foster from him.

He didn't like delays in his timetable, and he certainly didn't love that he'd had to leave his cozy headquarters and trudge out to the city's streets. His plague was doing its job out there—quite well actually—but he didn't want to be amongst the corpses decomposing in the gutters. He'd inoculated himself and his associates of course, but he didn't particularly want to see what his virus did to the human body. Mikale only wanted to bear witness to the repopulation that would happen after his disease wiped everyone out.

Darina would bear witness with him. She had a key role to play, though she didn't know it yet.

She will know soon.

Mikale regarded the girl still shaking before him. He reached out a hand and pushed her hair out of her face.

She jerked back, knocking over the chair as she stood, and Dugan was instantly in motion. He grabbed her arm, but Mikale gestured for him to release her.

"How can I make you understand we do not wish to harm you?" He tried using his gentlest tone, but his low, raspy voice didn't do gentle.

"Let me go. Leave my family alone." The girl's words cut in and out as she cried.

He hated to see her so upset. He did, but he'd had no other options. Foster had disappeared along with Darina. Emerge Tech was reeling from the fires his people had set inside its walls. His virus was spreading quicker than he'd imagined, and without Darina, he wouldn't be ready for the business of repopulation.

He was on a schedule here and Foster was shitting on that schedule.

"I can't leave you or your family alone, sweet girl. You are my only lead."

"Lead?" She shook her head and squared her shoulders a bit. It was the boldest he'd seen her look since plucking her off the street and bringing her here. "I don't understand. What do you want?" Her dark eyebrows lowered over beautiful blue eyes.

Why did he have to explain everything to everyone?

Wiping the sweat off his brow again, Mikale inhaled, prepared to spell it all out for her, but a rumbling overhead stopped him.

"He's here," Dugan said.

"Please don't hurt him." The girl let out a wail, but Dugan clamped his hand over her mouth.

"Be still now." Mikale pulled his weapon out of its holster and turned off the overhead light. He had one shot at this, and he hadn't waited all this time to have it screwed up.

The rumbling softened to a dull thudding followed by some metallic squeaks. After about five minutes, footsteps sounded outside the apartment door.

"Showtime." Mikale grabbed the girl and pressed the nose of his gun into her ribs. "I said I wouldn't hurt you, but you've got to cooperate. Understand?"

She nodded, her entire body nearly convulsing in his grip.

"Not a sound now. We want this to be a surprise," Mikale whispered.

A tiny whimper slipped from the girl, and he tightened his grip on her.

More footsteps thumped outside the door. The knob jiggled. A moment later a large shadowed figure filled the doorway.

"Mareea?"

A thud filled the quiet, followed by a grunt and what Mikale hoped was a body sliding to the floor.

"Dugan?"

"Mission accomplished, sir."

The dim overhead light came back on, and Mikale smiled victoriously at the man lying in a heap at Dugan's feet.

Mareea broke free of Mikale's hold and kneeled by the body, tears streaming down her cheeks. "Uncle Ghared!"

****

Darina listened to Zeke's steady breathing in the twin bed beside the one she occupied. The kid had cracked her up when he'd emerged from the bathroom and did a complicated running flip onto his bed, landing belly down.

"We'd never have enough room at home for me to do that stunt," he'd said, laughing and flopping over to his back. Propped up on one elbow, he smiled at her—a genuine smile, not one of the ones he often dug out for her.

She walked over to him and cupped his face. "You wouldn't have such red cheeks either at home. Did you turn the water all the way to scorching?"

"When was the last time we had a shower with hot water, Mom? How about never?" He'd shaken free of her hold and had run a hand through his damp hair. His bangs were getting too long, hiding his genetically perfected face.

"This needs cutting." She'd stepped closer and ruffled his hair until he squirmed out of reach.

"Mareea said she likes it longer." Worry had crept into his dark eyes. "You think she's okay?"

"She will be once Ghared gets to her."

Zeke chewed on his bottom lip, and Darina wondered if he was going to finally admit aloud to being interested in Mareea. Instead, he grabbed the pillow on the bed and bopped her with it.

"You asking for trouble, kid?" She'd jerked her own pillow off the other bed and retaliated.

Five minutes later, they were both breathing heavily and giggling. She hadn't had that much fun in ages.

Well, that much mother-son fun anyway. She recalled some different fun in Foster's library earlier. Staring up at the ceiling now, the guest room shrouded in darkness, she imagined Foster was with her, his body hovering over hers, his lips doing things to stimulate her every nerve ending.

That man can kiss.

The last time she'd been kissed—really kissed—she'd been playing a game. A game to get a free prosthetic hand. One she couldn't afford on her own. Her goals had been clear in her mind, but somewhere along the way, she'd let herself fall in love.

With a rich bastard.

Fisting the sheets beneath her now, she shook her head. How could she have been so foolish? Well, she'd paid the price. She'd learned her lesson. Rich bastards were not her type.

Kissing Foster, however, made rich bastards seem not so much like bastards. Words like *forever* and *happy* circulated in her mind when she thought of him. Even now, hours later, her lips still buzzed with the attention he'd given them. The rest of her body craved to know more of Dr. Foster Ashby.

That would be a mistake. Huge.

She angled her head back and looked at the wall behind the headboard of the bed. Foster was on the other side of that wall. Nothing but lumber, sheetrock, and plaster stood between her and him.

Maybe I should check on him.

She was, after all, in charge of keeping him safe. It wouldn't seem out of the ordinary if she made a nighttime survey in the name of security.

Folding the pillow around her head, she released a muffled growl into it. Going to Foster right now would be absolutely idiotic. Their worlds were barely in the same solar system. The clean, fresh scent of the bed linens beneath her and the vibrant colors of the property she'd toured today let her know she did not belong in Foster's life. She was used to musty, dark, and gray places. Places where broken asphalt crunched under her boots. Places where the odds were stacked against her.

Not this paradise.

But to have a taste of it? A taste to keep locked away in her soul to pull out on especially tough days in the city? She couldn't deny she wanted that. She couldn't deny she wanted Foster.

Looking over at Zeke and deeming that he was out cold, she sat up. She hadn't bothered getting under the covers. It wasn't as hot in Vermont as it was in the city, but something about settling in too deeply made her feel unable to react quickly if need be. She actually still had her shoes on and her weapon at her hip, though she'd changed her tank top and pants for ones that someone had left in the bathroom. Though the clothes weren't hers, they fit well, were comfortable, and clean. While she didn't make a habit of being filthy, city life didn't loan itself to regular laundry cycles or purchasing new clothes or showering with hot water. This was definitely as fresh as she'd felt in a long time.

A shame to waste all this freshness.

Foster hadn't minded the scents of the city that had stuck to her earlier. They hadn't stopped him from wanting her.

She stood, glanced once more at Zeke who hadn't stirred, and tiptoed to the door. After opening it, she slipped into the dark hallway. A flashlight beam instantly lasered her, and she froze.

"Everything okay, Darina?" Rasha asked.

Guards. Right. She'd forgotten about them. "Everything's fine. Just checking on you guys," she lied.

"All clear out here," Hydec reported. "Shift change in ten minutes."

"Why don't you two knock off early?" she asked. "I've got this covered for ten minutes."

Rasha raised her eyebrows. "You should be getting some sleep."

"I should be, but it isn't happening." Darina shrugged then tapped her weapon at her waist. "Go ahead. I'm armed and ready."

"Something tells me you're always armed and ready," Hydec said.

"Better than being defenseless and unprepared." A state she never found herself in. Never. Though Foster had made her feel both rather unexpectedly. "Now go on. Maybe you'll succeed in getting some sleep."

Rasha laughed. "Hydec will. Nothing interferes with his sleep."

"And you've tried to *interfere*." He hooked his arm around Rasha's shoulders.

"Oh," Darina said, "you two are... together?"

"The woods can get lonely," Rasha said with a sly smile and a quick glance back at Foster's door behind her. "A few of us here are paired up." She poked Hydec's ribs. "I was the only one who could tolerate this guy."

"Not nice, Rasha." Hydec waved a finger at her as if scolding a child.

"I'll make it up to you." She winked at him as he smiled. "We have an extra ten minutes thanks to Darina. That's all you'll need right."

"Ignore her." Hydec tugged on Rasha's arm. "She knows full well I can go all night."

Rasha nodded and laughed. "Actually, that *is* one area where his genetic engineering excelled."

"Believe it, baby." He grinned. "Good night, Darina."

The two of them walked down the hallway, their hands joined, their heads bent toward one another as they shared secrets in the dark. A great longing swelled in her chest, and she turned toward Foster's door.

To knock or not to knock? Was he deeply asleep in there? He'd had a long day, just as she'd had. Would he be annoyed if she visited? His subconscious might be still working on the cure while he slept. She didn't want to get in the way of his progress.

Did his genetic engineering excel in the area of lovemaking too? If one were to attempt to build a more superior human, wouldn't improving their sexual prowess be a fun enhancement?

Did he sleep in the nude?

Deciding she absolutely needed the answer to that last question, she turned the knob and eased the door open. The room was dark, but she could make out the shape of Foster's bed against the far wall between a set of windows. A lump in the middle of the king-sized bed let her know the man was a bed hog.

For some reason that made her grin.

The room smelled like the outdoors, and a quick scan revealed the windows were open to let in fresh nighttime air. Inhaling deeply, she stood in the doorway as the long curtains on the windows rippled in the warm breeze.

"Are you going to stay at the door or get your unbelievably sexy ass over here?" Foster's voice was low and whispery, sending goosebumps over her skin.

"You're awake."

"Did you actually think I'd be able to sleep knowing you were right next door?" Sheets rustled and a shadowed form became visible as he sat up in the bed.

Darina's eyes had adjusted to the dark enough to see his finger curling to invite her over to the bed. She swallowed loudly—too loudly—and hesitated. Yes, she'd been the one to bust into his room, but she'd expected him to be asleep. She'd expected to look to see that he was safe—and if he was nude—then pop back out of his room, returning to her own and facing a sleepless night alone.

His invitation changed things.

"Darina, I'm not going to bite… unless you want me to." He turned on a dim bedside lamp so she could see him grinning now.

Did she want him to bite her? Did she want those grinning lips on her body?

Hell yes!

Her legs took charge and carried her to the bed where she found herself climbing on where Foster's feet were under the sheets. On all fours, she continued up his body until her face was even with his and she straddled his lap.

"Hey, Doc," she whispered.

"Hey." He cupped her face and wasted no time feasting on her mouth.

She was just as hungry. For at least three solid minutes, they went between heated kissing to crazy intense kissing. Darina was more than pleased to find that when she'd rested her hands on Foster's shoulders, they were bare. If that impressive something poking her from under the sheet still covering his lap was any indication, the man was also bare from the waist down.

Shiver.

Foster's hand clawed at her tank top, pulling the strap off her left shoulder. He leaned closer and ran his lips along her exposed skin. When his teeth grazed her flesh, she tightened her thighs around his waist, and he groaned into her hair.

"I sincerely hope this isn't a really vivid dream." He sucked her earlobe into his mouth then tugged on it with his teeth. "And no one better interrupt us."

"I'll shoot them if they do." She was kidding. Maybe.

Darina closed her eyes and let her head drop back, giving him more of her neck to explore. He didn't disappoint as his mouth charted a course over what she offered.

She wanted to offer a hell of a lot more.

Foster's hands skated up into her hair, and he grabbed fistfuls of it, tethering her to him. He looked into her eyes for a minute, and Darina expected him to come to his senses or something.

"Please, don't stop." Again, she hated the begging in her voice, but being denied two times in one night was enough to have her throw out all her rules.

He traced a circle on her cheek and smiled. "I couldn't stop if I wanted to, Officer Lazitter... and trust me, I don't want to."

In a quick move that made her let out a little squeak, Foster swiveled her onto her back. Hovering over her, he quickly caught her lips again, and any demands about being on top faded from her consciousness.

She was only aware of one thing… Foster.

He peeled her tank top off completely, and she shimmied out of the rest of her clothes, making a point to rest her weapon within reach on the bedside table. Foster looked at the gun for a few seconds, a crease forming between his brows. Shaking his head, he rested on his elbows and gazed down at her, the dim light getting caught in his pale green eyes.

"Ah, yes. Right where we left off." He lowered and nibbled on her neck, along her jaw, and to her mouth.

"And Zeke's totally out in the other room."

"Another benefit to the seizure medicine. It promotes deep REM sleep."

"So you sleep that well too?"

"When thoughts of touching you aren't getting in the way, yes." His mouth turned up in a half grin, and she needed him inside her. Immediately.

In tune with her thoughts, he slid down her body and used that skilled mouth on her breasts, teasing low moans from deep inside her. He stroked her ready heat with his fingers, testing how badly she wanted him.

Had she ever been this charged with anticipation? Something about seeing Foster on this Vermont property, watching him interact with the people he housed here, and the way he'd shared his knowledge to help Zeke made her feel close to him. Closer than she should. She found it hard to believe she'd only met him early this morning.

He replaced his fingers with his arousal and slowly slid into her, filling her. Inch by delightful inch. They shuddered simultaneously, and Foster stilled for a second, his gaze connecting with hers.

In that moment, Darina saw this man was much more than a doctor trying to save the world. He was capable, perhaps, of saving her.

Chapter Nine

He had hoped Darina would come to him tonight. He'd gotten into bed, but sleepy was the last thing he'd felt. Every time he'd closed his eyes, visions of Darina in the library, ready and willing, had parts of his body refusing to settle.

Now she's here.

He was buried deep inside her, and no hologram could compare to having her wrapped around him so snugly, so completely, so perfectly. He'd had a few live partners in the past, but no one like Darina. From the moment she'd pulled him off the street in the city, he knew she wasn't like anyone he'd ever met. Strong, confident, smart. She was all of these and more.

Her fingernails grazed his shoulders as she pulled him closer and took him in deeper. Their bodies were so tangled, her legs hooked around his waist, his arms touching everything he could reach. Never had he wanted to be a part of someone so desperately.

"Foster." His name was a plea on her lips, urging him to give her what she needed, to take what he wanted.

He shifted, pulled out of her slowly, then thrust back in, causing her to let out a husky purr that gave him the fuel to continue, to take them both higher.

With a final series of thrusts, he drove into her and earned a full body shudder for them both. Breathing heavily, they went limp, and he lay cradled between her legs, his head resting on her shoulder.

She hugged him, her muscled arms locked around him in a way that made him feel as if he were important to her. It was silly to think what they had shared was anything more than two adults finding a release in pleasuring each other.

But it felt like more.

A great deal more.

"Nothing wrong with your genetic coding in this area, Doc," she said, her breathing still a bit labored.

He lifted his head and smiled at the satisfied expression on her face. Her eyelids were lowered, her lips slightly turned up at the corners as she ran her foot up and down his calf. The light scrape of her toes made him hard all over again.

"Oh, really?" She raised her head off the pillow to meet his gaze.

"Extra stamina came with the DNA." He gave her hopeful eyes.

"Be a shame to let it go to waste." She grabbed him and rolled them over so he was on the bottom now. "I'm in charge this time."

"Yes, Officer Lazitter." He raised a hand and pushed her hair away so he could see her beautiful face. "You have the most amazing lips."

"You haven't even begun to see what they can do." Her eyebrows tilted devilishly as she slid down the length of him, her nipples coasting along his chest, followed by the sweep of her hair.

She reached up to his shoulders and raked her fingers down his front until she arrived at where his prosthetic right leg began. Like her hand, the seam was hardly visible. You'd only find it if you were looking for it. The muscles in his real left leg were slightly bigger than what remained of his right thigh due to years of overcompensating when walking, but other than that, the evidence of his non-organic part was almost nonexistent.

"Do you ever take it off?" She ran her index finger along the seam, then flattened her palm against the prosthetic part of his thigh.

He shook his head. "When I had a lesser model I did because it wasn't comfortable, but I often forget this one isn't the real deal."

She flexed her prosthetic hand. "Me too. Thanks to you."

He reached down and threaded his fingers between hers. Pulling her hand up to his lips, he dropped a kiss on the back of it. "But you can't feel that, can you?"

"No, but I like watching you do it anyway." She grinned at him, and her face became more magnificent.

"I was working on adding nerve ending simulators into the fleshy outer layer of my prosthetic designs, but the Anarch ruined my plans."

"And Warres didn't help any." She clenched her teeth hard enough that he could hear them grind together.

"No, he didn't. I should be working on so many other things." Foster blew out a breath. "Instead, I'm trying to undo a situation that never should have happened in the first place." Even now he felt guilty for enjoying the pleasure Darina had given him. If he wasn't sleeping, shouldn't he be trying to find the cure?

"Recharging is okay." She grabbed his chin and made him look at her.

"What?"

"I can feel the guilt coming off you, Doc. Have you been working on that cure the way you worked on it today?"

He nodded. Every hour of every day had been consumed with trying to find the combination that would eradicate Warres's plague.

"Then you're giving it your all. Besides, this," she gestured between the two of them, "might be good for your brain." She tapped his temple. "Might kickstart a line of thinking you haven't considered yet. You know, like when you're trying to remember something, but the more you try to remember it, the more you can't retrieve it. The moment you work on something else, however, it just pops into your head." She snapped her fingers. "You know what I mean?"

"I do." He ran his index finger over her full bottom lip. "Does that make you the *something else* I'm working on?"

"It would, except..." she shifted lower and stroked his erection, "*I'm* working on *you*."

He wanted to reply with some witty comment, but her hands on him in that way made forming sentences impossible. Her hands were warm and strong and most welcome to touch him like that any time she wanted them to.

She tightened her grip and moved her hand back and forth until he could barely contain himself. When her mouth closed around him, stars flashed behind his closed eyelids, and his heart threatened to pummel his ribs to splintery bits. Her full lips were velvety and the heat of her mouth was a welcome sanctuary. Her tongue massaged him, coaxed him to steel hard, and brought him to the breaking point.

"Darina, please..." He had to be inside her. Had to. Immediately.

With a final caress of her lips against his tip, she released him and climbed atop him instead. "Ask for it again."

"Now. Please." One word demands were all he was capable of giving her.

"What do you want, Doc?" She leaned forward, her lips brushing against his ear. "Tell me."

"I want you take me into that hot, wet paradise between your legs." He impressed himself with that bit of poetry, considering the fact that all the blood in his body was definitely assembled in one area.

Darina's eyes darkened as a low growl rumbled in her throat. It was the most erotic sound Foster had ever heard.

With a few teases of his lips, she slid onto him, accepting him, making his fantasies come true with each movement of her body above his. Their flight to the summit was powerful and consuming and primal. He clamped his hands on her slender hips, holding her to him, pushing himself deeper, wanting to fuse their bodies into one.

When her insides clenched around him, milked him until he had no more to give, he had to bite his bottom lip to keep from tossing a victory cry into the quiet night. She must have known he was trying to contain himself because she took control of his lips, keeping him busy enough that he no longer wanted to sound off.

Instead, he wanted to kiss her everywhere.

Flipping her over onto her back, he ran his tongue down the valley between her breasts and around her flat stomach. Dropping feather-light kisses along her soft flesh, he enjoyed the taste of her, knowing it was a flavor he'd always crave now that he'd sampled her.

She dug her fingers into his hair, her nails scraping his skull in a way that had him feeling it in every extremity—even his prosthetic leg somehow.

He settled next to her, his arm draped across her stomach, hoping to keep her there.

"You know I can't stay, Foster." She pressed a kiss to his forehead.

He tightened his grip on her waist. "I don't know anything of the sort."

She laughed and her body shook beside him. Damn, he loved having a body beside him. More specifically, *her* body.

"I should get some sleep if I'm to properly protect you, Doc."

"You can sleep right here." Again he nestled closer, hoping she wouldn't be able to resist staying.

"You and I both know if I stay, we won't be sleeping." She patted his cheek and grinned at him.

"We can rest between not sleeping."

She angled her head to the digital clock he had beside the bed. "Shit. The new set of guards is already at your door."

"See? Too complicated for you to get past them now. Better hunker down right here." He liked this line of reasoning.

"Maybe another night. How would it look if I was found in here on the very first night?"

"Like I'm irresistible?"

She pushed him back with a light slap to the shoulder. "Maybe you are. I don't know how to explain falling into bed with you otherwise."

"You're probably just too tired to fight me off." He nibbled on her shoulder while his thumb caressed her nipple to a tight bud.

Darina arched into his touch. "I don't want to fight you off." She pressed her lips to his, explored his mouth for several glorious moments, then pushed away. "I have to go." She slid from his grip and pulled herself to sitting on the edge of his bed.

"Help me in the lab tomorrow?" He at least wanted to be sure she'd be with him all day tomorrow.

"Guarding you personally, remember?" She pointed to herself. "It's my job to be in your space."

Foster pumped a fist in the air. "Yes!"

Smiling, she stood and collected her clothes. She dressed in the dim light, and he enjoyed everything about watching her. Of course, he'd have liked it better if she were undressing to stay with him, but he was encouraged by the prospect of being with her tomorrow.

"What time are you planning to get up?" she asked as she stepped into her boots and tied them.

"When the sun does. I don't want to waste a moment. I'm close on this cure." He sat up and ran a hand through his hair, scratching at the back of his neck. "I'm just missing something." If only he could put his finger on *what* was missing.

Darina pressed her palms to the bed and leaned down to him in a quasi-pushup. Her bicep muscles caught his attention for a moment, then the way her tank top dipped over her breasts in that position stole all his focus.

"You'll get it."

She sounded so sure. Surer than he felt.

"See you in the morning, Doc."

After a quick kiss, she left. He heard her talk to the two new guards, saying something about investigating a sound inside the room. Then the night got super quiet again except for the crickets singing their summer song outside. He folded his arms behind his head and listened to those crickets until he could almost pick out the sounds of the individual insects.

Was Darina back in bed in the guest room? Had Zeke noticed she was gone? If so, was he asking her a million questions? What were her responses?

Did she want tomorrow to come as fast as he did?

****

Strangely, Darina slept like a newborn puppy after returning to the guest room. Nothing like a few rounds of amazing sex to make a girl sleep deeply. She couldn't remember the last time she'd slept like that.

Possibly she'd *never* slept like that.

In the shower now, she let the water beat against her skin. Zeke had been right. There was no sense in taking a lukewarm shower when a scorching hot one was available. Seriously, how did Foster return to the city when he had all this here in Vermont? She thought back to his Emerge Tech domicile and even with its state-of-the-art technology, it didn't compare to this place. She felt as if she'd been transported back in time to a much better version of living on planet Earth. It'd be hard to let it go when this gig was over.

Whenever that would be.

Foster had been so frustrated last night when he'd spoken of working on the cure. The man had dozens of other projects waiting for his brilliance, but this cure was sucking up all his time and energy. Darina wished she could help. Too bad she didn't know shit about mixing up medicines.

"You almost done in there, Mom?" Zeke knocked on the bathroom door.

"Almost." Though she wanted to stay in there forever. And have Foster join her. Now *that* was an image to get a girl through the day.

"Good. Hurry up. I'm starving and something smells tasty out there," Zeke said.

Darina finished in the bathroom, and by the time she emerged into the guest bedroom, Zeke was dressed in a pair of black cargo pants and a yellow T-shirt that gave his skin a healthy glow. She hadn't seen her boy look that well ever. When she'd found him, huddled under that pier, he'd been pale with gray circles around his bloodshot eyes. He'd had a seizure five minutes after she'd picked him up in the back seat of her squad car. Once his body stopped convulsing, he certainly didn't look better.

But now?

Now he looked like a vigorous teenager, ready to conquer the world. Or at least do some serious eating.

"C'mon," he said, tugging on her hand. "I don't want to miss whatever food is out there."

She let him drag her out of the guest room. The two morning guards, Vero and Tonner, still stood at Foster's bedroom door so she paused.

"Is he still in there?" she asked.

Vero nodded. "But I heard him moving around."

She was tempted to relieve them of their duty and start her day the way she wanted to, but Zeke was waiting for her in the hallway.

"Any problems during your shift?" she asked instead, deciding sticking to official business was best.

"Not one," Tonner said. "Do you think we're overdoing this protection thing?"

"Dr. Ashby almost got killed twice in one day in Boston," she said. "So no, I don't think we're overdoing anything."

"Of course," Vero said, throwing a glare at Tonner. "Besides, we're happy to do anything for Foster."

Tonner nodded, a penitent expression on his face. "That's true. He's given us so much."

The man was a giver. What he'd given her last night was one of the best gifts she'd ever received.

"Any news from the perimeter team?" she asked.

"No. Everything's been quiet all around," Tonner said.

"Good." Darina hoped things stayed quiet all around. "Let's keep up the designated schedules unless you hear from me."

"Got it." Vero gave her a little salute.

Working with genetically engineered humans who had been designed to be soldiers definitely had its advantages. The government may not want them, but the police department could certainly make use of them. Everyone she'd met on Foster's property had something to contribute. What right did the government have to create these people then decide they weren't good enough? She'd always been pissed at the treatment GECs received, but now, after meeting so many of them, it was even more ridiculous.

She caught up to Zeke, and they followed his nose until they got to the kitchen. Estoria stood by the stove, mixing something in a large glass bowl.

"Good morning." She didn't look as if she'd given birth only yesterday. Her stomach was flat, and she appeared well-rested.

"How are you feeling?" Darina asked.

"Empty." Estoria gave her sad eyes, but then collected herself with a big inhale. "Thought I'd try to fill the void with pancakes. You interested?" She glanced at Zeke.

"Yes, yes, a million times yes," Zeke said, clasping his hands together in a plea.

Estoria laughed. "If you want to eat them, you have to help."

"No problem." Zeke looked over the ingredients she had on the counter. "Tell me what to do."

Darina wandered to the big windows in the dining room while Estoria directed Zeke. Looking out, she surveyed the team surrounding the main house. No one was getting through that line of defense. Not with each one of them outfitted with weapons, genetic advantages—even if the government didn't think so—and the desire to pay Foster back for what he'd done for them. It was a damn fine team.

"Tell me you dreamed of me all night."

She turned to see Foster leaning against the doorframe to the dining room. Glancing to the kitchen, she said in a low voice, "Maybe, but the dreams didn't top the real thing."

Foster put his hand to his chest. "Wow. I think that's the best compliment I've ever received." He stepped into the room. "I know you probably want to keep a lid on what happened between us last night. I'll respect that."

"Thank you." A part of her, however, wanted to climb the tallest tree on the property and shout about how she'd been completely and totally satisfied by this man. That wouldn't do anything for the leadership she was trying to establish among the security team, though.

Foster came closer, his movements slow and graceful. He wore black cargo pants with a hunter green T-shirt that showcased his superior body and highlighted his eyes.

"The clothes Zeke has on?" She gestured to Foster's outfit. "Are they yours?"

He nodded as he came closer, his gaze zeroing in on her. "What's mine is yours."

"How hospitable." She raised an eyebrow when Foster came to stand right in front of her. She desperately wanted a good morning kiss, but with Zeke and Estoria right in the next room, she was afraid of getting caught.

"Are they making pancakes in there?" Foster asked.

"Yes." She loved how she had to look up a little to see his beautiful eyes.

"Estoria puts all her focus into her pancakes, so if she's teaching Zeke, all his attention is on the task as well." He reached out a hand and let his finger trail down the fat braid she'd wrangled her hair into today.

"So anything we might be doing in here would be totally undetected by them?" She ran her own finger along his bottom lip. "Is that what you're saying?"

"Exactly."

Before she could think about it too much, Foster's lips were pressed to hers. Heat instantly flooded her veins when he clamped his hands onto her shoulders and brought her body against his. She slid her arms around his waist and held on as if she planned to never let go.

Stupid. She'd have to let go eventually. Foster would find the cure. The world would be saved. Maybe she could catch Warres, settle the score, and end all future threats.

And that would be that.

Foster would have no need for around the clock security if Warres was caught. She'd have no reason to stay at his lovely Vermont oasis. She and Zeke would go back to the city, back to their little apartment. At least the plague would no longer be a threat to her or Ghared. Maybe, with the cure in place, the world could get its shit together. Maybe she could have a better life.

Lonely, but better.

Because she would be lonely. She realized that now as she kissed Foster. Something had surfaced with his sweet lovemaking, something that had made her understand she'd been craving companionship only a man like Foster could provide. But she couldn't actually *have* a man like Foster. They were too different. He was a brilliant scientist, and he'd be a hero once he found the cure. The whole world would know who he was. Know him and love him. She, on the other hand, was just an average cop. Only criminals would know her, and they certainly wouldn't love her once she caught them.

A low rumble sounded in Foster's throat now as he ended the kiss and rested his forehead against hers. "You make my knees weak. Even the one I built." He tapped his right thigh. Sighing, he said, "Let's have some breakfast... unless I can convince you to let me carry you back to my bedroom?"

"Breakfast, Doc. We need breakfast." She took a step back, but he caught her arm.

"Will you come to me again tonight?" His green eyes lasered into her. "Please."

A man who didn't hide what he wanted. Interesting. She couldn't say she knew too many men like that. It was refreshing to have Foster be so direct with her, but a voice in her head told her to keep her distance. Falling for him would be dumb. Super dumb.

"We'll see," she said, laughing at his pout. Damn, his lips were gorgeous.

His shoulders slumped as he let go of her arm. "You say that a lot."

"Yeah, and didn't you get what you wanted last night?" She arched an eyebrow at him.

A slow grin worked its way across his face. "Actually, yes, I did." He crossed his fingers. "Here's to hoping *we'll see* works in my favor again." He tugged her into the kitchen, dropping her hand as they crossed the threshold.

Darina paused, taking a moment to compose herself. If Zeke looked directly at her right now, he'd totally know she'd been kissing Foster... and loving every second of it. She didn't need her teenage son knowing that about her. She was Officer Darina Lazitter. Logical, practical, focused. She didn't do daydreaming or kissing or whatever she should call what she'd done last night with Foster, because it couldn't happen again.

But she wanted it to.

Oh, she was in trouble here.

"Mom?"

"Yeah." She snapped her gaze up to Zeke, now standing in front of her.

"I asked if you wanted blueberries in yours." He held up a handful of the berries. "They're from the property." He popped one into his mouth and dropped a few into her hand.

The berries actually made a sound when she bit into them. A snap that indicated their freshness, their perfect ripening. Juice shot onto her tongue and filled her mouth.

"Wow." She stole a few more out of Zeke's hand. "These are amazing."

"Let's put them in her pancakes, Estoria." Zeke walked back over to the stove. "I now know how to make pancakes, Mom."

"And he'll be in charge of making breakfast tomorrow." Estoria laughed at Zeke's wide eyes. "What? Did you think I was showing you how to make them for the hell of it?"

"She's tricky like that," Foster said, stealing a few blueberries and winking at Darina when he caught her watching him. "You're having a good time cooking with her and then *bam.* You've got the spoon in your hand, and you're doing all the work."

Estoria laughed again. "You make me sound like a manipulator."

"And?" He held his hands out to his sides.

She picked up a towel and threw it at him. "Jerk."

Zeke chuckled and looked at Darina. "They sound like you and Ghared." His face grew serious as he turned toward Foster. "You haven't heard anything from him, have you? About Mareea?"

Foster dug into his pocket and pulled out his tablet. He swiped his finger across the screen, causing Darina to remember his fingers gliding across her skin. She grabbed more berries and stuffed them in her mouth to focus on something else.

"No messages from him." Foster looked up at Zeke. "But that could be good news, right? Like everything's okay."

Zeke nodded, but Darina could tell the boy was still concerned. "If we don't hear anything by tonight," she said, "we'll contact Ghared. It might be good to have some information from the outside too."

"Sounds like a solid plan to me," Foster said. "Now let's eat so we can get into the lab."

He shot Darina a quick glance followed by a grin, which heated her entire body in two seconds flat. Apparently working on the cure was not the only thing on his agenda for the lab today.

How was she going to resist him?

Chapter Ten

"How hard did you hit him, Dugan?" Mikale asked, walking a wide circle around Ghared Timms's body still prone on the floor of the apartment. The apartment adjacent to Darina's.

Lucky bastard. Not that Mikale had any desire whatsoever to live in such squalor, but to be that close to Darina was definitely an attractive option. He'd be that close to her, only in the comfort of his private rooms back at headquarters. She was going to love being able to leave this lifestyle behind and fulfill her destiny with him. Together they'd rise to the top of the new world he built.

"Socked him in the jaw. No harder than I hit anyone else, sir." Dugan crouched and poked Ghared in the cheek.

Ghared moaned and slid his arm up to his head.

"Ah, it awakens." Mikale sidled up to Dugan and bent over Ghared's body as the man tried to wriggle up to all fours. "Nasty headache there, Mr. Timms?"

Ghared flicked icy blue eyes in his direction. Blood glistened on the man's bottom lip, and the early shading of a bruise had bloomed on his jaw. "Where's Mareea?"

"Oh, she got hysterical when you didn't wake up right away and started making too much noise. We had to quiet her. Too much noise and the lower class humans who live around here will come out of their holes to investigate. Can't have that." Mikale shined his flashlight to a corner of the room where Mareea was tied to a chair and gagged. Tears still streamed from her eyes, and her shoulders shook.

Ghared struggled to his knees, his eyes squinting in pain. "What do you want from us?"

"Information." Mikale swooped the flashlight beam to Ghared's face, and the man raised his hands to cover his eyes.

"Get that out of my face. The overhead lighting is enough."

"Of course you've grown accustomed to this dimness. You no longer remember what it's like to have things that work on full power." Mikale shook his head.

"Are you pitying me?" Ghared got to his feet now and Dugan took a step forward, but Mikale signaled him back.

"Yes. I do pity you. I pity the life you lead down here." He opened his arms wide to encompass the dingy apartment. "I pity the fact that it's only a matter of time before you catch my plague. I pity the fact that you'll be dead soon."

At that sentence, Mareea let out a wail that could be heard over the gag in her mouth. Choking noises emanated from her throat, and she hung her head forward so her hair covered her face.

"At least someone will mourn your passing before she joins you in death. Such a loyal niece," Mikale said. "She didn't want to call you when we asked. She fought us, but Dugan here can be very convincing."

Dugan reached to his back pocket and pulled out a wicked looking dagger. "She immediately understood her face wouldn't look so pretty after I got done with her."

Ghared charged toward Dugan, knocking the dagger out of the larger man's grasp. He pummeled his fists into Dugan's gut until the man couldn't stand anymore. With a few kicks to the ribs, Dugan was out cold, and Ghared turned his attention to Mikale.

"You're next." He stepped forward, but Mikale was ready. He had his gun in his hand and pointed at Ghared's chest.

"Dugan likes knives and the hand-to-hand stuff. Me?" He shrugged. "I like to have the technological advantage." He regarded the gun. "This is special issue. Military-grade. Developed for close combat and maximum damage. I developed it myself when I worked at Emerge Tech. Want to see a demo?"

Ghared put his hands up and shook his head. "Not today."

"Good, because I need you to do me a favor." Mikale had, after all, lured the man here for a reason.

"A favor?" Ghared smirked. "I'm not doing shit for you, man."

"Fine." Mikale marched over to Mareea and pressed the gun to her temple. The girl's muffled cry sent a shiver of anticipation over Mikale's body. "Do it for her then."

"If you hurt her..." Ghared's fists clenched by his sides.

"There'll be no need to hurt her if you cooperate." Mikale took a section of Mareea's long hair and combed his fingers through it. He remembered a time when women's hair smelled like fruit and was as soft as silk. This girl's hair was neither. It was cleanish, but it didn't shine. It didn't slither around his hand with a hushed whisper.

The time for a new order has come.

This world wasn't operating properly anymore. It hadn't been for a long time. The government and Emerge Tech said they were working on restoring balance, but it wasn't happening fast enough. The government couldn't be trusted to do anything right and Emerge Tech wasn't much better.

Mikale's plague was the only thing speeding up the restoration process and what re-grew in the aftermath would be better than anything of the past.

But he had to have Darina first.

"What do you want?" Ghared's voice brought Mikale back to the present.

"Your neighbor."

Ghared's eyes narrowed then widened as he looked at the wall joining his apartment to Darina's. "You want her?"

Mikale nodded once.

"Why?"

"She's destined to help me with my mission." He'd always known there would be a woman involved in his plans. He didn't know who until he'd seen Darina's picture. She'd stirred

183

something inside him, and no other woman would do now. It had to be her.

"If you think Darina Lazitter will help you with anything, you're insane." Ghared laughed. The man actually laughed. He stopped when the split in his bottom lip began oozing fresh blood, but his eyes still held amusement. "You obviously know she's guarding Dr. Ashby. She's chosen her side, dude, and it ain't yours."

"It's your job to get her to switch sides."

Ghared shook his head. "Warres, you don't know a thing about Darina. Once she's made a decision, there's no flipping her. Besides, you're a lunatic. She doesn't like lunatics."

"Then I guess today is the last day on this planet for you and your niece."

Mikale flicked the setting on his gun to maximum power and made a show of preparing to pull the trigger. Mareea squealed in her chair, water pouring out of her eyes like a faucet on full blast.

"Wait!" Ghared put his hands out. "There's no need to involve Mareea. What does she have to do with any of this? She doesn't know where Darina is. I'm the only one who does."

"Mareea is the incentive to get you to cooperate." Again, he pressed the gun harder into the girl's temple and twitched his finger on the trigger.

"I'll cooperate." Ghared took a step closer. "I'll do it, but you have to let Mareea go. Completely. She's out of here or you get nothing from me."

Mikale shook his head. "She's not going anywhere. You'll help me find Darina, but this girl comes with us. I may need her again to properly motivate you."

Ghared let out a growl, and Mikale had to admit he feared the man. Without a weapon, he would definitely not have an advantage. Ghared was bigger, more muscular, and had a fierce edge that was barely contained by his skin.

And were those skeletons beyond the barbed wire tattoo on his arm? Something about the hollow eye sockets of the skulls made Mikale uneasy.

But I have a weapon. As long as he had the gun and the girl, he had the power. He just needed it to stay that way.

"What do you say, Mr. Timms?" He wrenched Mareea to her feet, poking the gun into her side now. "Are you ready for our field trip?"

Ghared's expression wrestled with several emotions Mikale didn't care to waste time deciphering. The man clenched his teeth and wiped blood off his split lip. "Fine. I need gas for my hovercopter."

"Do you really think I'm going to allow you to chauffeur us?" Mikale rolled his eyes. "My pulsejet is charged and ready."

Dugan moaned from the floor as he regained consciousness.

"And it appears my driver is nearly ready to act as pilot." Mikale shuffled Mareea closer to Dugan and nudged the man with his boot. "Shake it off, Dugan. We've got to go."

Dugan rolled to his back and rubbed his eyes. "I think my rib is broken. I can't drive the pulsejet in this condition." He sat up, pain etched into his features as he wheezed on each inhale and exhale.

Mikale decided right then and there that Dugan wouldn't be around for repopulation. The man had been loyal and effective in his role so far, but if a mere broken rib could ground him, he wasn't worth the trouble.

"My offer to drive still stands," Ghared said.

Mikale shook his head. "Dugan is not my only associate. I have many loyal people." He dug out his tablet and summoned Trevis, his next in command. After a brief conversation with him, he said, "It'd be nice if I could handle all this myself, but it takes people to put plans like mine in place."

"People like Darina?" Ghared flexed his hands by his sides, and Mikale could tell the man felt something for the beautiful officer.

"Yes. She's a centerpiece to my plans. Her role is pivotal to its success."

"How so?" Ghared's eyes narrowed as if his tiny brain couldn't possibly understand the complexities of such a plan. Average people were so dull.

"She will be the mother of the next evolution of the human race." He knew Darina would see the importance of such a title.

Ghared paused, his entire body growing impossibly still as he stared at Mikale. "Wait a minute. You mean Darina and you... you're planning to use her to..."

"Reach my repopulation goals? Of course. I've looked into her, Mr. Timms. She's superior."

"No shit." Ghared shook his head. "But she's also not an idiot, Warres. She'll never agree to your demands."

"Well, I guess we'll find out exactly what her son means to her then, won't we?" Mikale gestured to Mareea, still blubbering next to him. "I gained your cooperation by threatening the one person you care most about in this rotten world. What makes you think the same won't work on her?"

"Because Darina is always ready. Always."

"She's not ready for me." Mikale smiled, thinking of introducing himself and finally being in Darina's presence. He couldn't wait to breathe the same air as her.

"Maybe not now," Ghared said, "but she doesn't hesitate. She'll react, and you won't know what hit you."

"I don't think that's the way it will unfold." Mikale's tablet chirped, and he glanced down at the screen. "Trevis is here. Let's move."

Mareea let out another mournful sound. Ghared stepped closer to her, but Mikale got between them. "No contact."

"She's my goddamned niece. I'll get as close as I want. You realize she's the only reason I haven't ended you yet, Warres, right?"

"If that's what you believe…" Mikale waved a hand at the ridiculousness of his statement. "But I think this gun has something to do with it as well."

"Go ahead and feel safe with that gun. That'll be your downfall. Trust me."

There was a look in Ghared's laser-sharp blue eyes Mikale didn't quite care for, but he couldn't let that rattle him. Nothing could detract him from his goal, his cause, his higher purpose. Finding Darina would bring him closer to that purpose, and this sub-human was going to get him to her.

Mikale shuffled Mareea toward the door and motioned for Dugan to take charge of Ghared. Dugan hesitated, his hand pressing to his busted rib, but one glare from Mikale propelled him into action. He'd retrieved his dagger and after brandishing it at Ghared, he'd gotten the man to walk ahead of him.

They made it outside undetected by any neighbors. One benefit of the current world status was that everyone minded their own damn business. No sense in getting involved in the problems of others when there were enough problems to go around for everyone. Blind eyes were easy to come by.

Mareea and Ghared were piled into the pulsejet where Trevis waited in the pilot's seat. Slowly, Dugan climbed into the copilot's seat as Mikale got in with his hostages.

"Let's review the numbers," he said to Mareea and Ghared. "Three of us to two of you, and my people and I are all armed in some form. Try something and one or both of you will end up dead."

"Then you don't make it to your destination." The smug tone of Ghared's voice stirred hatred in Mikale's gut.

"I always complete my mission. Maybe not the way I originally intended, but I do not accept failure."

"There's a first time for everything." Ghared settled into his seat, his muscled arms folding across his chest.

"Just give Trevis directions to Officer Lazitter's location."

The sooner he found her, the closer Mikale's plans would be to completion. That was all that mattered.

****

Foster wasn't accustomed to having a lab assistant as sexy as Darina. How could cargoes and a tank top make a woman's body so irresistible? It scrambled his brain, and he was in no position to have a scrambled brain.

Focus, focus, focus. If he didn't find the cure today, he was putting everyone at risk. It had once been just about the world's population "out there," but now, with him basically a refugee, hiding out in Vermont, all the residents on his property were in the line of fire as well. If they were discovered, they'd be confiscated by the government like contraband and dismantled faster than he could say *fuck you.* Couldn't let that happen. No way.

Shaking his head, he concentrated on the beaker in front of him as Darina held two ingredients for him. She stood close enough that her scent intoxicated him. Something a little fruity reached his nose, and he immediately identified it as the natural bath products Rasha made from herbs she grew on the property. He'd always liked the fragrances she'd experimented with, but combining it with Darina turned the aroma into something divine.

"Which one do you want first?"

"What?" He blinked at her, coming back from the erotic side trip his brain had taken.

She wiggled the two vials she held. "Which one first?" Her brows lowered as he stared at her. "Are you okay?"

He inhaled one final whiff of her and nodded. "Yes. I'm just finding it hard to keep my attention on the task today." He raised an eyebrow at her.

A slow grin turned up her lips. "Might I be the cause of that particular difficulty, Doc?"

"Most assuredly." He elbowed her. "I can't stop thinking about last night."

Her cheeks pinked and sexy mixed with adorable to create a look Foster would never be able to erase from his memory.

"It was no big deal." She shrugged and handed him the vial he'd reached for.

He paused in his work and gaped at her. "No big deal? You have nights like that all the time?" He didn't want an answer to that question. Especially if the answer was yes.

He poured the first vial into the beaker and stirred it.

"What if I did have nights like that all the time? Would you think me a tramp?" She flexed her prosthetic hand, an expression on her face that Foster couldn't exactly read.

"No." He took the second vial and added that to the mix. After pouring it all into a test tube, he slipped it into the centrifuge and turned it on, a low whir filling the lab. "I'd think that you've made some guys the happiest they've ever been in their lifetimes."

She rolled her eyes. "Does saying shit like that get you laid often?"

He put a hand to his chest. "You wound me, Officer Lazitter, with your suggestion that my words are not sincere."

She turned to face him, her shoulders squared to his. "Rich bastards will say anything."

Foster puffed out a breath and hung his head so his chin nearly touched his chest. "I thought we'd gotten past the I'm-a-rich-bastard stage."

"Why? Because you've seen me naked?"

"No, because we made love last night. It wasn't just sex. At least for me it wasn't."

She pulled her full bottom lip between her teeth and stared directly into his eyes as if looking for the truth. She needn't look too far.

The moment Foster had touched her last night, he knew what they were doing was way more than two bodies sharing physical pleasure. Darina had flicked a switch, turning on something he didn't think he had inside him. Something he'd thought his genetic engineering had purposely left out. He knew the government had toyed with creating soldiers without certain emotions. He also knew some GECs had emotional problems due to such experimentation. He had three on his property. They chose to live in cottages set apart from the others a bit, and he'd given them medication to deal with the highs and lows, but he often wondered about his own emotional range.

He was stoic.

He was level.

He never felt extremes.

Until last night when Darina lit something inside him that had been asleep.

"My experience with rich bastards tells me to be careful, Foster." She squeezed her prosthetic hand into a fist then released it.

"What experience have you had?" He took her hand and ran his fingers over her knuckles though she couldn't feel his touch there.

She watched his fingers move for a few silent moments then looked up to meet his gaze. Her eyes captivated him, swirls of brown and green that reminded him of the outdoors. They held him, made him want things he shouldn't want, things he probably could never have. Not if Darina kept thinking of him as a rich bastard.

"Your prosthetic limbs are expensive." She slipped her hand from his grip and turned it palm-side up. "But I couldn't be a cop with a sub-standard hand."

He had a feeling he knew where this conversation was going, and his jaw clenched as he waited for her to continue.

"I was in a pretty bad place after I lost my hand. Then the Anarch hit and pretty bad went to fucking terrible." She paced away from him, the fingers of her prosthetic hand coasting along the top of his worktable. "I had Zeke to care for and Ghared... well, he and I watch each other's backs, but I couldn't do what I wanted for both of them in the condition I was in. I couldn't be a cop."

She stopped walking when she was on the opposite side of the table facing him, and Foster didn't love that distance. He wanted to reach for her, but knew she was purposely giving herself space to say what she had to say.

"I needed money to get a better hand. Only one way a girl like me could get a large sum of money." She met his gaze, but looked away quickly. "I found a rich bastard and convinced him to fund my cause."

"And you were successful." He gestured to her hand, hoping to end this conversation, wishing she wouldn't give words to what she'd had to do to afford one of the limbs he'd designed. If he'd known her then, he would have made her a custom one on his own dime without hesitation.

"I suppose so, but that funding cost me more than I was willing to give. I was okay with handing over my body for a little while." She motioned down to herself. "It's just a physical shell after all. Then I got stupid and fell for him." Gripping the edge of the worktable, she steadied herself. "I was the only one who fell." She looked away, and when she looked back, anger heated her gaze. "I handed over my pride, my dignity, to some asshole. An asshole who didn't want my heart."

Foster instantly wanted to find said *asshole* and drag him from the back of a hovercopter. A low-flying hovercopter over the peaks of the White Mountains.

"I'm sorry you had to go through that, Darina." He slowly made his way to her side of the table. When she didn't shirk away from him, he tipped her chin up so she had to look him in the eye.

193

"I've said it before and I'll say it again. I'm not a rich bastard. I would never treat you like anything less than an equal."

She let out a snort. "Equal? I don't belong in the same room as you, Doc. There are so many levels between us."

Foster dipped his head down and brushed his lips against hers, softly, gently. In two seconds, the kiss became something more, something big. She reciprocated his efforts, her arms wrapping around his waist when his hands cupped her face. Her hips ground against his and flashbacks to their adventures last night filled his mind. Adventures he wanted to indulge in again and again.

When he pulled back and looked at her bright eyes, her swollen lips, her flushed cheeks, he said, "Did that feel as if there were levels between us?"

She shook her head. "No, but it's a trick."

"How could you think that was anything but genuine?" Her reluctance to believe they could be on equal ground frustrated him.

"Your kind are incredible actors." She shrugged and stepped back so they no longer shared the same space.

Foster thrust a hand out to the worktable littered with vials, beakers, and ingredients. "I know science, not drama. I couldn't fake the feelings I have for you if I wanted to."

"Feelings?" Her eyes narrowed. "What feelings?"

Shit. He wasn't prepared for this conversation, but her guarded stance with her hands on her hips told him he wouldn't be permitted to ignore or reschedule the question for another time.

"Human feelings, Officer Lazitter," he said. "Ones I didn't think I was capable of having. Ones I've never had before. Ones I was sure had been left out of my genetic code." He ran his hands through his hair. "Do you know what I woke up thinking this morning?"

"That you had to take a piss?"

"No. That I couldn't wait to see you. Couldn't wait to be in this lab with you. Even after we'd spent that time together last night, it wasn't enough. I wanted more. I still want more."

She didn't say anything for long, silent moments, but he couldn't take his eyes off her until she responded in some way. He couldn't toss his newly found feelings out there and have her ignore them.

Finally, she stepped closer and pressed her palms to his chest. She stared at her fingers as she splayed them out against his T-shirt. Her left hand was warm, but her right hand sent no heat his way.

He put his hand over her real one, gave her time, waited.

"I want more too, Foster." She turned her hand around and gripped his, the fingers of her other hand tracing along his tattoo. "I'm just afraid we won't be able to have it."

He dropped a light kiss on her forehead and loved when she leaned into him for a hug that was somehow more intimate than what they had done last night.

"I'm going to make sure we have it." He stepped back and looked at the worktable. The centrifuge had stopped spinning. "Shall we see what results we have?"

Darina nodded and tugged him to the other side of the table.

Foster removed the test tube from the centrifuge and sent a silent prayer to anyone who was listening that he'd found something useable this time. More than anything he wanted to keep his promise to Darina. He wanted them to have a shot at happiness together. He wanted to be able to focus his attention on her. He wanted her to believe.

He prepared a Petri dish with a sample from the plague-inflicted powder he'd collected on the streets. As Darina looked on, he stuck a medicine dropper in the test tube and drew up some of the solution. He slid the Petri dish under the microscope across the room, and with a hopeful look at Darina, he released a few drops of the solution onto the sample.

"How can so much be riding on a few drops of liquid?" Darina came to stand beside him by the microscope. "I mean, it's crazy. That medicine you gave Zeke will change his life, yet it doesn't look like anything important."

"It's easy to make," he gestured to the Petri dish, "unlike this cure."

He leaned forward and put his eye to the microscope. Encouraged by the pink coloring and texture of the sample, he increased the magnification, holding his breath as he observed. If he'd finally found the winning combination, he'd send his recipe for it to Emerge Tech—if it were still standing—and get it distributed right away.

Then maybe he'd have some time. To pursue other endeavors. Work on the genetic problems of his friends here in Vermont. Get back to adding nerve endings to the prosthetic limbs.

Show Darina exactly what feelings he had for her. Show her until she was absolutely convinced he wasn't a rich bastard.

He blinked a dry eye and focused on the view in the microscope. Pink had gone to black as he'd daydreamed.

"Fuck." He pounded his fist on the worktable and had to fight the urge to sweep everything to the floor in a fit of rage.

Darina's hand on his shoulder made him lose the urge.

"Clearly I'm not as damned smart as everyone thinks I am." He marched away then pivoted to face her again. "Maybe we'd have better luck if we searched for Warres and made him tell us how he manufactured the disease. If I knew what he used to create it, I wouldn't be taking all these aimless shots in the dark. I'm trying to think like him, but I'm not that diabolical."

Darina surprised him by smiling. "Diabolical? You?" She shook her head. "Nope. You don't have that blackness in you."

She came to him and pulled him in close. He wasn't sure he wanted to be consoled right now. The anger was rather refreshing.

"And we don't want Warres here. Not with all your people about. He wouldn't think twice about reporting all the GECs."

This was true. Mikale was willing to hunt him down. Finding a load of GECs and reporting them for dismantling would probably delight him.

"However," she continued, "if you want to meet with Warres at another location, we can probably make that happen." She stared up at him. "It'll involve using yourself as bait though. How do you feel about that?"

"I feel as if it might be our only option."

Chapter Eleven

"Give me your tablet." Darina held out her hand. Having Foster anywhere near Warres—or being near him herself—was not on the top of her list of ways to spend an afternoon, but it made sense. Draw the asshole out of his safe haven. Let him think he was getting what he wanted then turn the tables on him. Taking down Warres would bring her great satisfaction… not to mention potentially save the world.

Foster dug in his pocket and slapped the tablet into her palm. His disappointment over his failed attempts made her heart ache. He took his job of saving the planet seriously, but that was too much of a load for one man to bear.

"Why don't you have a team of scientists working on the cure?" she asked as she tapped in Ghared's number. If they were bent on bringing the enemy to them, there was no need to worry about tracing phone calls.

Foster rubbed his eyes and leaned against the worktable, his fine backside resting on the edge. He folded his arms across his chest and Darina was a little irritated by how much she wanted those arms folded around her.

One night of sex and I'm hooked on the man.

So not like her. She hadn't gotten stupid about a man since…

She couldn't allow that to happen again, but as Foster had said, last night was more than sex. They'd shared their bodies in a way that went way beyond mere physical urges. They'd become a part of each other, and Darina didn't think she'd ever be able to shake the feelings she was developing for Foster.

"We had a team working on the cure, but none of them understood what was happening to victims' organs once the plague had time to mature inside them."

"But you do?"

"Yes. It's a breakdown of the organs at a DNA level."

"Which is why it's so hard to reverse." She gestured to the microscope with the latest failure still in it.

Foster nodded. "And then people were also afraid to work on the cure."

"Afraid of getting it?" She understood that fear.

"And afraid of dying from it." Foster turned back to his table. While he appeared to go in for another round of experimentation, Darina tapped the tablet to call Ghared.

She watched Foster while the phone rang. He was bent over the microscope now, taking another look and mumbling to himself. How she wished she'd met him ages ago. Maybe her life would have taken a different path. Perhaps she never would have gone on that ride with Ghared that resulted in the loss of her hand.

No hand loss, no rich bastard, no embarrassment, no pieces of her soul shriveling and dying.

A sigh of resignation escaped her throat. She had not met Foster ages ago. She had done what she'd done to get her hand. Her life was what it was. She couldn't turn back the clock and get a do over.

She only had the future and it was time to steer her path in a slightly different direction once this job was over.

"Why is he not answering?" She stared at the still ringing tablet.

Foster looked up from the microscope. "Does he usually answer right away?"

"Well… yeah. When I call."

"He runs to do your bidding?" His eyes narrowed at her, and she knew she had to answer this question carefully. He was already upset about the cure. The splash of jealousy in his question was seed enough to turn into something messy and ugly.

"Ghared's a part of our family. Zeke and I have depended on him for many things just as he's depended on us. I'd answer his call immediately too."

Foster glanced to the tablet, still attempting to establish a connection to the outside. A muscle in his jaw ticked, but when he looked at her, his face had relaxed. "I'm glad you have… someone like him in your life. I'd hate to think you and Zeke have been alone out there all this time."

His concern touched her, even if a little jealous flare still flickered in his beautiful green eyes.

"And you've had all the people here. I know they depend on you keeping them hidden, but I can tell they give you something you need too."

"They do. While Carielle took wonderful care of me, she wasn't really my family. I started in this world without a family, but I like to think I've built something resembling one here." He met her gaze directly. "I want the real thing though. I want a family that is truly my own."

She swallowed around the tightness in her throat. His sincere admission of what he wanted, his vulnerability, reached deep into her.

Darina wanted to be the one to make his wishes come true, but did they live in a world where anyone's wishes came true anymore? Besides, GECs couldn't have children. Not biological ones anyway.

She entered Ghared's number again and when he didn't answer, she tried Mareea's number. No answer there either. "Something's wrong."

"How can you be sure?"

"Cop instinct." She sifted out a breath. "You're not going to like what comes out of my mouth next."

He straightened and waved his hand. "Hit me with it."

"I have a bad feeling Ghared and Mareea are in a situation." She gestured to the door of the lab. "We need to evacuate this property."

"Wait. You think our location has been compromised? I thought you trusted Ghared."

"I do. With my life. With Zeke's life. He wouldn't willingly do anything to betray us, but he may not have had a choice. If someone got his hands on Mareea, Ghared would do whatever it takes to spare her. Even give up my location should someone want it."

"Warres wants it if he knows you're guarding me."

"With the reach that man has, the probability he knows is high. While drawing Warres here was our next plan of action, I want it to be *our* plan of action. Not on his terms. If I'm to properly do my job of guarding you, Doc, we have to leave... or..." She pulled on her bottom lip.

"Or?" Foster joined her on the other side of the table.

"Or we make it *look* as if we've left." The pieces of a plan fused themselves together in her brain. "If Warres has Ghared and Mareea and he's made Ghared give up our location, he's probably thinking he'll waltz in here and grab what he wants."

"Me."

"You." She clenched her teeth. "What he doesn't realize is when I guard something, I consider it mine, and I've never quite mastered the ability to share."

Foster's smile warmed her from head to toe. "I don't want to be shared." He came to stand in front of her and kissed her, but as much as she enjoyed that, the taste of him clouded her thinking. Now was not the time for clouded thinking.

She stepped back, and his pout almost made her launch back to him. "I can't think tactically with your lips on me."

"Now you know how I felt." He held up his hands, but didn't look sorry that he'd distracted her.

In fact, he looked rather pleased with himself and the effect he had on her. "Do you want me to assemble everyone in the great room, and we can brainstorm how we want to leave the property without actually leaving?"

His ability to shift from kissing her to helping her was impressive. Her body, however, hadn't quite forgotten what it was like to have his lips on her yet.

"Yes. Everyone needs to be part of the plan in order for it to work and we need to get organized quickly. We don't know what kind of a jumpstart Warres might have." Her experience so far told her that everyone living there would be on board. They'd do anything for Foster.

She understood now why they'd want to.

Foster opened the lab door to find Estoria on the other side, toting a tray of food. "Oh," she said with a startled look on her face. "I was coming with some lunch for the two of you. If finding a cure is as exhausting as giving birth, I figured you'd be starving." She balanced the tray on one hand, plucked a strawberry from a bowl, and popped it into her mouth. "Repairing the cells of a seriously worn out vagina stirs up an appetite."

"Repairing cells…" Foster repeated.

When Darina turned to look at him, he had this crazed expression on his face as if he were doing some fevered calculations in his head. "What?"

He clamped his hands on her shoulders almost painfully and gave her a little shake. Realizing his roughness, he released her and raked his hands through his hair so it stood out on either side of his head.

"Repairing cells." He laughed. "All this fucking time, I'm struggling to revive the cells of dead organs, and I have a cell repairer right here." He thrust his arms out to Estoria. "She *grew* female reproductive organs in place of the ones I removed. She's got the code I need to unlock the cure." He smacked a hand to his forehead. "The answer's been here all along."

"Some genius you are." Darina smiled and poked him in the chest.

"Sometimes genius takes time." After setting the tray of food down, he grabbed Estoria by the hand and tugged her toward his worktable. "Time is what I need now. Go and meet with the others. You'll have their full cooperation. Come back and fill me in when you're done. Hopefully, I'll be done by then too."

"I don't like the idea of leaving you here," Darina said. Clearly, now wasn't a time to get brainless. Especially if Warres *was* on his way to Vermont.

"Rasha and Hydec were in the great room when I passed by with the food tray," Estoria said.

"I'll send them in." Darina walked toward the door, but turned back. "Foster?"

"Yeah?" He looked up from the empty beaker in his hand.

"Good luck."

He smiled. "I don't need luck. I've got science."

Darina hoped that was true.

****

"Vermont? Foster Ashby is hiding in Vermont?" Mikale shook his head as he gazed out the window of the pulsejet. The leafy treetops spread green over much of the landscape, but here and there cleared spaces broke up the woods. In one of those cleared spaces, Foster thought himself safe as he worked at stopping Mikale's plague.

Can't have that.

No. Foster had to be ended. Today.

But Vermont?

"You're not lying to us now, Mr. Timms, are you?" Mikale wrapped a section of Mareea's hair around his hand and yanked. "Because if you are…"

"I don't make a habit of lying when my niece's life is on the line." Ghared hadn't moved much in his seat. His arms remained folded across his chest, his legs looking as if they didn't quite fit in the space behind the copilot's seat. The hollow eye sockets of those tattooed skulls on his arm watched everything. The man knew how to look intimidating.

But he doesn't have a weapon. I do.

Mikale didn't like having so few advantages over an opponent, but if he didn't lose his focus, he'd be victorious. That was the only outcome he'd accept.

"About two miles east of here," Ghared said, "you'll see a series of open fields. Set this rig down in the northernmost field."

Trevis made the course adjustments as Dugan assisted, and Mikale went back to looking out the window. He assumed Darina was armed, but was Foster? The Dr. Ashby he'd known at Emerge

206

Tech wasn't a violent man. He'd had no love of war and weapons, but had the state of the world changed him? Had he felt the need to protect himself? Clearly, Emerge Tech had felt the need or they wouldn't have hired a bodyguard for him. Hiring a bodyguard had to mean Foster wasn't capable of keeping himself safe.

Weak. Though Foster's mind had always been strong, his willingness to fight had always been nonexistent. Suited Mikale just fine. He was coming into the Vermont hideout with three weapons: two associates with fight training and Darina's supposed best friend to get her to comply. She'd probably hand over Foster without a second thought. He was just a job after all. According to his intel, this Ghared Timms was important to her. If she had thoughts of refusing Mikale's demands, he'd send Mr. Timms to live amongst those damned skulls on his arm.

Mareea wiggled closer to Ghared, but Mikale tightened his grip on her. "A pretty girl like you should relish the attentions of an older, more experienced man."

Ghared shifted forward in his seat now and glared around his niece at Mikale. His blue eyes were as sharp as lasers, and Mikale had to fight to not look away.

"It'd be in your best interest to keep your mouth shut, Warres. Say something like that again to her and you're not going to like what your face looks like afterward."

Mareea sniffled, her body shaking slightly against Mikale's. Her fear aroused him almost as much as picturing what he was going to do with

Darina once he had her. Maybe he'd keep Mareea too. Just to piss her uncle off.

Grinning, he watched the fields come into view. He wouldn't have to wait much longer to have both Foster and Darina in his possession. His plague would continue to flourish. His repopulation plans could enter the practice round—and he wanted lots of practice. His dream of building a better world would be in its final phases. His mother would be so proud of him.

Today was a good day.

Trevis switched to silent mode and lowered the pulsejet in the field Ghared had indicated. He turned around and looked at Mikale.

"What's the plan, boss?"

"Bind these two and tote them along. Locate Ashby and Officer Lazitter."

Trevis and Dugan nodded and got out of the pulsejet. The back doors opened, and Mikale climbed out, dragging Mareea behind him. Ghared got out on his own. By the time Mikale had rounded the pulsejet with Mareea, Dugan was on the ground in a pool of his own blood.

"Oops," Ghared said, an amused tilt to his lips. "I must have slipped getting out. Your man was kind enough to break my fall."

Drawing in a breath, Mikale pressed his weapon into Mareea's side, making the girl cry out. Her mouth was still gagged, but her wail bounced off the nearby trees just the same.

"Hush." Mikale shook the girl. "You'll ruin our surprise arrival." He looked at Ghared, then gestured to Dugan's lifeless form. "Do something like that again and you'll get a hole in you."

"You can try." Ghared braced his legs, geared up for a fight. "You didn't actually think I'd lead you here and let you get Foster and Darina, did you?" He let out a raspy laugh. "I just needed a ride back."

He made a move to charge Mikale, but Trevis had crept up behind him and landed a kick to the back of Ghared's left leg. The snap that sounded made Mikale cringe and Mareea scream around the gag as Ghared sunk to the ground.

"I said no screaming, sweetheart." He shook Mareea and more tears poured down her cheeks. Her eyes were bloodshot and puffy, her nose red. Crying was never attractive. He bet Darina never cried.

Ghared attempted to get to his feet with grunts of pain, but Trevis leaned down and punched him in the jaw. The sound of Ghared's body thumping face first into the soft dirt brought Mikale great pleasure.

Time to get more pleasure out of this trip.

"Bind him," he told Trevis, "and give me something to secure this one." He jostled Mareea, who had gone limp at the sight of her unconscious uncle.

Once Ghared and Mareea were secured with magnetic cuffs, Mikale said, "He's going to be too much trouble to move around now."

"Sorry." Trevis gave him a regretful glance.

"Don't be. You did the right thing. He needed to be controlled."

Trevis beamed at Mikale's praise, and though the large man wasn't bright most of the time, he knew how to fly a pulsejet, take orders, and bring a man like Ghared Timms down to his knees. Plus, he was loyal as hell.

"Secure the cuffs to the pulsejet," Mikale said. "We'll leave him behind. This girl should be enough leverage. The good officer will know if we have her, we also have her uncle."

Trevis did as he was told, and Ghared's hands were clamped above his head to the pulsejet. "What about Dugan?" He gestured to the body mingling with dirt and blood.

"Leave him," Mikale said. "Dust to dust."

Nodding, Trevis took control of Mareea so Mikale could lead. As they walked away, Ghared released a pained moan.

"Too bad I won't get to see Darina fuck you up, Warres. Should be a great show." The man smiled then passed out again.

"Is it possible we've underestimated what we're up against, boss?" Trevis asked.

"No." There would only be one kind of fucking going on between him and Darina. The kind he'd been dreaming about. The kind he never got from the women he bought.

Mikale led Trevis and Mareea toward a series of cottages. They stuck to the tree line, using it as cover as they approached. His sharp eyes scanned everything. His ears listened for any indication that their appearance had been detected. His fingers were poised over the trigger of his weapon, ready to blast anything in their way.

But the place was a ghost town. No voices sounded. No engines ran. The huge water wheel they'd come upon was still and silent. The only noise was the stream rippling as it passed over rocks and the rustle of leaves when the warm, summer wind blew.

"You think Timms screwed us?" Trevis asked.

"Possibly. Always hard when you have to rely on your enemies for information." But being here *felt* right to Mikale. As if he could smell Foster, sense Darina. They were close. He knew it.

All he had to do was find them.

****

Foster ripped open the door of his lab, making Rasha and Hydec whip around. "Where is Darina?"

"Not sure," Hydec said. "We've all been ordered to burrow into our holes. Just Rasha and I are out and about, guarding your ass."

"I'm out and about too." Estoria peeked from behind Foster and waved to her friends.

"Our orders are to keep you in the lab until we hear from Darina," Rasha said.

Foster shook his head. "No, I need to find her right now." He stepped beyond Rasha, but Hydec got in his path.

"I'm going to have to advise that we follow Darina's orders," the taller man said. "She threatened us with bodily harm if we allowed you to leave."

"And since when are you intimidated by a woman half your size, Hydec?"

"Since I saw the wild look in her eyes at the thought that something could happen to you." Hydec glanced at Rasha. "It's the same look I'd get if I was trying to keep her safe."

Foster looked at Rasha then at Hydec, knowing exactly the look he was talking about. He'd seen it pass between them before, but they were true partners. He'd found them as a readymade set. They'd been together for years. Surely, in only two days' time, Darina wouldn't have had that expression for him, would she? The thought seemed crazy, but he wished it to be true with every cell in his genetically engineered body.

But if Hydec wasn't going to let him out, they weren't getting out. "All right. Fine. We'll stay here, but when do you expect to hear from her?"

Rasha looked at Estoria and the two women grinned.

"What?" Foster turned to Estoria.

"Nothing. You just seem a little… eager to see Darina." Estoria's smile deepened.

Foster pointed over her shoulder into the lab. "I'm eager because of what we've found in there, Essie." That was at least half true although his mind did wander to the way Darina's lips felt against his own. He shook his head to clear the sensations. He had to keep his head on the goal.

Though maybe he now had additional goals.

"You mean you did it?" Hydec's eyes widened.

"*We* did it," Foster said, sliding an arm around Estoria's shoulders.

"I didn't do anything except bleed for you." Estoria indicated the tiny pinprick on her forearm. "You're the one who worked your magic."

"Magic I should have figured out sooner than this." Foster ran a hand through his hair in frustration. "All the people who could have been cured…"

"Don't do that," Estoria said, resting her hand on his shoulder. "You've been working on this cure around the clock. Most people never would have made the connection you did between the disease and my genetic code."

"Hopefully, Emerge Tech still has the capability of mass producing this cure."

"If not, we'll find another way, Foster." She gestured to the test tubes on the worktable. "You've got the blueprint now. That was the hard part."

"I'd still like to test it on a live victim of the plague, but I'll need to go back to the city for that." Foster grabbed his tablet and tapped like wild for a few moments then he shoved the tablet into his pocket. "Everything I need is on here."

"All that's left to do is keep you and that tablet safe then," Rasha said, "which is what we're going to do." She entered the lab with Hydec and closed the door. "We wait here until Darina signals us." Motioning to Foster, she said, "Lock us in."

He went to the keypad by the door and entered the security code. The door was a sturdy barricade, but he hated the idea that Darina was on the other side of it. He wanted her in there with him. Zeke too. He'd seen the look on her face when he talked of wanting a family. A look that said maybe she wanted to expand hers.

Turning back to the test tube full of a potentially successful cure, he hoped he could create a world where a life for him and Darina was possible. Assuming she didn't die out there protecting him.

They waited in the lab for what seemed like an eternity before Foster said, "Couldn't we take a peek out there and see what's going on?" The not knowing was killing him. He'd worried about his people on this property before, but this was different. Darina meant something different to him. Something more.

"I'll go," Hydec said. "Lock this door behind me. If I'm not back in ten minutes, Rasha, you should—"

"You'll be back," Rasha interrupted, refusing to hear anything about him not coming back.

Hydec gave her a quick nod and Foster let him out. "Be careful."

"Always am." Hydec readied his weapon and disappeared in the shadows of the quiet main house.

Foster was tempted to step out of the lab, but Rasha tugged on his arm as if reading his mind.

"It's not worth it, Foster." She pulled him back and closed the door herself. "Set it."

He entered the security code again, effectively sealing them in. He hated the separate feeling being in the lab gave him today. Normally he didn't mind being sequestered from the world, but today there were people on the other side of the door that he simply couldn't lose. There was a cure to administer. There were lives to save.

And a woman. A woman to possibly love.

Chapter Twelve

Darina's legs cramped in the crouched position she'd been in as she watched Warres, Mareea, and one of Warres's men skitter along the tree line like field mice.

Rats. At least two of the approaching people should be classified as low-life rats. Seeing Warres in the flesh made Darina's fight instinct flare inside her.

"We have to get Mareea," Zeke said from beside her. He had his own weapon, which he knew how to use thanks to Ghared. She'd disagreed with teaching him at first, knowing firsthand what these weapons were capable of, but Ghared had convinced her, and now she was happy the kid could defend himself.

Zeke got up from his crouch, but Darina grabbed him and yanked him down. He fell on his butt and gave her one of those teenage looks.

"I agree that we have to get her, Zeke," Darina said, "but we have to be smart about it. Both of those guys are armed."

"I know you're right, but Mareea... I... she..." He scrubbed a hand down his face and blew out a frustrated breath.

Darina squeezed his kneecap. "I know, buddy." She knew because she felt the same way about Warres getting his hands on Foster. And Ghared.

Where is Ghared?

If this asshole had Mareea, and he had found this location, Ghared had to have been involved. If he hadn't answered Darina's call, he could be hurt.

Or worse.

That thought nearly had her sprinting from her cover just as Zeke had attempted. Ghared had been there for her and Zeke for years. She loved him as much as the two brothers she'd lost. She wouldn't lose him too. If she had her way, she wouldn't lose anyone today. After Deo and Dixon and her parents had died, she'd been so alone. They had been such a tight family. She'd been fortunate to be raised with loads of love and nurturing. She hoped she was giving Zeke a similar experience, even if the world around them sucked. She also wished someday the world wouldn't suck so much, and she could have what her parents had between them.

In the surrounding cottages, the rest of the GECs were armed and hiding as well, waiting for her signal to show themselves, force Warres to drop his weapon, and rescue his hostage. She took comfort knowing Foster was locked away in his lab and guarded by two competent people. Hopefully, he'd found the cure by now and was just waiting for Warres to be contained.

Closer, closer.

She needed this prick to be close enough to surround. Then she could overpower him with her team, free Mareea, find Ghared. She'd love to take Warres down execution style, but if Foster needed him to get the cure, she didn't want to deny him that opportunity. Her fingers twitched on the trigger of her weapon, while her prosthetic hand fisted in her lap. Ending Warres would feel so good.

Long time coming.

Warres continued walking toward the cottages. He turned back to his associate and yanked Mareea from the man.

Zeke bristled beside Darina, but she clamped a hand on his shoulder, keeping him down. A low growl sounded from Zeke's throat, and Darina knew she wasn't crouched next to a boy anymore. A young man—a young man in love—waited in the shadows now. One who was prepared to do what it took to make sure Mareea was not harmed.

"He's using her as a shield," Zeke whispered.

"Which means he doesn't entirely believe this place is abandoned." Darina turned back to the two GECs in the cottage with them. "Yolase, tell Roben to reduce their numbers."

Yolase, who'd told Darina her genetic engineering included telepathy, closed her eyes, her blonde brows lowering in concentration. When she opened her eyes, which were a lovely shade of violet, she said, "Done."

A moment later, Warres's associate dropped to the ground, causing Warres to whip around, holding Mareea close to his chest. His own weapon was jammed up under Mareea's chin, but he wouldn't kill the girl. Not yet.

"Mom…"

"Stand down, Zeke. Rule number one in catching bad guys is study their reactions."

"What if his reaction is to kill Mareea?" Zeke's voice cracked on her name.

"He won't. If he kills her now, he has nothing to bargain with, and he wants to bargain."

"For Foster."

Darina nodded and swallowed loudly, her throat growing tight. "What Warres doesn't know is there will be no bargains today."

Warres turned in a circle, dragging Mareea around. The girl let out a muffled cry, while another growl sounded from Zeke.

"I'm looking for Officer Darina Lazitter," Warres shouted.

What? Why isn't he asking for Foster?

"I know this place isn't empty, folks." He pressed Mareea up against his body. "I know you've got eyes on me. Weapons too." He glanced at his fallen man. "And you've taken out one of my best men. Trevis was beyond loyal. You owe me something now."

"We don't owe that asshole anything," Zeke mumbled.

"Although, I guess what I've done to your friend Mr. Timms might balance the scales," Warres said.

Darina was on her feet, but Zeke pulled her down. "We have to be smart, Mom, remember?"

A few moments of silence stretched on as Warres rotated, covering himself with Mareea's body and squinting at the cottages.

"Interesting," he yelled. "Mr. Timms made me believe you were a force to be reckoned with, Officer Lazitter. I didn't figure you'd cower." He unzipped Mareea's ratty hooded sweatshirt and slid his hand inside. "It's okay though, I have something to play with to pass the time."

Mareea let out a wail and Zeke bolted out of the cottage.

"Zeke!" Darina ran after him.

The sunlight was blinding at first, her eyes having not adjusted from the darkness of the cottage. Nothing was wrong with her hearing though as that weapon blast echoed in her head. When she blinked everything into focus, Zeke was on the ground halfway between the cottage and Warres's position.

"Zeke!" Darina's stomach roiled with anguish... and anger. She dropped to her knees at Zeke's side and he looked up at her with panicked brown eyes.

"Get Mareea..."

He passed out, and Darina took in the blood gushing from the hole in his chest. She looked back to the cottage she'd been hiding in. Yolase sprinted out, pulling off the T-shirt she had on over her tank top and kneeling beside Zeke.

Pressing the T-shirt to the wound, she said, "We've got this."

A second later, Hydec appeared and hoisted Zeke up into his arms. He didn't say a word, but jogged back toward the main house with Yolase right behind him.

Foster will help Zeke. Yolase's voice bounced around in Darina's head. She had to believe that or else she'd come unglued.

Turning to Warres, she said, "Let Mareea go." She held up her hand in a fist and the area became flooded with GECs prepared to do whatever she asked of them.

"I'll let her go," Warres said, "but only in exchange for you." He looked around at the people surrounding him. "And if any one of them tries to fire on me, I'll kill her."

"And if you kill her, they will let loose with their weapons, Warres. There'll be nothing left of you."

"Oh, I don't think that's the way it'll go, officer." He gave her a smile—one that made her flesh crawl. "See, I know Dr. Ashby is working on a cure for my handiwork. I know he'd love to have me alive to interrogate. If you kill me, my virus will still be going strong out there." He brandished his weapon, indicating beyond the trees on the property. "There is no way I can lose here."

"If that's what you believe." She shrugged as if to say he was stupid, which he was. "I agree to your exchange anyway. Let the girl go, and I'll come with you." She holstered her weapon and put her hands out to her sides.

Warres gestured for her to walk toward him. As she did so, the rest of the team took a step forward.

"The rest of you don't move." Warres threw an arm around Mareea's throat, his gun still pressed under her chin.

Darina made a motion with her hand for everyone to stay put. Once the exchange was made, they would know what to do. They'd planned for this scenario before hiding.

She continued walking. When she was a mere yard in front of him, he released Mareea and pushed her to the ground. Mareea made quick eye contact with Darina, then scrambled to her feet and ran in the direction of where Zeke had been taken.

"Okay, so now what?" Darina asked. "You have me. Where is Ghared? What did you do to him?" She had to keep him talking while a few members of the team crept forward behind him.

"Mr. Timms most likely has a broken leg and is bound to my pulsejet at the moment. I'm sure his arms ache by now as they've been above his head all this time."

Ghared is alive. And the pulsejet was somewhere on the property, so finding him should be easy.

"Well, let's get to the pulsejet then. We are leaving, right?" She walked closer as if to start them on their way, but Warres shook his head.

"We will leave. Eventually. First I need to stop the good doctor. He seeks to undo my work, and I simply can't have that."

"Foster isn't here."

"Of course he is. Don't lie to me, Officer Lazitter. It's not attractive." He stepped closer to her. "You know what else isn't attractive?"

In a move her mind barely registered, Warres grabbed her and jabbed a syringe into her shoulder. Something burned under her flesh as he released whatever was inside.

"My virus isn't attractive. What it does to a body isn't attractive." Warres turned around quickly and pointed to the handful of GECs that had left the perimeter to pursue him. "I said none of you were to move." He shook his head as Darina slumped against him, her head swimming. "You didn't listen, and now I had to infect Officer Lazitter. Kill me and you'll kill her too. Only I can stop the virus from taking her. Just me."

Darina blinked rapidly, but the red spots before her eyes didn't disappear. She was aware of Warres supporting her and hated that any part of her was touching any part of him.

She'd gone down that road before…

"Now someone is going to tell me where to find Foster Ashby or things are about to get really bad," Warres said.

No one budged, and Darina felt a measure of pride in the team she'd organized. They were level-headed and loyal and not going to take Warres's shit. The government made a stupid decision in casting off these genetically engineered gems.

She was glad she and Ghared had made a deal years ago that if anything happened to her, he'd take care of Zeke. If anything happened to Ghared, she'd agreed to watch out for Mareea. Other than Zeke, she didn't have any other affairs to get in order.

She could die today.

Not that she wanted to. Living—even in this craptastic world—was preferable to checking out for good. She had to believe Zeke would be all right and she wanted to be part of his future.

She also wanted Foster to be a part of *her* future. If that was possible.

Darina fought to stay conscious and tried her hardest to ignore the fiery pain coursing through her body as the virus spread. The pain turned into an unbearable itch beneath her skin. She scratched her flesh but couldn't reach deep enough. How long before her organs broke down? How long before her insides looked like the image Foster had shown her on his tablet?

As she closed her eyes and wished she had the strength to beat the shit out of Warres, a hum overhead made everyone look up.

"Ah, my reinforcements," Warres said. "I'm not a lone wolf, Officer Lazitter. I always bring at least part of my pack. Mr. Timms was kind enough to lead us here, and I was smart enough to relay those directions to my associates. If you don't take me to Foster, they will land and kill everyone here. If you don't take me to Foster, I won't give you the cure I already have for my virus. The cure you now need desperately."

"I'm right here, Mikale."

Darina managed to look toward the main house. Her vision wavered as if her eyeballs were swimming in their sockets. A dim outline of Foster standing on the deck with Rasha and Hydec on either side of him came into focus. Blood stained Foster's shirt.

Zeke's blood?

She prayed enough blood was still inside Zeke. He needed to live. He deserved to live.

"Darina and I will both go with you," Foster said. "Call off your men."

"And why would you agree to go with me, Foster?"

"Because I don't want any fighting here."

Warres shook his head. "No. I think it's something else." His face came into view as he looked down at Darina. If she had the energy, she'd

223

rearrange that face as she'd dreamed about doing for so long.

Too long.

Turning in a circle again, Warres surveyed Foster's people. His eyes widened at Kivin, a beautiful woman with skin the color of freshly polished copper. His gaze shot to Oraslo, an eight-foot tall man who loomed above the others. Nevianne stood beside Oraslo with her yellow, snake-like eyes.

"Oh, Foster..." He turned to face the main house. "You've been keeping secrets." He laughed. "I wondered why you'd be in Vermont. Men like us could go anywhere in the world. We have the means and the connections." He grinned, and Darina wanted to send her foot into his teeth... or his groin. Either one would work. Both would be best. "But you're keeping a low profile here in the woods. You and your GECs. My, won't the government love receiving this tip?"

Hell no. These people had put their safety on the line to defend Foster. Their loyalty would not be rewarded with dismantlement.

Because she was too weakened from the virus eating up her insides, Darina did the only thing she could think of to distract Warres.

She raised her arm.

The one with the prosthetic hand.

Warres's gaze went to the tattooed stars and his eyes bugged. "It... it can't be."

"I never thanked you," Darina whispered, "you fucking rich bastard."

****

That ring of tattooed stars rocketed Mikale to the past. To a young, beautiful woman with a hideous excuse for a prosthetic hand. He'd been in the city helping Emerge Tech restore technology where he could after the Anarch attack. After a particularly long shift, a bunch of ET employees stopped in some hovel for a drink. Personally, he'd been willing to wait to kick back until they all were safely behind Emerge Tech's walls, but his friends assured him the drinks were better on the outside. He hadn't cared all that much about drinking. Besides, Foster was waiting for him. They'd both agreed to put in a few extra hours working on adding nerve endings to the prosthetics they'd developed.

It had been dark inside the establishment, but the place was full. As he sat with his comrades and swigged some concoction, a young beauty nursing a tall glass of beer caught his eye. She stared, her striking hazel gaze combing up and down the length of him. She had straight, jet-black hair that framed a simply exquisite face. He couldn't have ignored her if he'd tried. She was magnetic.

"I'm Mikale," he said when he'd worked his way over to sit next to her.

"Dee," she said. "I could use another drink, Mikale."

He quickly bought her another one, and they did that getting-to-know-you flirting thing for a few hours. When he'd looked up, his colleagues were gone, but she wasn't. She hadn't budged.

Fingering his shirt, Dee said, "I'll bet a guy like you could show a girl a great time."

That was all the invitation he'd needed. He'd bundled her into his Podster, secretly jetted her to Emerge Tech, and they'd taken full advantage of each other's bodies. Mikale had never enjoyed such physical pleasures. Dee was… gifted. She was willing to cater to his every desire—even the ones where things got a little rough. He'd loved the way she let him dominate.

They'd had encounters several times a week for a few months—a few glorious months. She'd been his little secret. Foster never approved of the women he kept as company, and Mikale had stopped introducing them to him. He spent money on Dee. Loads of it, but she always reciprocated with physical escapades he'd only dreamed possible.

One night, while she was stroking his arousal, she cursed her prosthetic hand, wishing she could more skillfully caress him. It didn't take long for him to make the decision to get her a new hand. A fully functional hand that could properly jack him off.

In celebration, the next time they'd been together, Dee had used that hand to make him come hard and repeatedly. He had doubts he was going to survive that night. Giving her that hand had been worth every penny.

The next day, she'd asked to get a tattoo to hide the slight seam the prosthetic caused on her arm. Emerge Tech didn't have any tattoo studios inside its walls, so he'd escorted her outside to the city where tattooing was really the only art form that had survived the Unplug. He'd stayed by her side as the stars were added to her flawless skin, getting aroused watching the ink mark her. In the last two stars on the inside of her wrist, she had the letters M and W added, one above the other so they connected and only the two of them would know what it meant.

It'd been a sweet gesture, and he'd known Dee was falling for him. Falling hard. But he wasn't a one woman kind of man. Never had been. He had many interests. No single woman—not even Dee— had all the skills he needed to be truly satisfied.

A set of gorgeous twins with the longest legs in creation walked into the tattoo studio. He'd also been screwing them at the time. They instantly plastered themselves to him, and he showered them with the same dominant handling he showed all his women.

Dee gaped at him, silent accusations screaming from her eyes. Hell, he'd never claimed to be exclusive to her. He'd considered it. She was amazing after all, but she wouldn't be enough. He knew it. Why had she assumed she was the only woman in his life?

She'd let the tattoo artist apply ointment to the ring of stars and bandage her arm.

Then she'd taken off.

She knew the city streets well, and he'd searched for her, but it was as if she'd never existed. He'd put her out of his mind and buried himself in plenty of hot, wet pussy to make her a distant memory.

Until right now.

Staring down at Darina and taking in those stars again, he let out a roar. "You're Dee."

"In the flesh," she whispered, "except for this." She waved her prosthetic hand. "But you already know that."

"Where have you been?" Her hair was a different color and curly, her face more mature and far from pleased to be in his presence, but now that he looked at her, live and in person, how could he have not known she was Dee?

"I've been right under your nose apparently."

He reached out to take her hand and pull her to her feet. "Well, plan on staying there."

****

Foster couldn't hear what Darina and Mikale were saying, but from the looks of it, she'd shocked him good with some news. Mikale looked downright confused, and Foster took that opportunity.

"Yolase, tell them to close in and take control of Warres," he said.

She closed her eyes and the team slinked closer. Before anyone could get their hands on Mikale, though, a pulsejet roared overhead. Two retractable arms lowered. One grabbed Mikale around the waist and the other gently scooped up Darina. The pulsejet flew toward the main house and deposited Darina on the deck.

"What do you want me to do with this piece of shit?" came Ghared's voice.

Foster squinted up to the cockpit where the man stared down at him. "Leave him with us."

Hydec and Rasha stepped forward, ready to get their hands on Mikale who squirmed like caught bait in the fingers of the retractable arm.

"The sky is full of my associates," Mikale yelled.

"For the moment." Ghared turned to the pulsejet's control panel and a few seconds later, Podsters were falling to the ground, shaking the earth. "Never underestimate the power of a tech geek. Child's play for me to hack into the navigation systems of your fleet, Warres. Child's play."

Looking to Foster, he said, "Save Darina. You don't want to know what I'll do to you if you don't." With that, he turned the pulsejet around to face Warres's associates now pouring out of their downed crafts and fighting with GECs on the ground.

While chaos ripped up the woods, Foster gathered Darina into his arms. Her body was burning up and her eyes were hazy. He had to work fast.

"Rasha, Hydec, bring Mikale inside. We'll question him after I've tended to Darina."

Nodding, the two GECs took control of Mikale and dragged him inside.

"Foster…" Darina's voice was hoarse as her eyes fluttered.

"I have you." He squeezed her to his chest as he bolted for his lab. "Yolase, assist me?"

"You got it." She followed him inside.

"Zeke…" Darina gripped a handful of his shirt.

"He's going to be fine. You'll see him soon."

"No, I don't think I will." Her eyes rolled up then shut, her body nearly motionless in his grip.

Foster kicked open the door of his lab and set Darina down on his worktable. She immediately curled her legs into a fetal position, her hands over her stomach as if she were holding herself together.

"The virus is already attacking her organs," Foster said. "Take some blood, Yolase. That way I have a sample of the virus."

Yolase set to work and Foster was thankful for her calm presence. He was anything but calm. He was pretty sure he'd found the cure, but if he hadn't—if the cure didn't work—he was about to lose the best thing that had ever happened to him. Not only had Darina put her ass on the line to keep him safe, she'd also shown him what was possible between a man and a woman. She'd gotten him to dream about a future where he wasn't alone. Where neither of them were.

He wanted that future. Desperately. For the both of them. And Zeke. He wanted them all to be that family he craved so much.

Foster set his emotions aside and thought like a scientist. He pulled out his tablet and with his notes, mixed what he sincerely hoped was the cure.

Darina let out a howl from the table and her body convulsed. Yolase did her best to hold her down, but Darina was stronger.

"Hurry, Foster. She's in serious pain here." Yolase climbed on the table and struggled to restrain Darina. "You're going to be okay, Officer Lazitter. You're going to be okay."

When Foster came over to the two women, Yolase's eyes were closed, and Darina's body had relaxed some.

"Nice work, Yolase."

"What good is telepathy if you can't use it to take away someone's pain?"

She eased off Darina and Foster drew the cure up into a syringe. Finding a prominent vein in her right arm, he pushed the needle in and released the cure. He set the empty syringe down and moved Darina's sweat-soaked hair off her forehead.

"Come on... come on..."

Her breathing grew shallow, her chest barely rising and falling. Her eyes remained closed, and Foster reached back for a heart monitor. Hooking her up, he and Yolase both gasped when Darina's heartbeat hardly registered on the small screen.

She was nearly flat-lined.

"No. *Hell*, no." Foster opened a package of electripads and yanked off Darina's tank top. Adhering the pads to her chest on either side of her heart, he activated them.

Darina's body arched up from the table as the current flowed through her, but her heart rate didn't improve.

He was losing her.

Losing her to Mikale Warres and his virus.

With a frustrated growl, he set the electripads off two more times. When a high-pitched whine sounded from the heart monitor, Foster climbed onto the table and straddled Darina's limp body. Gathering her torso, he crushed her to his own chest and buried his face in her hair.

"You can't die. You cannot. Zeke needs you. Ghared needs you," he said, his voice strained. "I fucking need you."

Her body was so hot in his grip, almost too hot to touch, but he didn't release her. Couldn't release her. Not now. Not ever.

"Come on," he said again. "Don't leave us." He bent down so his lips were right at her ear. "Don't leave me."

He sat up and let her body rest back on the table. Her face was pale, her chest hardly moving at all. The heat was quickly leaving her.

"Doesn't the virus take longer to attack the body than this? I mean, she was only injected minutes ago." Yolase's voice startled him. He'd forgotten she was there.

"Maybe he put a different strain in her." He looked up at Yolase. "Where's the blood you took from her?"

She pointed to a vial on the worktable.

Foster climbed off Darina and took the vial. Mumbling to himself, he put a sample of her blood on a slide and examined it under the microscope. "Dammit. It is different."

He tore open his lab door and shouted, "Bring him in here!"

Moments later, Rasha and Hydec appeared with Mikale between them. Foster immediately grabbed Mikale by the neck and slammed him into the wall. Rasha and Hydec took a step back. They'd never seen him behave like this. But then again, he'd never had someone he was truly terrified to lose.

"What did you put in her?" he demanded.

A cocky smile slithered over Mikale's lips. "Something a little special."

"Tell me what's in it now." Foster banged Mikale's head against the wall and tightened his grip on his neck.

Mikale made a choking sound as his face turned red. "Can't... breathe..."

Yolase put a hand on Foster's shoulder. "You can't get the information you need, Foster, if you kill him."

Right. Of course. But the temptation to rip this guy apart was hard to ignore. Foster had spent most of his life wanting to help people, but right now all he could think about was squeezing Mikale's neck until it broke.

Somehow he loosened his grip. "If Darina dies..."

"What do you care if a whore like her dies?" Mikale asked, rubbing his neck.

Foster hadn't consciously decided to launch his fist into Mikale's face, but after he'd done it, he was glad he had. Seeing blood pour from the other man's nose and upper lip was surprisingly satisfying.

"You've had enough experiences with whores, Mikale, to know Darina is far from one." Foster had known that when Mikale wasn't working with him on something for Emerge Tech or one of their own projects, he was with a woman he'd hired. He didn't approve of it, but he'd turned to hologram programs to get off himself, so was he much different?

He shook his head. He *was* much different. He hadn't played with the emotions of real women. Holograms didn't get attached. That was why

Foster had always felt so empty after being with one.

Being with Darina hadn't left him feeling empty. Totally the opposite in fact. He'd never been so filled as when he'd made love with her.

She absolutely couldn't leave him now.

"Tell me what you put in her, Mikale. Tell me and maybe I won't let my friends here shoot you full of holes. They'd love to, you know."

"Was saying that just the other day," Hydec said as Rasha nodded.

"The whore means something to you." Mikale looked over Foster's shoulder to where Darina still lay motionless.

"Stop calling her a whore."

"But she is one, Foster. She was my whore. She fucked me so good, and I bought her that hand."

Foster stumbled back. Mikale and Darina had been together?

Rich bastard…

The words echoed in Foster's head. Mikale was the rich bastard. That news socked him in the face worse than a punch. Why hadn't Darina told him it was Mikale?

Why had she lied?

"Mikale, we used to be best friends," Foster said, trying his hardest to contain the burning rage boiling inside him. He'd never been this furious… or desperate. Conflicting emotions swirled like a tornado around him. He wanted Darina to live, yet he was shocked to find out she'd been with Mikale, that he was the rich bastard upon which she judged other rich, intelligent men. He wanted Mikale to die, yet the man had been his closest comrade for years before getting fired from Emerge Tech.

"We *were* best friends, Foster," Mikale rasped, one of his hands massaging his windpipe. "Then you forgot about me when I needed you most."

"I didn't forget about you. Emerge Tech made me choose between you and getting the globe up and running again. What would you have chosen?"

"I would have listened to my heart instead of my unfeeling brain. I would have realized that joining me on the outside meant we could have continued our work together. That we could have saved the world on our own, free from Emerge Tech. We would have found a way, Foster. I know we would have. Together."

Mikale's eyes were tear-filled now and Foster's throat tightened as he realized Mikale was probably right. Mikale had managed to build himself back up on the outside alone. He'd lost his grip on reality with his virus and repopulation plans, but with Foster's assistance and friendship, perhaps the two of them could have achieved their common goals without Emerge Tech.

Running a hand through his hair, Foster said, "I made the choice I thought was right at the time. I can't undo it. I wish I could. All we can do is move forward, but I need you to help me save Darina now."

"I'm not helping you do shit, Ashby."

Suddenly, Mikale cried out and put his hands to his skull. He gasped for breath and slumped against the wall. "Make it stop! Make it stop!"

As Foster looked on in confusion, Yolase approached, her eyes closed. Her breathing was labored, but she kept moving closer to Mikale. Her body trembled, but it was Mikale who slid down the wall into a heap on the ground.

"The cure is...." He rattled off a list of ingredients then passed out.

Foster turned to Yolase, who Hydec had to grab and support. "What did you do?"

"Bombarded his mind with unpleasant images from his own subconscious. Wasn't sure I could do that, but there's a first time for everything." She shivered. "Don't want to do that again." She looked at Darina. "You have a cure to make so let's get to it. Darina's still alive, but barely."

Foster quickly mixed a new cure and tested it on Darina's blood sample. With one drop, her blood was pure again. He got a fresh syringe and sucked up the cure.

"Please work." He injected Darina once again, his gaze going immediately to the heart monitor.

The beeping still sounded as the image on the screen showed a faint ripple representing Darina's heart rate. After a few moments of agony watching the faint ripple grow into a steady up and down, it flat-lined completely.

"No!" He still had things to say to her, and she had truths he needed to hear from her lips alone.

Foster slapped his hands on the table with an echoing smack and Darina sat up with a gasp. She sucked in deep inhales, her eyes wildly searching the room.

"What the hell?" she said, her voice not much more than a rasp.

Foster pulled her into his arms and squeezed until she shoved him back.

"Need some air, Doc."

He cupped her face. "You can have all the air you want. Later."

His mouth crashed down on hers, and at first, she struggled against him. Within seconds, though, she'd softened into the kiss, her full lips matched his fervor. She slid from her position on the table so her legs were on either side of his body, locked around his waist. Her arms came around his shoulders as his own raked up and down her back.

She was alive. She was in his arms.

"She likes being whipped." Mikale's voice grated on Foster's ears, ripping him from the sweet oblivion of Darina's kiss.

He tore his lips from Darina's and marched over to Mikale, dragging him up from the ground by a fistful of his shirt. "The woman you were with is not this woman." He thrust his arm back to Darina still sitting at the edge of the table. He didn't care if she'd left out who had purchased her prosthetic—who she had seduced to get it. What did it matter? All he cared about was that she was alive.

"The woman you were with was desperate to care for her son and her friend and her damn city. She wanted her life back. You were a means to getting that life back. Nothing more."

"If that's what you want to believe." Mikale smiled through the blood still dripping from his mouth. "Enjoy her. I did."

Foster grabbed Hydec's weapon and shoved it into Mikale's gut. Before he could pull the trigger though, a blast sounded and Mikale crumpled to the ground.

Looking over his shoulder, Foster saw Darina holding her weapon out.

"I've wanted to do that for a while." She looked at Mikale's body. "I hope you didn't still need him."

"No one needs him." Foster looked to Rasha and Hydec who picked up Mikale and headed for the door of the lab.

"I'm pretty sure it's going to take some extra fuel to get the waterwheel going again, don't you think, Hydec?" Rasha asked.

"Absolutely. Be a shame to waste any wood when we have this here body that'll burn just as nice." Hydec threw Mikale over his shoulder and carted him out of the lab.

Yolase followed Rasha and Hydec out, turning only to say, "I saw what Warres wanted you for, Darina." She shuddered, rubbing her hands up and down her own arms. "He had some grand repopulation plans. You did the right thing ending him." She slipped out of the lab and closed the door.

Alone now, Foster turned to Darina. "I'd like to make sure that virus is out of your system completely."

Silently, she offered him her arm and he drew more blood. After a few minutes at his microscope, he returned to her with a wide smile.

"Free and clear."

"Thanks. Though that word doesn't seem like enough." She hopped off the table, taking a moment to make sure she was steady on her feet.

"Darina, I want—"

"Can I see Zeke?" she interrupted.

"Of course."

Holding off telling her that it didn't matter what she'd done with Warres, that he wanted her anyway, Foster led her out of the lab and to the guest room. A battle raged outside between Warres's associates and the GECs, but he couldn't leave Darina. He wouldn't. Not after he'd almost lost her permanently.

Inside the guest room, Estoria and Mareea sat by the bed where Zeke rested.

Darina came to the bedside and lowered next to Zeke. She brushed hair off his forehead and cupped his cheek. "He's going to be okay?" she asked Foster.

"Yes. The blast hit him above his heart. I was able to repair the damaged tissue." Foster came to stand behind her. "He should be back to a hundred percent in a few days. GECs don't take a lot of time to heal."

"He woke up once," Mareea said, looking up at Darina. "He asked for you."

Darina smiled and pressed a kiss to Zeke's cheek, lingering a moment as if making sure he was breathing. "Are you all right, Mareea? Warres didn't... do anything to you, did he?"

Mareea shrugged. "Bruises only." A few tears dribbled down her cheeks, which she quickly brushed away with the sleeve of her sweatshirt. "When I think of what he could have done to me or that he almost killed Zeke…" The girl buried her face in her hands then appeared to shake it off. "My uncle? Where is he?"

"Most likely kicking ass out there." Darina reached for Mareea's hand. "Zeke cares about you."

"I know. He took a shot to the chest to prove it." Mareea took Zeke's hand and held it in her lap. "I feel the same way about him."

Estoria got up and put her hand on Foster's arm. "Why don't we give them some time?"

He wanted to say no. He wanted to say he wasn't leaving Darina's side. Something about the way Darina hugged Mareea and snuggled up to Zeke, however, made him feel like an outsider looking in on a place he didn't belong.

Nodding, he let Estoria tug him out of the guest room.

"They've been through a lot. All three of them," Estoria said, "but don't give up, okay?"

He didn't want to give up, but was it already too late?

Chapter Thirteen

Darina needed a few moments to make sure Zeke was, in fact, all right and that she was strong enough after having one of Mikale Warres's viruses inside her body. She'd never wanted another thing of Warres's in her body after seeing those two women throw themselves at him in the tattoo studio. He hadn't turned them away. Hadn't asked them to stop fondling him. He'd accepted whatever they were willing to give him.

As he'd been doing the entire time he was with me.

Which shouldn't have bothered her. After all, she was using him too. She needed another hand. Another hand cost money. Warres had money. It was a simple equation, but she'd let her emotions get caught up in the exchange. She'd imagined getting the new hand and staying with him. He lived a good life, a life she wanted. She'd dreamed of introducing him to Zeke and living together within Emerge Tech's walls, safe and sound.

She'd been foolish.

Rich bastards didn't know how to love or respect or think of anyone but themselves. When she thought of the things she'd done simply because Warres had said it would please him, she wanted to beat the crap out of herself.

And now Foster knew she'd prostituted herself with Warres. He'd understood and accepted when she'd first told him what she'd done to get the prosthetic hand, but certainly now that he knew *who* the rich bastard was, he wouldn't want anything to do with her.

How could he? She'd fucked the enemy. Literally.

She closed her eyes in a lame attempt to push everything out of her mind. When a blast sounded outside and rocked the main house, however, she couldn't continue hibernating in the guest room.

"Take care of him for me?" she asked Mareea.

"Sure. Where are you going?"

"I assembled that team outside. Be downright cowardly of me to stay in here, wouldn't it?"

"Cowardly is the last word anyone would use to describe you," Mareea said. "You and my uncle don't know how to be cowards."

Yeah. She and Ghared were cut from the same cloth. They both knew you had to make sacrifices. And when the fight was over out there, they'd haul ass back to the city and keep making those sacrifices.

She'd been stupid to believe she could actually have Foster. He was the light. She was the dark.

Besides, he'd found the cure, and Warres was dead. Her job as his bodyguard was over.

Weapon ready, Darina ran outside into the fight and took down as many of Warres's associates as possible. The GECs had done a fine job without her, and within an hour, the enemy was either dead or captured. Ghared was already organizing a convoy to fly prisoners back to the city to hand over to the government.

"These GECs were instrumental in fighting Warres's crew," he told Darina as he struggled out of the pulsejet. He winced as he put some weight on his injured leg. "Some of them are willing to come back to the city with me and plead for citizenship. I think they have a real shot of getting it if we back them."

"I'm in," Darina said. "We wouldn't have been able to accomplish what we did here today without them. I'm pretty sure once the government realizes Warres is dead and we have the cure, they'll give us whatever we want."

"Well, you know how the government likes to make everything hard," Ghared said.

"True, but it's worth a shot. The GECs can always go back into hiding if necessary." Darina surveyed the field in front of them. Trees had come down when the aircrafts fell, and the ground was torn up. The woods looked like a battlefield, and her heart broke a little knowing Foster's sanctuary had been treated so harshly. But, knowing how the people who lived here worked together gave her confidence the oasis would be restored to its former glory. "How many casualties are we facing here?"

"No GECs died today. They were made to fight, just like they said." Ghared pointed to a pile being assembled at the western side of the field. "Those are Warres's men who didn't make it."

Roben jogged over to them. "The prisoners are loaded, and we're ready when you are, Ghared." He gestured to Ghared's leg. "Let me get Foster to tend to that." He was gone before either Ghared or Darina could stop him.

Ghared glanced back at the main house then to Darina. "Zeke and Mareea are all right?"

"Yes."

"And you and Foster?"

"There is no me and Foster."

"Yeah, right."

Darina folded her arms across her chest. "If I say there's no me and Foster, there's no me and Foster."

Ghared shook his head. "Whatever you think is keeping you apart isn't. You deserve him." He gestured to the land around them. "You deserve this. You know, when it was pretty and shit."

What did Ghared know? He had no idea she'd been with Warres. The rich bastard was still nameless to him, and she'd keep it that way. She'd already lost Foster. She wasn't losing her best friend too.

Foster appeared on the deck of the main house, and Darina helped Ghared navigate the steps up to him.

"Your niece is asking for you," Foster said. "I'll fix you up then you can see her."

"Sounds like a fine plan to me."

Darina made a move to shift Ghared's weight to Foster, who stood ready to accept it, but Ghared wouldn't let go of her.

"Nope. You're coming with," he said. "You know how I cry like a baby when I have a boo-boo."

She couldn't stop the laugh that rushed out of her. "You're an idiot."

"Smartest idiot you've ever known." He tightened his grip on her as they followed Foster into the main house.

Foster skillfully set Ghared's broken leg, ran his tablet program over it, and immobilized it in a sturdy brace. His hands worked efficiently yet tenderly, reminding Darina how Foster's hands had felt caressing her body. She so wanted to feel that again.

"Keep the brace on for a week," Foster said to Ghared. "You should be fine after that." He gave Ghared a washcloth to clean the dried blood on his face. Ghared still had that same wild look he always had, but he didn't look as beat up anymore.

"Thanks, man." Ghared tested his weight on the braced leg then shook Foster's hand.

"No problem. Thank you as well. Rasha told me some of the GECs are going to the city with you. I'll miss them, but I'm happy they have this opportunity." Foster picked up a test tube. "Do you know if Emerge Tech is still operational?"

"It was when I left the city. That fire only destroyed the one building where your domicile was."

Foster released a slow breath. "Good. I'm going to send them my formula for the cure then."

Ghared took the test tube and squinted at its liquid contents. "This is it? This will save the world?"

Foster nodded as he took the tube back. "Looks rather unimpressive, doesn't it? But if Emerge Tech makes more and releases it into the water supply, it will reverse Warres's virus in current victims and prevent new outbreaks. They can share it globally so other countries can do the same."

"Rock and roll, you mad scientist, you." Ghared clapped Foster on the back. Turning to Darina, he said, "I'm going to stop in to see Zeke and Mareea then head back to the city with whoever is coming with me. You'll keep an eye on Mareea?"

"We're all coming with you, Ghared." Darina purposely didn't look at Foster.

Ghared, however, glanced at Foster then lowered his voice. "Take a few moments, Darina. Don't make a rushed decision."

"I need to come with you. I need to get back to my *real* life." She had a little trouble swallowing around the lump in her throat.

"Can Zeke be moved?" Ghared asked Foster, who had crept closer.

"I'd feel better if he wasn't, but medically, there's no reason why he can't be moved."

Darina did look at Foster then. Mistake. A billion different kinds of hurt swam in his lovely green eyes. Kind eyes. Though she'd slutted with Warres years ago and hadn't known Foster then, Darina felt as if she'd betrayed Foster now.

In a monumentally unforgiveable way.

She had to leave.

"Maybe the kid should rest." Ghared clamped his hand on Darina's shoulder, and tears burned at the corners of her eyes.

She had to clear her throat before speaking. "He can rest at home. Back in the city."

"If that's what you decide…" Ghared let his voice trail off as he regarded Foster again. "I'll be by the pulsejet. Take off time in ten minutes."

Ghared turned to limp out of Foster's lab, and Darina followed him, but a hand on her shoulder stopped her.

"Don't go," Foster said. "We need to talk."

Ghared hesitated for a minute, looking back at Darina.

"I'll be right there," she said.

He nodded once and continued out.

"What's there to say, Foster?" She faced him, but stared at her dirt-covered boots. "Warres was right. I was his whore. How could you ever want to look at me again, never mind touch me?"

He rested his hands on her shoulders, electrifying her entire body. All she wanted to do was collapse against him and have him never let her go.

But she couldn't even look him in the eye.

Foster tipped her chin so she had to look up at him, but she shrugged out of his grip before their gazes connected.

"I have to go. My job was to protect you. The threat on your life is over. I don't need to be here."

Not giving him the chance to say anything or stop her, she jogged out of the lab and up the stairs. She fought back the tears threatening to spill out. Officer Darina Lazitter did not cry.

But her cheeks were wet.

With an angry swipe at the traitorous tears, she made her way to the guest room. Inside, Zeke didn't stir on the bed nor did Mareea, her body half in a chair and half on the bed beside Zeke. Darina stared at the young pair, Mareea's hand resting atop Zeke's. She hated to disturb either one of them, but they had to get out of there. The longer she stayed in Vermont... with Foster... the harder it would be to leave, but she didn't belong on his land, in his home.

In his heart.

Dr. Foster Ashby was the kind of man who saved the world. A simple cop who'd whored it up with one of the globe's most wanted was not the woman for him. He may have thought differently, but fortunately Darina was thinking clearly. Logic wouldn't let her give in to what she wanted because, as she'd said before, she and Foster weren't in the same realm. The Universe didn't operate in such a way that they could be together. They were at opposite ends of a spectrum, brought together in the middle only for a brief moment.

A brief, amazing moment. One that Darina would treasure... and mourn... always.

****

Foster stayed in his lab after sending his cure formula to Emerge Tech, his hands pressed to the worktable, wondering what to do next. Why had he said Zeke could be moved? Why the hell was he so damn honest? One little lie and Darina would have stayed. She never would jeopardize Zeke's health.

But she would rip your heart out...

His chest actually ached. Foster rubbed at the source of the pain, but knew there would be no alleviating it. The hurt was deep down in his soul.

"She was merely doing her job," he said aloud to the empty room. The good officer had protected him, shielded him from Warres, and now his life wasn't in danger. That was a good thing.

Only it didn't feel like a good thing. Not at all.

A soft knock sounded on the lab door, and he opened it, hoping Darina had changed her mind.

Estoria stood on the other side with her hands folded across her chest.

"Want to tell me why Darina is piling Zeke and Mareea in a pulsejet piloted by Ghared?" She tapped her foot, and the noise rattled around in Foster's head as he stared at her feet. "Hey." Estoria stepped closer and grabbed his hand. Giving it a squeeze, she said, "Foster?"

"Yeah?"

"What's going on?" She tugged him back toward the table and made him sit on a stool.

"Officer Lazitter has completed her job. She's heading back to the city." His voice sounded robotic to his ears.

"And you're just letting her go?" Estoria's eyebrows rose as she regarded him.

"It's her choice to make, Essie." He stood and began cleaning his worktable to have something to do.

"Not if she makes the *wrong* choice, Foster. Then it's up to you to make her see, make her stay. You don't want her to go, do you?"

He shook his head. "But I need to respect her wishes." He held up a hand when Estoria opened her mouth. "Darina finished guarding me. She finished her job. *I* was just a job."

"No way." Estoria wagged a finger in his face. "I saw how she looked at you. You mean more to her than a job."

Foster drew in a breath, held it, then let it gush out in one long stream. Shit, he was tired. Almost getting caught by his enemies, being with Darina, nearly losing her to that injection Mikale pumped into her, having a battle on his normally peaceful slice of Vermont, and watching Darina walk out of the lab weighed down on him.

"I need sleep."

"The Foster Ashby I know never needs sleep."

"Maybe you don't know me at all. Maybe no one knows me." He was being a jerk. He knew it. He wanted to be left alone. "Is there anything out there," he pointed to the lab door, "that needs my immediate attention?"

"No. Hydec and Rasha have taken charge of assembling teams to fix any damaged structures, and a few other volunteers are firing up the chainsaws to cut up any fallen trees. The woodshed ought to be full to the brim by the time they're done."

He picked up his tablet and shoved it into his pocket. "Good. I'll be in my library." He made a move to walk past Estoria and out of the lab, but she stopped him.

"You're really not going to go after her?"

"I'm really not."

Estoria made an exasperated noise, but Foster continued walking. She was often full of good advice that he usually accepted. Today, however, was different. She hadn't seen how Darina had squared her shoulders. How she had hardened her eyes. How her lips had formed a tight, determined line. Darina thought he didn't want her because she'd been with Mikale. She thought she had to leave now that she'd protected him successfully.

She was wrong on both accounts, but no matter what Estoria had imagined seeing in Darina's eyes and regardless of the strong spark he'd felt between them when they'd made love, he couldn't keep her. She didn't want to be kept. She wanted to go back to her life in the city, so he'd let her. He'd been fine on his own all this time. Nothing had to change.

Except that everything has changed.

Darina had unleashed emotions in him— ones that had made him feel wonderful. Ones that made him see there was more to life than science and working and solving other people's problems. Ones that only came about when two people were so right for each other. Why didn't Darina feel that?

Foster knew he hadn't been imagining the passion and the compatibility. That had been as real as the sun shining outside. He wasn't one to see things that weren't there. He didn't hallucinate. He didn't ignore the truth. Scientists relied on acute observation and systematic analysis. If he applied both of those to his feelings for Darina, more than enough evidence existed to support the notion they were meant for each other. In fact, he'd go as far as to say he could *prove* they belonged together.

As a police officer, didn't she live by evidence as well? She used observation and analysis. She saved people with her skills. She thought they lived different lives, but that actually wasn't true at all. They had a great deal in common. Enough that he couldn't see a reason why he should let her go.

All his genetically engineered life, he'd done things for everyone else. He'd been constructed to serve, put others' needs first, solve complicated problems. The time had come to consider what he wanted. To get what he wanted.

He wanted Officer Darina Lazitter.

"If she needs proof," he said as he entered his library where he'd first touched Darina, "I'll give it to her."

Chapter Fourteen

Two weeks had passed since Darina had been in Vermont. Two long weeks of feeling alone and aimless. She was busy with police work, but she could hardly focus on what she was doing. She'd helped with cure dispersal efforts as soon as Emerge Tech began releasing it. That made her miss Foster. She'd assisted in the incarceration of Warres's associates. That made her miss Foster. She'd worked closely with Ghared on presenting citizenship cases for the Vermont GECs, and guess what? That made her miss Foster. It was as if she couldn't make a move without thinking of him.

"Damn annoying," she mumbled as she shoveled her cold breakfast of artificial oats into her mouth. A far cry from Estoria's pancakes, as Zeke had pointed out nearly every day since they'd left the woods. The kid was dying to make the pancakes himself, but the city wasn't up and running enough to get the necessary ingredients.

Soon.

The signs were all there. The world was on the brink of hopping back on the tracks and forging ahead. People were recovering from Warres's plague. No new cases had been reported last week. Some major gains had been made in cranking up the power levels across the nation. Darina could easily envision eating a better breakfast in a brighter domicile in the not so distant future.

Still wouldn't compare to eating breakfast after sleeping beside Foster all night long.

She finished the last bite of her breakfast and sighed.

"Something weighing on your mind, Mom?" Zeke rested his hand atop hers on the table where they both sat.

"No." She stared into the chipped glass holding her water.

"Bullshit."

That word snapped her head up and her eyes connected with Zeke's. She'd never had to talk to him about swearing, though she and Ghared swore like thugs around him on an almost continual basis.

"Excuse me?" She sat up straighter, her hand slipping out from under his.

"You heard me." Zeke pushed his own breakfast aside. "Bull. Shit. When are you going to admit that you miss Foster?"

"I don't—" She stopped when Zeke held up a hand.

"You do. I even miss the guy, and I certainly didn't lock lips with him... among other things."

Heat instantly fired Darina's cheeks, and Zeke laughed.

"Yeah, I knew. What am I, blind, Mom?"

"No... I just... I didn't..." How she wished for spontaneous combustion right now.

"It's okay that you locked lips and such with Foster." Zeke tilted his head so his hair moved out of his face. "I've locked lips with Mareea. On several occasions."

"And such?"

Now his cheeks pinked a little, and Darina was equal parts afraid of his growing up and proud of the young man he'd become.

"Not yet," Zeke said, and Darina let out the breath she'd been holding. "We have plenty of time for 'and such.'" He grinned.

"So?" she asked.

"So... what?" A little creased formed between Zeke's dark brows.

"So is Mareea a good kisser?" If he was going to knock her on her ass with his questions and statements, she could do the same to him.

"Mom, we were not discussing me. We were talking about you and Foster." He leaned back in his chair and folded his arms across his chest.

"I'm going to take that as a yes then."

The right corner of Zeke's mouth twitched up in a slight grin as the boy no doubt imagined his lips pressed to Mareea's. Young love. Darina hoped the kids didn't get their hearts broken. It hurt. She should know.

Two weeks of no contact with Foster had been torture. Which was totally stupid because she'd only spent days with the man in the first place. But shit, there had been some amazing moments during those particular days. She'd reviewed her decision to leave Vermont a million times and knew she had done the right thing, but why did it have to hurt so badly? Why couldn't she forget Dr. Foster Ashby?

"I figured you needed time," Zeke said. "Time to figure out that you love him. Why is it taking you so long?"

"It's not taking me long." She sipped her water, but her throat remained dry. "I figured out I loved him after day one of guarding him."

Zeke's eyebrows shot up. "You did? Then why are you here without him?"

She hoisted her arm onto the table between them and waved her prosthetic hand. "You know this isn't real."

"Yeah, but what does that have to do with anything?"

"Mikale Warres bought it for me."

Zeke's eyes bugged. "You knew Warres before he unleashed his plague?"

Darina nodded, not sure if she could continue, but she had to make Zeke understand why Foster couldn't possibly want her. She didn't want to give the kid hope. He liked Foster too, but there was no place for a genius doctor in their lives. He'd get bored with them.

"It was a desperate time. I needed a better hand than the one I had. I couldn't take care of you or do police work." *And then I fell in love with the selfish, unfaithful prick.*

She flexed her hand, watching the ring of stars waver on her skin. The M and W carved into the last star made her sick to her stomach. How could she have been so naïve to think she was the only woman Warres was seeing at the time? He was handsome. He was rich. He was brilliant. He could have had literally any woman he wanted… and so he had *all* the women he wanted. At the same time. Thinking of that now made her blood boil. She usually didn't act that foolish.

Except that now I've fallen in love with Foster. Another man who was way out of her league on all accounts. He was more handsome and brilliant than Warres and probably richer. Why couldn't she find someone on her level in the city? Why did she and Ghared only have sibling-like feelings for each other? *He* was on her level. On paper, they made a great pair. In real life, however, they didn't spark.

"So what if Warres bought your hand?" Zeke's voice brought her back to the present. "I still don't see why that means you can't be with Foster."

She stood and paced away from the table, her fingers pressing into her temples. No easy way to say this. "I had... Warres and I... we were... well, we were together for a time."

Zeke's nose crinkled. "Like you were a couple?"

She nodded once, hating that any of this was true about her.

A complete body shudder coursed through Zeke and a look of complete disgust came over his features. "Eww, Mom. Why?"

"He wasn't a madman back then." *Just a man with an insatiable appetite for sex who had made me feel a little exotic.* He'd had some different tastes when it came to what he liked in bed, and Darina had learned she didn't mind catering to those tastes... until she realized she wasn't the only dish at his buffet.

Zeke waved his hands. "Okay, whatever about Warres. That was the past. I still think you could have Foster now if you wanted him." He stood and walked over to her. "For once in your life, think about what you want, Mom. You're always worrying about everyone else. What about you?"

He leaned forward and pressed a kiss to her forehead, and for a moment, she felt as if they had reversed roles. He was the parent, she the child.

"I'm meeting Mareea," he said. "There's some activity at what remains of the old high school two streets over."

"Activity? What kind of activity?" Darina fingered her weapon tucked into the holster at her waist.

"Easy now, Officer." Zeke laughed. "No need to go all cop on me. The activity is of the rebuild nature. With things looking up on the health, power, and technology fronts, some of us were thinking we could get the learning front going too."

Was there no limit to this kid's greatness? And now that he hadn't had any seizures, thanks to Foster's medication, Zeke was unstoppable. He would do great things with his future. Darina was sure of it.

"Let me know if you need any help." She stepped closer to him and ruffled his hair.

He swatted at her hand and spent a few seconds trying to right the disheveled strands. A haircut was definitely in order, but she knew better than to suggest it.

"We're making lists of action steps, materials, and so on right now, but I will definitely take you up on help when we figure out what we want to do." He walked away then turned back to her. "Until I need your help, though, I think you need to talk to Foster."

She followed him to the door where he tugged on his boots and squatted to tie them. Before Zeke could open the door, Ghared busted in.

"Good," he said. "You're both still here." A look of relief washed over his face.

"What's going on?" Darina stepped around Zeke and looked up at Ghared.

He scratched at his bearded jaw and puffed out a breath. "Some lunatic that lives by the old high school is apparently refusing to drink the water. Claims he's got Warres's plague but doesn't want the cure. He looks pretty fucked up. Boston PD is trying to contain him now."

"Mareea's at the high school." Zeke pushed past Ghared, ready to rescue his girl.

"No, I'm not." Mareea came around the corner of the hallway leading to Darina's domicile. "Uncle Ghared got to me before I left to meet your sorry ass." She lightly punched Zeke in the shoulder, and a big, goofy grin blossomed on Zeke's lips.

He folded Mareea in his arms. "My sorry ass is right here, so you're exactly where you should be."

"And I should be at the high school," Darina said.

"I'll go with you." Ghared turned to follow her, but glanced back at Zeke and Mareea. "You two stay here, and don't do anything stupid." He narrowed his eyes at Zeke.

Zeke gave him a salute while Mareea rolled her eyes.

In the hallway, Darina said, "He can't get her pregnant you know." Not that she wanted to recognize the fact that her teenage son would be having sex, but it was inevitable.

Ghared stuck his fingers in his ears and shook his head. "At the top of my list of Things I Never Want to Discuss."

"They're young adults in love, Ghared, what do you think they want—"

"If you finish that sentence, I will push you into the street, and there's actually some traffic now. You'll be flattened, and I'll have some peace."

"Fine. Deny what you know is going to happen."

"I'm not denying anything. Mareea and Zeke will be little kids forever. They don't fall in love, they certainly don't *make* love, and I don't have to start giving Zeke the get-your-hands-off-my-niece stare of death. End of discussion."

"Wouldn't you rather have her with a kid like Zeke than some jackass you don't know?"

"I don't want Mareea with anyone. She was playing with a torn up teddy bear like just yesterday."

"Sorry, buddy, but both of them grew up while you weren't watching." Darina broke into a run toward the high school where two police jeeps were parked at odd angles to the crumbling building.

"Mr. Jarkins, the cure is for real. Take it, and all your problems are solved," an officer said to the man pacing by the front steps of what remained of the high school building.

"He looks like total shit," Ghared whispered to Darina as she assessed the situation.

"But he doesn't trust the cure is real." She couldn't blame him. After living the way they had for so long, nothing seemed real anymore.

Things are changing, though.

And thank heavens for that.

She moved toward the closest officer whose gun was trained on the sick man. "Mr. Jarkins, is it?"

The man stopped pacing and met her gaze, his left eye filled with blood. A vein in his neck was particularly swollen, and Darina recalled when Warres had injected her with a virus strain. The all-over burn that had coursed throughout her body was like nothing she'd ever felt. She had to make this guy understand that taking the cure was his best course of action.

"I know you're thinking this cure is bogus, but it's the real deal. I watched Dr. Ashby make it myself. He's an amazing scientist." Saying Foster's name caused a soul-deep ache in her chest. How she wished their story had a different ending. One where they got to hold each other for as long as they both shall live.

"The cure works?" Mr. Jarkins asked as he rubbed the back of his neck. "How can you be so sure? What if it kills me?" The man's hands shook, and he sat on one of the school's steps, cradling his head in his hands and mumbling things Darina couldn't quite hear.

"Taking this cure is your best option. If you don't take it, you will certainly die from Warres's plague. That's a definite. If you take the cure, you have a shot at living." She folded her hands across her chest and regarded the man. "I know the pain you are in right now, Mr. Jarkins. I've been in similar shoes, but Dr. Ashby was there with his cure and look at me now." She gestured from her head to her toes. "All my organs are fully functional."

"And doesn't her hair look great?" Ghared added, earning a laugh from the nearest officer.

"More than her hair looks great," another voice said from behind her. A voice she knew. A voice she couldn't forget.

Slowly, Darina turned around and blinked at what surely had to be an incredible illusion of some kind.

"Foster?"

****

She was every bit as beautiful as she was two weeks ago. Maybe more so. Tank tops and cargo pants would forever be Foster's favorite outfits on a woman.

And Darina would forever be his favorite woman.

He fought the overwhelming urge to run toward her, scoop her up, and twirl her around. She definitely wouldn't appreciate that. Especially because she thought she was working.

Instead he walked calmly to her, his heart beating faster the closer he came. How he'd managed to wait two whole weeks to see her was a mystery, but he'd wanted to give her time. Time to realize she couldn't live without him.

From the look on her face maybe he'd waited exactly the right amount of time. She hadn't blinked since turning around and seeing him there.

Slowly, Estoria, Roben, Pike, Rasha, Hydec and several other GECs came out from nearby buildings. Each of them was holding a bouquet of bright orange daylilies they'd harvested from the Vermont property. They lined up on the crumbling sidewalk, instantly turning the gray city into something magical.

At least Foster hoped they did. He needed some magic.

Glancing around Darina, Foster looked at the man now lounging comfortable on the steps of the building behind Darina. "Thanks for your help, Natik."

"Not a problem." Natik stood and motioned to his eye and neck. "Can we fix this up? I don't want to scare the piss out of my wife."

"Of course." While Darina was adorably confused, Foster dug out his tablet and scanned away Natik's symptoms. Within seconds, his eye was no longer filled with blood and the swollen neck vein had shrunk to its normal size.

The two men shook hands and Natik gave Darina a friendly smile. "Just wanted to let you know I totally would have taken the cure because you told me to. I could feel your sincerity. You must be an amazing police officer. Especially if you've managed to turn this guy's head. I worked with him at Emerge Tech. *Nothing* but science turns his head."

"Until now," Ghared said.

"Until now," Foster agreed, still loving how dumbfounded and quiet Darina was. He'd hoped to surprise her, and he was pretty sure he'd nailed it.

The two officers gave Foster a nod and drove off as Natik strolled down the street. Ghared hung around, giving Darina a nudge.

"A speechless Darina... interesting," he mused.

"Is this a good thing or a bad thing?" Foster asked.

"Can't say for sure." Ghared grinned. "It's never happened before."

Darina blinked and glared at Ghared. "What is going on here?"

"And she's back." He rested his hands on her shoulders. "Maybe I lied a little bit." He held up his thumb and index finger, an inch or so between them.

"Lied?" She squinted down the street in the direction Natik had headed. "Mr. Jarkins wasn't really infected?"

Foster shook his head. "I wasn't sure you'd come to meet me if I asked."

"But he knew you'd come to help out a fellow citizen," Ghared added.

"Real nice. Use my sense of duty against me." She folded her arms across her chest and looked between Foster and Ghared.

"Oh, don't get all pissy," Ghared said. "This guy wants to talk to you, and I say you let him."

"And who put you in charge?" Now her foot tapped, and Foster found her even more attractive when slightly pissed off. Shit, he'd missed her.

"I did." Zeke came to stand next to her, Mareea holding his hand.

Darina whirled around to look up at her son. Foster got a little thrill out of tipping her world on its axis. She deserved it. She'd done it to him with her simple presence.

"Foster contacted me, and as soon as I determined he was as miserable as you were," Zeke pointed at his mother, making her go a little cross-eyed as she followed his index finger, "Ghared and I decided it was time for an intervention." He kissed Darina's cheek. "Make the best of this opportunity, Mom."

"Wait, you weren't heading to the high school? Our whole exchange back home was—"

"Somewhat fictional? Yes." Zeke gestured between him and Mareea. "We do have a plan to rebuild the school, but there's no meeting today. Forgive me?"

Darina shot a look at Foster—one that made his blood rush around his body, cyclonically. "I suppose so."

"Good enough for me," Zeke said.

With that, Zeke and Mareea, followed by Ghared, wandered away as if they were out for a casual stroll through the newly alive city.

Darina slid her hands in her pockets and gave Foster a head-to-toe sweep with her eyes that he felt everywhere. "How are you?" Her voice was soft, none of her usual confidence anywhere to be found.

Foster smiled. "Fine. How are you?"

Her lips twitched up as she fought not to smile. "I'm well. Except for the liars I apparently raised and decided to befriend."

"Liars with your best interests at heart." Foster took a step closer to her. He wanted nothing more than to occupy her space. He longed to touch her as he had back in Vermont.

"Oh yeah? And what best interests are those?" She took a step closer too.

"Me. It's in your best interest to be with me, Darina." He reached out now, letting his hand trace the contours of her cheek. When she closed her eyes and didn't jerk away from his touch, Foster's heart swelled in his chest. "I couldn't take being away from you another minute."

"Really?" She pressed her face into his palm, bringing her hand up to cup his hand. "I hardly noticed you weren't around."

"Is that so?" He moved his hand to her waist and tugged her so her hips touched his.

Her hands snaked up his chest and hooked on the back of his neck, her thumb running gently over his tattoo. "Well, maybe I wondered about your wellbeing a little."

"Good to know." He leaned his head down and caught her lips. As soon as they made contact, the fireworks crackled to life all over again.

When she ripped herself free of his kiss, of his grasp, he couldn't breathe.

"We can't do this, Foster." She paced away from him, squeezing her eyes shut.

"Why the hell not? I know you feel something for me. That kiss told me so."

"I feel more than *something* for you, dammit." She puffed out a frustrated breath. "But there's no way you could possibly want to look at me, touch me, call me your own. Not after I've been with Warres. I've made terrible mistakes." Her gorgeous eyes filled with unshed tears, and she swiped at one escapee.

Time to make her understand. Once and for all.

"I most definitely want to look at you," Foster said, an edge of anger outlining his words. He had to get it into her thick skull that she was everything to him. "I certainly want to touch you. I don't care about the past or Warres or anything except being with you. Now. Tomorrow. Forever. Do you know why?"

"You're crazy?"

He grinned and slid his hands around her waist corralling her in his arms again. "No. It's because I love you, Officer Darina Lazitter. I love you. We've only known each other mere days, but I've thought about you every second of every day during the two weeks we've been apart. I feel as if I've been searching for you for an eternity. Now that I've found you, I don't want to let you go." He gestured to himself with his left hand. "You promised to keep me safe, and here I am. But I'm in danger again. In danger of being heartbroken without you. I want to be with someone who keeps her promises. Keep me safe again, Darina. Safe in your heart. Please."

Foster didn't give her a chance to reply. Instead he captured her mouth with his and what started out as a slow, gentle kiss turned into something feral and scorching. He grabbed the back of her legs until she hoisted both of them up and wrapped them around his waist. It was as if she were willing to crawl inside his heart, and he was all for that notion.

She broke the kiss, cupped his face, then freed her legs. Taking his hand, she led him down the street without a word. When she stopped in front of a broken-down apartment building, Estoria and the others who had followed a short distance away rested the lilies by her door, hugged her each in turn, then continued down the street. Darina unlocked a door and pulled him inside, shutting the door behind them.

"You really want me?" she asked.

"More than anything." He held his hand up as if taking an oath. "Say you want me too."

She shrugged one shoulder, smiling slightly. "I guess so. Why not?"

Foster poked her in the side then worked her tank top off along with her pants. Dropping kisses along her exposed flesh, he said, "Let's see if I can turn that 'I guess so' into something a bit more definitive."

"You can try."

****

Turns out his attempt was so good he'd convinced her to return to Vermont with him after they'd made love in her domicile.

Then they'd made love again.

In his bedroom now, with Darina cuddled close, Foster watched sunlight grow brighter around the blinds on his windows. The brightness made him feel as if everything was finally in order in his life. A few weeks ago, he'd almost lost Darina and his GEC friends, not to mention the damage to the property Warres's associates had caused. That had sucked. On the other hand, he'd saved Darina. Last night he'd told her he loved her, then spent the night showing her how much. That had been amazing.

So amazing that he…

"Darina?" he whispered.

She shifted beside him, her naked body rubbing alongside his naked body in such a way he didn't ever want to leave the bed.

Or put on clothes ever again.

"Hmm…" Her throat vibrated, and he felt it against his chest where she rested her head.

"I have some thoughts on how we should start this day." He let his hand glide over one of her nipples, teasing it to a tight bud.

"You scientists are always thinking."

He felt her lips turn up in a smile as she dropped kisses along his shoulder, across his collarbone, and up his neck until she reached his mouth.

Lifting his head slightly, he caught her lips, and they kissed as if they were having each other for breakfast. He never wanted to eat anything else.

"How do you feel?" he asked when they stopped for a breath.

"I feel horny." She rose to her knees and straddled him, his hands automatically going to her hips, sliding up her curves, kneading her full breasts. "Tell me you feel the same."

"Around you? Constantly." He threaded his fingers with hers and tugged until she had to lower her chest to his. "What are you going to do about it?"

She scooted back a little so her hot center rubbed against his hard and ready erection. Her head went back when he groaned and arched his hips to grind against her.

"I'm going to say something I've never said to a man before." She stopped moving long enough to make eye contact. Her face was serious as she hooked her hair behind her ears and licked her lips.

"Let's hear it." Foster braced himself, not sure if he was going to like what came out of her mouth. He didn't want anything to destroy the fantastic buzz he had going.

"I love you, Foster." She pressed her hand on his chest when he made a move to sit up and embrace her. "Let me finish. I love you because you stopped Zeke's seizures then tended to him when Warres shot him. I love you because you tended to Ghared and his busted leg. I love you because you've housed GECs here for years and made them feel a part of a community when the world told them they weren't good enough. I love you because you cured me and the globe. I love you because you make love with the exact right mix of tenderness and wildness. I love you because you came back for me." She wiggled on his hips and grinned. "But most of all, Doc, I love you because you make me feel alive."

She moved her hand now and allowed him to sit up. He gathered her in his arms and squeezed her wonderfully naked body against his. Raking his hands up into her hair as she smoothed her hand over his tattooed neck, he lightly bit a trail along her shoulder.

When he reached her jaw, he pressed open-mouthed kisses up to her lips. Pulling back for a moment, he stared into her hazel eyes, getting lost in the green-brown whirlpools.

"And here I thought I was going to have to provide you with a bunch of evidence on why we should be together." He cupped her face and brushed a gentle kiss to her cheek. "I love you for the same reason, Darina. You make me feel alive too." Grinning, he swept his gaze over her naked body. "Oh, and because you're the sexiest thing I've ever laid eyes on."

She laughed and lightly slapped his chest. "Keep saying stuff like that and you'll wake up like this every morning."

"That's the plan." He wrapped his arms around her and rolled her to her back so he was on top now. "Which brings me to my next question." He ran his fingertips along her side, over the smooth expanse of her stomach, and up around her breasts. "Will you and Zeke stay with me? I know we have to go back to the city for work and rebuild efforts, but wherever I am, I want you two there as well. I want you to be my family."

Darina reached her hand up and smoothed his hair back, her touch gentle yet possessive. And possess him she did. Not a doubt in his mind that he wanted to belong to her and have her belong to him.

"As luck would have it, Doc, you're just who Zeke and I have been looking for all these years to join our team." She walked her fingers up his chest and hooked her hands on his shoulders, bringing him down toward her. "Now make love to me, and let's start this day out right."

Foster didn't need to be told twice. He stroked her nipples with his tongue until she blissfully writhed beneath him. Caressing her center, he found her more than ready for him. He held her gaze as he slid into her, inch by inch, and found the home he'd always been looking for.

She widened her legs, accepting him deeper, her nails raking lightly along his back. With each rhythmic thrust, he claimed more of her, came closer to merging his soul with hers, destroying the emptiness they'd both endured.

That emptiness would plague them no more.

Foster basked in the warm hold Darina had on him. How had he ever been satisfied by a hologram? Those programs didn't come close to what Darina made him feel, how she fit snuggly around him, her insides contracting until he couldn't stop the freefall, didn't want to.

She cried out his name before they climbed higher and erupted in a shower of trembling sparks that danced before Foster's eyes. He collapsed beside her on the bed, still buried deep inside her as the aftershocks stroked him.

"I could lie here forever with you," he whispered into her ear.

She turned to kiss him as he slowly slid out of her. A sexy groan rumbled from her throat, and Foster wanted to make love to her again. She turned to her side and traced her fingers along the tattooed spirals on his neck.

"You said these meant survival, right?"

He nodded.

"Well, here's to surviving then."

"Oh, we're going to do more than survive," Foster said. "We're going to thrive."

Epilogue

One month later...

Darina hummed as she helped Estoria and Rasha in one of the many gardens on the property. Not once had she imagined she'd be covered in dirt on purpose, but tending vegetables had become a favorite activity of hers when she and Zeke were with Foster in Vermont.

They divided their time between the city and the woods. Spending time with Foster brought her so much happiness. Watching Zeke and Foster together made that happiness grow exponentially. She'd always wished for a father for her son, and Ghared had done a fantastic job of filling that role for many years, but the connection Foster had made with Zeke was something more, something special.

"Hey." Estoria's snapping fingers made Darina blink up at her. "Quit daydreaming and harvest those veggies." She grinned and arched her back. In the past month, Foster had figured out how to stop Estoria's continual cycle of pregnancy. She wouldn't give birth to another stillborn baby nor suffer repeated conception.

Darina smoothed her hand over her own stomach and wondered what it would be like to give birth to a child. She glanced back at the main house. Did Foster wonder about that too? GECs were sterile, but with a brilliant man like Foster, anything was possible.

Right?

After giving Homer an extensive petting when he'd loped over to her in the garden, she pulled up a few carrots, adding them to her basket. Homer nosed around the basket and she couldn't resist giving the dorse a few to nibble. He lowered to his belly and gave the treat his full attention.

She continued harvesting, loving the soft warmth of the earth on her hands... well, one of them anyway. Maybe someday she'd be able to feel the dirt on her prosthetic hand.

But she wasn't complaining. She had no reason to. Her life was finally perfect, and each tomorrow promised more perfection.

"Darina!"

She looked up, and Foster waved her toward the house. Just looking at him caused a magnetic pull. She loved being near him. Dusting off her hands and the knees of her pants, she jogged to the deck.

"What's up?" She climbed the steps and allowed Foster to wrap her in a hug. He smelled like soap and whatever it was he used to sterilize his lab instruments.

"You have a call from Ghared."

She stiffened in his arms. "Is everything okay?" Zeke and Mareea were staying with Ghared in the city this week while the kids worked on the high school rebuild.

"Zeke is fine. That much he assured me, but he said he had other news." Foster shrugged and took her hand, leading her into the house.

With Foster standing close behind her, she picked up her own tablet from the kitchen counter and tapped it to life. Ghared's face filled the screen. The crease between his icy blue eyes told her the 'other news' was something big.

"Hey, Ghared. What's going on?"

He swallowed and looked away for a moment. The cinderblock walls of the Boston Police Department behind him filled the screen.

"It's not so much news *I* have as one of Warres's men has." Ghared had been working with the police and the government to handle the prisoners they'd captured in the Vermont battle.

"What does that mean?"

"I'll let him tell you."

Ghared's face was replaced with that of a dark-skinned man. His brown eyes were wide and nervous as if he expected Mikale Warres to jump out and beat him.

Thankfully, that wasn't going to happen. Not ever.

"Go ahead," Ghared said from off screen. "Tell her. Tell her what you told me."

The man looked her in the eye. "Deo Lazitter is alive."

My brother? Alive?

"Not possible." She shook her head.

"That's what I said too." Ghared was back on screen. "But then this guy handed me these."

The view got wobbly as Ghared turned his tablet. When it settled, Darina gasped.

"Dog tags?" Foster asked.

Ghared came back on screen. "Yeah. Deo's dog tags."

Darina felt Foster's hands on her shoulders, and it was a good thing he was there. She needed something to anchor her.

"Where did you get those?"

"Warres's guy said he got them off Deo himself. Said he'd been working undercover in Warres's circle with Deo."

"Working *with* Deo? Undercover?" It was as if Ghared were no longer speaking a language she understood. "How can this be true? Why didn't we know?"

"I don't know, Darina," Ghared said, "but I'm sure as hell going to find out."

If you enjoyed *SAFE*,
please consider leaving a review
on Amazon and Goodreads
and recommend my books to your friends.
Thank you!

If you have a book group,
I'd love to interact with you!
Email me at cdepetrillo@yahoo.com or message
me through Facebook for options.

Other Books in The Shielded Series
Sci-Fi Romance

PROTECTED (Book Two)

SECURE (Book Three)

*Check www.christinedepetrillo.weebly.com
for release dates.*

Read on for a peek at *PROTECTED!*

PROTECTED Sneak Peek

Chapter One

"If I ask you to tell me a million times, you'll tell me a million times." Ghared Timms slammed his fist down on the aluminum table separating him from one of Mikale Warres's associates.

The late Mikale Warres, that is.

Thanks to the kickass woman sitting beside him, Officer Darina Lazitter, the globe's most wanted chemist, Mikale Warres, was dead, exterminated August 2025. With his demise, the world had been saved from Warres's fatal plague—one that reduced victims' organs to ash. Darina's mate, Doctor Foster Ashby, had found the cure to the plague and the population was recovering, slowly but surely. Things were turning around. With people no longer fighting the disease, they were beginning to rebuild after the Anarch, a techhead terrorist group, had unplugged the globe a few years ago. Power was being restored. A second chance emerged from the rubble, and the city of Boston was as the heart of the revival.

But everything wasn't tied up neatly with a big, red bow just yet.

"These belonged to my best friend." Ghared held up a set of dog tags on a long silver chain and motioned to Darina. "To her brother. We've thought he was dead all this time and when you announce he's alive, we need every goddamn detail you have."

They'd been at it for a few days, trying to get all the crumbs out of this guy. Aven Demaris swore he'd been undercover—with Deo—inside Warres's organization on a government-backed mission to bring Warres down from within. As unbelievable as it sounded, how else did Aven have Deo's dog tags? How else was he able to describe Deo right down to the yellow-eyed wolf head tattoo on his left arm? How else had he been able to predict Warres's organization would name Sasha Boisette as Warres's successor?

And how much did that suck?

Taking down the head of the beast and capturing several of Warres's associates should have been enough to shut down the enemy. Curing the plague should have been enough. So many things should have been enough, but they weren't. With this new chick in charge, one could only guess what nonsense would come from the enemy now.

Things have to get worse before they can get better.

That was something Deo would have said and right now it sounded damn true.

"Can I have a drink?" Aven cleared his throat and Ghared saw red.

"A drink? You want a drink?" He shot to his feet causing Aven to flinch in his seat. The slightly smaller man was handcuffed and wearing a gray prison jumpsuit like all the other captured associates. He had been granted a private cell, however, until the validity of his tale of undercover work could be determined.

As of yet, the government had offered no support to Aven and with each passing day, Ghared grew more reluctant to believe his best friend was still alive.

But he couldn't give up. If a shred of possibility existed that Deo wasn't dead, Ghared would search to the ends of the Earth to find him. For Deo, for Darina, for himself.

"Ghared…" A wisp of warning simmered in Darina's voice.

"I'll get you a drink." He closed his hand around Aven's throat and lifted the man off the chair, knocking it over in the process. A loud metallic clang echoed in the cinderblock interrogation room followed by a shuffling as Ghared dragged Aven over to the wall and pinned him against it. "I'll get you a drink as soon as you start making some sense. You might have trouble swallowing that drink when I'm done with you though."

Aven's face grew purple as the man sputtered for oxygen. A little over the top. Ghared hadn't begun to tighten his grasp. Plenty of air still getting in. No need for the theatrics.

"So far, you haven't given us anything concrete besides the dog tags." Ghared increased the pressure slightly and Aven's eyes bugged. "You've given your word too, which is shit to me. The only thing I know for sure about you is that you were counted among Warres's associates during the battle at Foster's Vermont place. That doesn't put you on my list of Top Ten People I Trust, asshole."

Aven slapped at Ghared's hand, trying to get free. His attempts were no more troublesome than a mosquito's attack.

"Ghared, you should let him go." Darina uttered the words, but she never looked up from her tablet. Her attempt to be the "good cop" would have had him laughing. If he were in the laughing mood.

He was not.

"I'm done playing nice, Darina. This guy doesn't have anything more for us." He used his icy blue gaze to send a physical ripple of fear through Aven. That was kind of fun. "I say we end him."

Aven released a strangled whimper, his gaze darting to Darina in a silent plea for help.

"End him. Doesn't matter to me. I've got the cell space to hold him indefinitely, but ending him is much more efficient." She gave Aven a bored once-over with her hazel eyes, then returned her focus to her tablet. God, she was good. Ghared almost believed she didn't give a dorse's ass if Aven told them something of value or not.

He knew, however, Darina had not slept since he'd called her to say Deo might be alive. He saw it in the dark circles around her beautiful eyes. He'd heard it from Foster who was concerned. He'd also heard it from Darina's son, Zeke, and his own niece, Mareea. Everyone was worried about Darina and what it meant if Deo was, in fact, alive. He tried not to get his hopes up, but that was a hard thing to do.

To have Deo back…

Well, shit, that'd be like having a wish granted.

Letting out a growl, Ghared pulled Aven forward a bit so they were eye-to-eye. "I'd love to make this your last day, but maybe there's something you forgot to tell us. Something important. Something that makes you indispensable."

Aven nodded as much as he could with Ghared still gripping his throat.

"Let him go," Darina said.

Ghared released him and Aven slid to the floor, panting like a dog who'd run twenty miles. Uphill. On a humid, summer day.

Darina slid her own chair back and stood. She walked around the table to join Ghared on the other side and folded her arms across her chest as she glared down at Aven still on all fours and sucking in air.

She reached down and pulled Aven up by his hair. The man let out a screech and Ghared found it harder and harder to believe the guy was capable of undercover work or of being partnered with Deo.

Grow a set, dude.

"Why is it the government hasn't backed your tale, Aven?" Darina pushed him into the chair Ghared had righted. "Why is there absolutely no record of this undercover mission?"

Aven rubbed his cuffed hands over his neck, and Ghared wished he'd been able to crush the jackass's windpipe. All this interrogating wasted valuable time. Time he could be out there… somewhere… finding Deo.

"I already told you." Aven's voice was scratchy, strained. "I don't have the clearance to discuss the details with you. The mission is highly classified. Only a handful of people know about it."

"And most of that handful is unreachable, right?" Darina sat again and pressed two fingers to her temple. This was wearing her down.

Maybe I shouldn't have gotten her involved.

When this shitbag first mentioned Deo, Ghared had toyed with not saying anything to Darina until he had more information, but that felt too much like lying. He tried hard not to lie to Darina, the person who had become his best friend in Deo's absence. They'd been surviving in the hellhole the world had become by having each other's backs, and if he wanted help finding Deo, Darina was it.

As he studied her now, though, he reconsidered. "Maybe you should take a break, Darina."

She glared at him with those sharp green-gold eyes and he put his hands up in surrender. Right. Darina was no more willing to take a break than he was.

"Maybe we should shift our focus," she said to Ghared.

"To what?" He sat beside her again, but his gaze never left Aven. How he wished he could inject the dude with something that would have him blubbering all his secrets. Maybe Foster could whip up a special serum or some shit that could do just that. The guy was a genius after all.

Darina clasped her hands in front of her on the table and leaned forward. Aven's gaze dipped down to the tops of her breasts showing at the neck of her fitted T-shirt, and Ghared nearly jumped the table to rip the guy's eyes out.

A hand on his forearm stopped him. "Easy." Darina sat back, aware of what she'd showcased to Aven. Was that part of her interrogation strategy? If so, Ghared didn't like it. Darina was like a sister to him, and no one but Foster was allowed to look at her as if he needed her to breathe. Ghared wasn't even sure he was okay with Foster looking at her like that, but he didn't get to have a say on that. He did want Darina to be happy.

Bringing Deo back would make her happy. It'd make him damn happy too.

"Tell us about Sasha Boisette," Darina said.

Aven stretched out his neck, his dramatic performance as the victim nearly wrapping up. He rested his cuffed hands in his lap and looked at the ceiling. At first, Ghared didn't think the guy was going to answer, and he was more than prepared to beat a response out of him. He was itching to pound on something. Aven would make a great *something.*

"I guess you'd call her Warres's adopted step-sister. His mother took Sasha in when her own parents abandoned her. No one knows what happened to them, but Laurette Warres took pity on the girl and raised her with Mikale." Aven swallowed loudly and let out a cough as if his throat was sandpaper dry.

When neither Darina nor Ghared made a move to get him that requested drink, Aven continued. "Sasha is beautiful. Like unreal beautiful. Some of us suspected she was a GEC, but Mikale swore she was not a genetically engineered castoff."

"Like we should believe anything that asshole said," Ghared muttered.

"I agree," Aven said, "but GECs have a least one flaw. That was why they got cast off and were deemed unfit for military duty, but Sasha... well, there isn't anything flawed about her." His cheeks reddened. "She's as perfect as they come."

Darina shot a quick look to Ghared before asking, "Were you intimate with Sasha Boisette, Aven?"

The man let out a breath in one long rush. "No, ma'am. I was undercover in a government-supported mission, as I've stated repeatedly, with your brother, Deo Lazitter, and had no time for sexual activities."

"Not because you didn't want to have sex with Boisette though." Ghared found it more and more unbelievable Deo would be partnered with this dick.

"You can judge, but I'll bet one look at her would have you going hard too, man."

"Doubtful." Ghared had searched for Sasha on his underground online channels but found nothing. She didn't exist to the world until word had gotten out she was Warres's successor. Regardless of how beautiful she might be, Ghared liked to think he was more in control of his hormones than this average human sitting across from him.

Aven smirked. "You think you're better than me?"

Ghared shook his head. "I *know* I'm better than you."

"You gave up looking for your best friend." Aven pointed to Darina. "Her brother. You were told he was dead and you took that as truth. Meanwhile, Deo has been alive. I'd like to say alive and well, but that's most probably not the case."

Darina gripped the edge of the table and leaned forward again. "What does that mean?"

"Deo's cover had been compromised just before Warres made the trip to find Ashby. Warres found out Deo was working for the government and hauled him out of the rooms we shared at headquarters."

"Where did they take him?" Darina asked.

"A place called the Pit. It's their version of a prison."

Ghared's well of hope was running dry. Quickly. "How do you know he's still alive then?"

"Because if I know anything, it's that Deo Lazitter is one tough bastard."

"Finally, something we can agree on." Ghared leaned back and folded his arms across his chest for a moment. Then he took Darina's tablet and opened a sketch program. "Now show me the layout of Warres's headquarters and don't leave anything out." He slid the tablet toward Aven.

"What are you planning?" Aven asked.

"None of your damn business. Now draw." He arrowed his index finger to the tablet.

Aven got busy sketching, and Ghared felt Darina's eyes on him.

"What?" He didn't mean to bark at her, but his patience was nearly gone.

"You're thinking of going in there." She motioned to what Aven was drawing. "I don't know if Boston PD will approve of that, Ghared."

"I'm not a cop, sweetheart. I don't need Boston PD approval. I just need a way in and a plan." He hoped to have both in the next five minutes.

Check _www.christinedepetrillo.weebly.com_ for release dates on all upcoming novels.

Books in The Maple Leaf Series
Contemporary Romance

What Readers Are Saying:

"I was expecting a short, simple story, what I got was a well-written, slow-burning romance with just a touch of suspense and a whole lot of pancakes."

"I could imagine I was in those woods..."

"The premise is simple -- sophisticated city girl hooks up with rugged, outdoorsy Vermont guy, but the author creates such depth that I can't stop reading."

More Than Pancakes (Book One)
More Than Cookies (Book Two)
More Than Rum (Book Three)
More Than Pizza (Book Four)
More Than Candy Corn (A Halloween Novella)
More Than Cocoa (Book Five)
More Than Biscotti (A FREE Christmas Novella available on my website only)
More Than Peaches (Book Six)

Check www.christinedepetrillo.weebly.com for release dates.

Other Available Titles by Christine DePetrillo

Alaska Heart

Firefly Mountain

Kisses to Remember

Abra Cadaver

Lazuli Moon

Night Eternal (gothic poetry with author Joseph Mazzenga)

Salvation Eternal (gothic poetry with author Joseph Mazzenga)

The Vampire Diaries: Blood Angel (a Kindle Worlds novella)

Young Adult Romance writing as Christy Major

Run With Me

Sail With Me

Co-writing as Goodwin Reed

A Less Perfect Union

About the Author

Christine DePetrillo tried not being a writer. She attempted to ignore the voices in her head, but they would not stop. The only way she could achieve peace and quiet was to write the stories the voices demanded. Today, she writes tales meant to make you laugh, maybe make you sweat, and definitely make you believe in the power of love.

She lives in Rhode Island and occasionally Vermont with her husband, two cats, and a big, black German Shepherd who defends her fiercely against all evils.

Find Christine's other titles at
www.christinedepetrillo.weebly.com.
Connect on Facebook at
www.facebook.com/christinedepetrilloauthor,
on Twitter at @cdepetrillo,
and at The Roses of Prose group blog on the
4th and 14th of every month at
www.rosesofprose.blogspot.com.

Made in the USA
Lexington, KY
10 August 2018